HAGGARD
HAWK

Marcus Barr

Marcus Barr

Pen Press Publishers Ltd

© Marcus Barr 2006

All rights reserved.
No part of this publication may be reproduced, stored in or
introduced into a retrieval system, or transmitted, in any form,
or by any means (electronic, mechanical, photocopying,
recording or otherwise) without the prior written
permission of the publisher

ISBN 1-905621-00-0
978-1-905621-01-9

First published in Great Britain in 2006 by

Pen Press Publishers Ltd
39 Chesham Road
Brighton
East Sussex BN2 1NB

A catalogue record for this book is available from
the British Library

Printed and bound in England

Cover design by Jacqueline Abromeit

Haggard Hawk: *a wild hawk in full plumage*

Marcus Barr comes from an army family and was brought up in London. He was educated at Haberdashers Aske's and, after a series of unfulfilling jobs, went to East 15 Acting School where he began writing seriously. His first plays were produced while he was still a student but on leaving drama school he began writing for television, inspired by the likes of David Mercer, John Hopkins and Dennis Potter. His first half hour television play – submitted entirely on spec - was produced in 1978.

Shortly afterwards he went to work at the BBC and became a script editor, preparing and contributing to such classics as *Z Cars, The Brothers, Duchess of Duke Street* and many, many more. In 1980 he went freelance and has since written several stage plays, some radio, and literally hundreds of television scripts, most of which are still being shown on satellite channels in Britain and all over the world. His favourites include *Lovejoy, Maybury, Boon, Forever Green, Poirot* and, most recently, *Midsomer Murders*.

He lives in a thatched house in a Buckinghamshire village with his wife and two German Shepherd dogs, a stone's throw from the inspiration for Nathan Hawk. Like Hawk, Marcus has four grown up children who have flown the nest. Theoretically.

Marcus Barr is a pen name.

- 1 -

Julie Ryder came into the kitchen and said to her husband, "The sea bass for table seven? And the fish cakes?"

"Behind you, my love, ready to go. The Falconers, I think you said? May she in particular choke on it."

"Amen to that."

Julie took the plates from beneath the muslin hood and went. Jim checked the next order. Fillet of lamb with the asparagus tips, broccoli and sauté potatoes. Quite a change from the stuff he'd been dishing up at Grendon Prison for the past eighteen months. No matter how hard he'd tried to pep them up a little, shepherd's pie and cauliflower cheese hadn't unleashed his creative flare. Very little in prison had.

Not that life inside had been unbearable. In fact, after a few weeks of settling in and then a spell in re-hab, he'd begun to think of his prison sentence as a well-earned rest as opposed to the well-deserved punishment the judge had meant it to be. He still wasn't sure why the jury at Aylesbury Crown Court had found him guilty of course, but conducting his own defence probably hadn't helped. The prosecuting counsel, a witty and spiteful woman in her late thirties, had torn him to shreds on a daily basis. While working for Taplin Seafoods, she claimed,

Jim had led a sales drive in Europe which "had cost a bomb and failed to deliver so much as a sparkler". Over a period of five years, fees to bogus consultants, money for advertising and public relations, had simply disappeared. There was close to two million pounds unaccounted for.

It was a crime Jim would gladly have committed had he thought of it, had he been certain he could have got away with it. Somebody else thought of it, somebody else got away with it and Jim paid the price. He was given three years for something he hadn't done.

However, instead of descending into bitterness during those early weeks at Grendon he'd begun to think of ways to turn the whole business to his advantage. He'd be out in eighteen months, dry in the alcoholic sense of the word, de-toxed of speed and cocaine and he would track down whoever had fitted him up. He would sue the police for wrongful arrest. He would sell his story to the papers, he would write a book, go on lecture tours. He would make a fortune.

He used to lie in the bath on Fuller Block just before bed time and dream of how he would spend the money. Nothing fancy or risky, he promised himself, just good old-fashioned self-indulgence and security. In the early days of his sentence that had meant a house in the South of France with blue chip shares back home to provide an income. Then for a while he considered a hotel in Portugal until he discovered that two of his less than amiable fellow prisoners had had the same idea. Finally, with parole in the offing, he turned to the travel sections of the Sunday papers for inspiration and settled on a vineyard in Tuscany, offering as it did the three essentials of life: sun, wine and dusky women. Which begged a question. Would he be going there with or without Julie?

Julie came into the kitchen again and started dusting off a bottle of Jacob's Creek.

"The Falconers," she said. "They'd like a bottle after all."

"Don't tell me they're making up again?"

She shook her head. "He just wants to get her into soft focus, I imagine. What are you staring at?"

"Nothing. Sorry."

Although Julie had lost weight and generally taken good care of herself while Jim had been inside, the ugly truth was there for all to see. She would soon be the spitting image of her late mother whom Jim referred to as Mrs Tiggywinkle on account of her being round and prickly. Tuscany without Julie then.

Jim being in prison had rather suited Julie too. It had given her chance to do some of the things she had neglected over many years. She had got her figure back for a start, or as much of it as she had a right to retrieve at her age. She had dyed her hair Autumn Chestnut. She had begun to read again too, the romantic novels she'd missed out on as a girl, travel books about places she still hoped to visit, a few biographies of people she would rather have been. More importantly, with no husband to persuade her otherwise, she had proved that she was the most capable woman she knew. Three years ago The Plough was a murky little pub with a slipping thatch, rats in the cellar and half a dozen regular customers. A re-thatch, a few hanging baskets and a first rate restaurant had improved the look of the place. Adverts and glowing articles in the local press had brought in the punters, ready and willing to spend.

Certainly Jim had played his part in all that. When they first arrived here, refugees from the charges against him, Julie's name went above the door as licensee and he ran the kitchen, earning high praise from people who knew about food. Julie wasn't impressed, though. She believed that anyone who could read a recipe could knock up a decent meal. Believing also that her husband would soon be taking his well-earned rest she got him to teach her nephew, bean-pole Tom, from the very book Jim himself had used as a bible: *Mrs Beeton's Cookery Book*. It proved Julie's theory beyond a shadow of doubt. By no means the sharpest knife in the box, nor come to that a fluent reader, Tom's fish cakes were, said Sharon Falconer, a dinner to die for. Sadly for most people who knew Sharon it was a compliment not a declaration of intent.

At the Falconers' table Julie uncorked the bottle wondering just how bad things were between them. It was common knowledge that Martin loathed his wife but had hung in there for the sake of the children. The children were now nineteen and twenty. Time for the parents to move on perhaps, under the watchful eye of the Winchendon Gestapo.

She went to pour Martin a taste and he gestured for her not to bother with such niceties. She filled their glasses.

Martin was really quite a good looking chap, she thought, for a farmer. She especially liked the soft blue eyes, made all the more inviting by his boyish haircut. There were no signs of weather-broken veins on his face yet, no leathery hardness to his hands, no stoop to the shoulders. If he ditched his wife he'd have no trouble finding another. In fact he could start his search for one right here with Julie herself.

She headed towards the bar pausing only to whip up two of her teenage staff. They had an untidy habit of leaning at the cash till in moments of inactivity. Giselle Whitely did so in a manner made all the more provocative by the length of her legs. Beautiful legs, Jim had said the first day she came to work at The Plough. Beautiful girl, lovely body...

Julie's angry recollection nearly surfaced into words. Soon, when weekend leave matured into full-blown parole, her self-regarding fool of a husband would return home to ogle the waitresses, bombard them with *double entendres* and, yes, occasionally touch them up. And if he wasn't doing that you'd find him at the bar lecturing customers on everything from global warming to rheumatism via family values, foreigners and food. Anything you cared to name, Jim Ryder had a view on it and would share it with you against your will.

Why had that bloody judge given him such a paltry sentence? Didn't two million pounds merit chucking the key away? She broke off from her inward tirade unable, for one reason and another, to be *too* self-righteous about the missing money...

At the bar she retreated into the warmth of her long term regulars. The poshing up of the place, maintained Uncle Elvis, hadn't sent him elsewhere for his nightly pint or five. No, sir. This was the pub for him so long as Julie ran the place. Jack the Wood still showed his face here after a hard day. So too did Stef the Window Cleaner, when his partner allowed it. Tonight he was well and truly off the leash and had a set of fishing rods with him to prove it. The local angling club was holding a night match down at the river. If he caught that pike he'd been after for a year, Julie would gladly pay him the market price for it.

Yet for all the welcome she gave her regulars they knew their status had diminished. Once, when Charlie Brigham held the license, they had been its only visible means of support. Today, perched on rocky stools, living sculptures each with his own plinth, they were mere examples of local colour to brighten the lives of wealthy punters who came to eat in the restaurant.

"Good week, Jack?" Julie asked him.

"Not bad," he answered. "Not bad at all." Nothing was bad in Jack Langan's world. "Jimbo been given a release date yet?"

"Four weeks come Monday."

"Be good to have him home, I expect," said Stef.

She gave him an all purpose smile and then, as a means of steering the conversation away from her husband, she nodded across at the table in the corner.

"Who're those two? Any idea?"

Uncle Elvis turned to where two men in their twenties sat chain smoking from a packet of cigarettes, open before them in the launch position.

"Dunno," he said, "but I 'spect they're in the Guinness Book of Records. For making a pint last."

The taller one with the dark, curly hair and thin face must have heard the remark for he looked up and challenged Elvis's affable smile with a hard stare. His squarer, tougher looking companion, clearly recognising the signs of impending trouble, laid a hand on the other's wrist.

"Chill," he muttered.

The thin face heeded the advice. He took a breath, looked away from Elvis and he and his companion went back to whatever they had been talking about.

As usual, Uncle Elvis was the last man standing, if only just, after his five pints. As Julie urged him out of the door he protested undying love for her, promising to step in should her ponce of a husband ever do the dirty. She thanked him and said she would think about it.

As she bolted the door she watched Elvis through the quarter light weave his way across the car park and climb the slight hill past the terrace of thatched cottages. Odd to think that such a robust and powerful man, fifty years old at least, was now going home to his mother. How did they get on, Julie wondered, how did they talk to each other? Just as they had done forty years ago? Can I go out tonight? As long as you're back by...

The echoes flooded back to her, her own voice drowning out her mother's. Why do you treat me like a child? Why don't you like my friends? What have you got against them? Then finally her mother's voice surfaced. It's not all your friends we dislike. Just James Ryder.

The clock in the restaurant chimed a quarter past eleven as Jim emerged from the kitchen, shaking out his whites. He folded them neatly, even though they would be going into the wash the moment he reached home.

"Drink?" he asked, quietly.

It was meant, for the umpteenth time this weekend, as a kind of shorthand for thanking her. She chose to hear only its literal meaning.

"I thought you'd given up."

He smiled. "Well, special occasion..."

"Maybe at home."

He watched her at the cash till as, with practised fingers, she scooped the coins into a bag then rolled up the notes and snapped an elastic band around them. She clipped the cheques and credit card slips together and put them in her bulging shoulder bag.

"The stuff in the safe?" Jim asked.

Julie patted the bag. "All done."

She really had come into her own, he thought. She could manage the staff, the suppliers, the bank, the bills, the bolshie customers.

"How much are we turning over?" he asked.

"In a week? Twenty to twenty-five. Can we go now?"

He led the way back through the kitchen. Spotless. Not a knife out of place, not a ladle facing the wrong way, pans shining, hobs ready for use tomorrow lunchtime. Jim hadn't always been that fussy. In that regard, prison life had changed him for the better, Julie thought. Living in small spaces meant you had to be clean and well organised.

She called up the spiral stairs to the bed-sit above, her voice piercing the low hum of a football match on television.

"I'm off now, Tommy. If you're short of things to do in the morning, Gizzy, run a duster over those pictures in the restaurant."

There was no reply, just the swell of applause as somebody scored a goal. Julie took a deep breath, preparing to shout again and changed her mind.

She double locked the kitchen door behind them and led the way to her car. There were only splinters of mist tonight, breaking away from the stream which ran beside the beer garden. The air was still, the sky above starlit to the same magical degree as any night in one of those books she'd been reading. The kind of night people said they remembered...

As they drove out of the village and began the journey home, Jim tried again.

"You've done well, girl," he said. "Bloody well."

"I had no choice."

"What I meant was ... what I mean *is* ... thank you. Home to come back to, business to be part of, most of the guys I'm with ... eye teeth."

She reached out and patted his leg.

"You're welcome. Not that I did it for you. I did it for me."

"Well, sure."

"And just so as we understand each other it's still my name over the door."

There was a long pause before he found the courage to say: "You don't want me back, do you? You've enjoyed it, being on your own."

She turned and smiled at him, often her way of expressing agreement.

He said: "All I can promise is ... I'll try."

They reached Winchendon Castle, so-called for its crenulations, but in truth a rich man's folly set with ammonites he had pilfered on his travels. They stared out from the walls of the beleaguered ruin, once a mark of Victorian wealth, now a dumping ground for old fridges and the like, standing forlorn at a crossroads. Julie turned out of the village and began the gradual climb up to The Ridge.

Jim switched on the radio and found a local news programme and began to talk back at it. Who, at this time of night, he asked, gave a damn for Councillor Stuart's campaign to remove the bollards from outside the Crown Court? The interviewer certainly didn't. You could hear him sipping coffee in the background as the Councillor waffled on. Jim knew that court well. He had turned up at it every day of his trial, convinced that the jury loved him and would find him not guilty.

Julie tensed up as the road began to weave its way through Penman Wood. It belonged to Penman Manor whose vast, lumbering house dominated the south side of The Ridge. The wood unsettled her for some reason, perhaps because its one time good order and formality had been allowed to run wild. With Jim in prison she drove this part of her journey home without a glance to right or left, at the mercy of her imagination. Suppose the car ran out of petrol, or broke down, or a tree fell across the road, what would she do? Would those pillared pines, tall as a church and holding up between them their canopy of branches, beckon her in? Would she go, despite her fear, walk in among the Gothic shadows and be lost forever?

"Steady, girl," said Jim. "Bit fast for this road."

She slowed down as the final bend, marked by a lone chevron, came into view.

Once, and only once, she had stopped, right here, to test her resolve. She'd switched off the engine, wound down the window, expecting to hear sounds of the night. An owl, perhaps, a twig breaking beneath some nocturnal creature. There was only silence.

As they came out of the bend Jim asked in a puzzled voice: "What's all this about?"

Julie braked sharply, coming to a halt ten yards or so from a car slewed across the road, blocking the way completely. Its headlights were full on, the beam returned by the trees in its glare.

"He's been going too fast," said Jim. "The back's broken away."

"Where are the people?" Julie asked.

"We should see if they're okay."

Clearly, he didn't want to. There was something uncomfortable about that car, its position across the road, not touching either verge. No damage.

"Be careful," said Julie.

Jim nodded and reached under the driver's seat for the tyre lever which Julie kept there. Tapping it nervously in the palm of his other hand he walked towards the car.

A breeze unsettled the tall grass at the verge, then lifted into the trees with a gentle hiss. A chilly breeze for August but then they were high up here. The road followed the backbone of a long hill before dropping down to Dorton where the Ryders lived. The radio was on, the same station he had been listening to, the coffee sipping presenter taking those who cared through tomorrow's front pages. The dullness of the headlines had a calming effect, something about French lorry drivers.

Julie got out of the car.

"What can you see?" she called out.

"Stay in the car."

She approached him, drew level and for the first time in quite a while, she took his hand. They peered in through the side windows, Jim opened one of the doors and left it standing wide before announcing:

"Nothing."

"I still don't like it," said Julie. "We shouldn't have..."

They turned back to her car, alerted by a movement there. From the trees beyond it had come two figures, hooded with balaclavas. The taller of the two men leaned over the open driver's door, levelled a shotgun at them and asked as calmly as if he were asking the time:

"The money. Where is it?"

Only the radio presenter spoke, warning them of unsettled weather now that summer was nearly over.

The man asked again: "Where is it, lady? We mean business."

A young voice. Twenties and Irish. Belfast. Unafraid.

"In the boot," said Julie.

The man walked to the back of the car, yanked at the handle. "Open it," he said.

There was determination in the voice now. But they aren't going to kill us, Jim thought, or they wouldn't be wearing hoods.

"I said open it."

The determination had become anger. Controlled anger. The man raised his shotgun. As Julie made to approach the boot, so Jim snatched the keys from her hand.

"Not on your fucking Nellie!"

He threw the keys as far as he could into the trees. The shorter man looked at him for a moment, took aim and fired. Jim fell.

"You got another key?" asked the taller man.

"No," Julie yelled.

"Find his then," said the man. "On your fucking hands and knees!"

Julie stared at him, fancying that she recognised the framed eyes, the moody mouth. She turned to run, the man steadied his shotgun and fired. Julie arched backwards and fell.

The shorter man stooped and took the bloodied tyre lever from Jim's hand, stepped over his body and went to the back of Julie's car. He tried to wrench open the lock but it wouldn't give. He threw down the lever, stood back and fired. The other man fired a second shot and the boot sprung open, as if aghast at the intrusion. He reached in and took Julie's bag.

They got into their car. The taller man started the engine and drove away.

- 2 -

All in all it had been quite a pleasant evening. The company was reasonable, food excellent and I'd managed not to upset anyone. In fact I'd been pretty friendly given that I'd put away a bottle and a half of Mouton Cadet, the life blood of village England. I hadn't meant to drink so much. I'd meant to stop at a couple of glasses but with Angie Mitchell's hand on the corkscrew you don't stand a chance.

We were saying goodbye to her in the yard at Hayfleet, a barn conversion just off The Ridge Road. There was a breeze whipping up and making straight for the alcohol in my face: that sting you get, half way between a slap and a palm full of aftershave. Angie was arranging people's lives for them.

"Laura," she said, "I wonder if you could drop Nathan off. I'm not saying he's pissed but well..."

"Certainly," said the prim and sober doctor. She was on call, she'd told us, not that she drank much anyway. "Where do you live?"

"Er, Beech Tree Cottage. I think." I was trying to be witty but it was pearls before swine. "It's Winchendon. Are you going that way?"

"Apparently."

"All settled then," said Angie.

She turned to Allan and Petra Wyeth, the other two guests, and air-kissed them all the way to their car. I knew them as neighbours, a strange couple, at the back of the queue when looks were handed out but well to the fore on brains day. In fact between them they had enough intellectual power to launch a star fleet which is exactly what their Beetle sounded like as it pulled out of the Mitchells' yard.

"What was the name of his company, the word he kept saying as if we all knew what it meant?"

"*Eruditio*," said Geoff Mitchell. He was more pissed than I was and had a slight tussle with the Latin pronunciation.

"What does it mean?" I asked.

"No idea," he said. "I was hoping you'd tell me."

We collapsed, like real blokes, into a fit of giggles - we may even have hugged, I choose not to remember - until Angie slapped her old man over his bald head.

"Enough," she barked and the world fell silent. She turned to me and I backed away. "Lovely to see you, Nathan. Goodnight."

I got into Laura's car, a feminised Saab smelling unnervingly of both peach essence and surgical spirit. She rescued her medical bag from the front seat, just before I sat on it, and turned to me with a look devoid of all bedside manner.

"If you're going to throw up, give me notice. I'll stop the car, you can do it by the roadside."

"I could always walk," I said, huffily.

"Not in a straight line. And certainly not all the way to Winchendon. Seat belt."

I scissored the air with my hands in protest.

"It's the law," she insisted, "and you were a policeman, weren't you?"

She reached over and fastened me in and after we'd thanked our hosts repeatedly Laura Peterson hared off at a reckless twenty miles an hour.

At the Dorton observatory we turned onto The Ridge Road and I tried some polite conversation.

"Nice people," I said.

She nodded and slowed down to take a bend, passing the steering wheel through her hands like they teach you at Driving School. Most people do it right up to the day of their test and then forget it, but Laura Peterson had more staying power.

"Geoff and Angie," I said, in case she hadn't understood me.

"I knew who you meant."

Maybe I *had* upset someone and just hadn't been aware of it. It wouldn't have been the first time. I rolled down the window.

"You want me to stop?" she said, anxiously.

"No, just fancied a breath of fresh air. Tell me, Doc, what's the best thing for a hangover?"

"Temperance," came the stodgy reply. "Or, failing that, two pints of water before you go to bed. What was that?"

She'd heard the same thing I had. Gunshot, about a mile up ahead of us.

"Rabbits?" I said. It was meant to be another joke but came out plain daft. I tried to recoup by asking in a serious voice, as if I gave a damn: "Do people shoot rabbits round here?"

"Well, of course they do, but not in the middle of the night. It's more likely to be an engine back-firing. Allan and Petra's Beetle."

There was a second shot.

"Put your foot down," I said.

She did, all the way up to thirty. We drove for ten seconds before I said:

"Try another gear."

She was about to come back at me, tell me it was her car and she could drive it however she pleased, but she was sidetracked by two more shots in rapid succession.

"Phone?" I said, snapping my fingers.

"Why? We don't even know what's..."

"I know something's wrong. Where is it?"

"And I know you've drunk too much, so less of the snapping fingers."

She mimicked the way I'd tried to bring a touch of urgency to the situation. Meantime, I'd found the phone on the dashboard and was dialling three nines.

"Good evening, Doctor Peterson. Which service?"

"Police."

"One moment."

I could feel the disdain beside me and see, reflected in the windscreen, the shake of the school marm head despairing of the wayward pupil. It lasted until the final bend in the road. Coming out of it, Laura braked and I grabbed the wheel, steering us into the long grass.

Ahead of us a dark car, no lights on, unidentifiable, was pulling away all too carefully. It dipped out of sight below the brow of the hill, descending to the main Oxford road. The headlights came on and it tore like hell into the night. Give chase, I thought, but at twenty miles an hour we might just lose it. Besides, Laura was already getting out of the car, hurling instructions at me:

"Bring my bag! There's someone lying there."

I reached behind for her medical bag and followed her, taking the phone with me.

She stooped to the lifeless body of a man lying in a slick of his own blood, his rib cage torn open by the shotgun blast, his face caught in the headlights of Laura's car. A hideous, carnival mask, mouth overshadowed by his chin, eyes blacked out by his cheek bones.

"I know this man," I said. "Jim Ryder, The Plough. Where's his wife? They'll be together. Where's Julie?"

"She's here," Laura said.

She crouched down in the long, dampening grass verge and put a hand to Julie's neck.

"She's still alive."

She went to work as the emergency operator asked me for more details.

"It's a shooting," I said. "Ridge Road, Penman Wood. Ambulance and police."

"Could I...?" the girl began.

"Don't waste time taking my details. Just do it."

Forget two pints of water. Give me a double shooting any day, guaranteed to render you stone cold sober in an instant.

A minute or so later I heard the ambulance leave Aylesbury and head towards us, followed by a police patrol car, both doing speeds Laura Peterson had only dreamed of.

I didn't arrive home until dawn and made the mistake of slumping into an armchair where I must have nodded off. I woke with a start, counting murders. I'd worked on thirty-three in some capacity or other, from DC through to Sergeant and onto Detective Chief Inspector. Jim Ryder's was the thirty-fourth lifeless body I'd stood over asking myself the same question: Why do I feel so alive now that this poor bastard isn't? I was asking it even though catching Jim's killer would be none of my business. I could stand over as many bodies as I liked from now on, get the same rush and it would all lead nowhere.

Maybe that's what woke me, the sense of leaving things behind, of going past milestones at Laura Peterson speeds, slow enough to read every last detail on them. I was on the verge of depressing myself badly when two pints of water started knocking on my bladder door.

He was there again in the downstairs toilet, The Stranger, watching me from the mirror. Not a bad looking bloke, even with the time-lines carving up his face and the greying hair cut short to hide its recession. But he'd chubbed up lately, maybe a stone or more, dispersed over his frame, yes, but easily caught in the glare of the bathroom scales. I breathed on him and he disappeared behind the mist.

In the kitchen Dogge awoke and looked me up and down.

"Fancy a walk?" I asked.

Across the meadow behind the cottage I could see the all night fishermen who'd escaped from their wives to sit in discomfort on the river bank. Stefan Merriman would be there, having deserted his exotic partner for the sake of a spliff or two and a flask of metallic tea. Most men in the village couldn't understand why he left her alone so much, and prey to passing lotharios. I thought I knew why. It seems an odd thing to say about someone that all they have is beauty but in Bella's case it was true. There was little more to her, saving an endearment born of familiarity, than her stunning good looks.

At the gate I looked back at the cottage which had cost me just about all I had. I wasn't sure how I felt about her these days, this old lady placed in my care until some other admirer rode by looking for peace and quiet. First thing they should do is repair the shawl of thatch before it fell any lower round the old girl's shoulders. I couldn't afford to. Did it feel like home yet, Beech Tree Cottage? Not really. Maggie would have loved it, of course. She would have done it all differently, but she would have loved it. I guess that's why I'd bought it.

Dogge growled, the street-wise rumble she reserved for other creatures she hated, in this case Will Waterman and his sister, Prissy. I wasn't too keen on them myself. Pass by Will and his sister's front gate any time of day or night and one of them would be out there in a flash to check you over, usually on the pretext of putting rubbish in the wheelie bin. They must've kept a stash of it by the door for emergencies.

This morning, though, they weren't being nosy, they were off on holiday. Prissy was herding the pygmy goats she kept tethered on the green into the horse-box. Will was hitching it up to the Range Rover.

"Morning, Nathan," Prissy said. "Thought we'd get an early start."

"Devon? You'll be there for breakfast, Priss."

"That's the general idea."

Will began, as ever, to fill me in with bits of his life story.

"Only thing I really liked about National Service, the early rise. I remember one morning in Aldershot..."

The guy sure had seen the world

"Key, Will?" He looked at me. "You want me to keep an eye on the place?"

"Yes, yes, mate, thanks. I'll drop it in before we take off. Rotten luck about Jim and Julie, eh?"

It had happened just six hours previously but the Watermans already had chapter and verse on it, probably from Prissy's old nursing mates at The Radcliffe Infirmary. Be that as it may, it wasn't going to spoil their holiday.

At the far end of the slumbering village there was life in the attic rooms of The Plough. The curtains had been pulled back, young voices were chattering on the radio, water was running down a drainpipe. A police panda parked on the shingle at the front had a young copper fast asleep in the passenger seat, head back, cap over his eyes. As I slipped past him he smacked his lips, groaned like an old man and slept on.

Julie was fond of her nephew, Tom Templeman, and not simply because he'd run the restaurant for the past eighteen months. Her feelings went beyond that, partly to do with having no kids of her own, she once told me. Sure, Tom wasn't very bright, but he had a gentle warmth and a modesty you couldn't accuse most kids of.

So, Julie gave bean-pole Tommy the top half of The Plough and Jack Langan turned it into a bachelor pad for him. He made a nice job of it too. He built a set of spiral stairs, winding them round a central beam until they surfaced halfway along the attic. Behind a partition wall he managed to create a bedroom, a kitchen and a bathroom. You could see his mark on the place wherever you looked, from the brushed plaster finish, to the oak flooring, to the carved hand rail at the stair well.

Tommy loved the place, of course, and things went well between him and his aunt Julie until Gizzy came on the scene. Giselle Whitely, eighteen years old, mouth like a well-oiled machine gun, legs like a giraffe, all topped off with a kind of Scandinavian beauty. She begged a job waitressing and Julie obliged, unaware of Gizzy's big plans, big laughable plans that she was dead serious about. She was going to make Tom the best chef in the world this side of Marco Pierre White.

Julie Ryder turned a blind eye to many things. You have to if you're a publican or life doesn't roll along smoothly but when Gizzy moved into the flat and started putting ideas into Tom's head, Julie decided to act. I don't think she'd got round to the fine detail but I know there'd been an almighty row a week or so previously and Gizzy's days at The Plough were numbered. My own view of Julie was one of respect more than affection. I couldn't say I disliked her but I wouldn't have wanted to cross her. But Gizzy had, though she seemed totally unaware of the fact.

I was met at the top of Jack's stairs by WPC Greene, teeth bared.

"Friend," I said in a soothing voice, arms raised. "How are the kids?"

"I haven't got any."

Was she being funny, or were IQ levels falling in the police service?

"Not *your* kids. Tom and Gizzy."

"They're fine. Who are you? How did you get in?"

"You left the door open, so I turned the handle and pushed. I'm ex DCI Hawk. I live in the village. I'm a friend of Julie Ryder."

"None of that's a reason to be here. Leave."

So much for my all-conquering charm.

"And what'll you do if I refuse? Call a copper? There's one outside, asleep in the panda."

She didn't like it but could see this wasn't the time or place for a confrontation. She glared at me and I walked round her.

Tom was half buried in a sofa, the cushions rising up either side of him like quicksand. A police surgeon had checked him over, Greene eventually told me, and then had knocked him stupid with something. Pity he or she hadn't done the same to Giselle Whitely who'd stood up when I entered, though not out of respect.

"What the hell do you want?" she asked.

"To talk to Tom without any help from you."

She came at me with pure teenage strop. It's our own fault. We wanted them to stand up to authority figures and now we're rattled when they do.

"Go to hell!" she said. "He's not saying anything more till he's spoken to his lawyer."

"Less of the Hollywood, Gizzy. The boy Delia could be in trouble and for Julie's sake, if not for his own, I plan to help him."

"It's Nathan," said Tom, with a slow, clockwork turn of the head. "Hi, Nathan, d'you hear what they did to...?"

"Why could he be in trouble?" Gizzy asked.

"Same reason you think he needs a solicitor. Someone gets murdered, the first place they look is home and family. Then someone tells them about the dust up you both had with Julie last week and well..."

The eyes were flashing, shoulders forward, mouth ready to savage all comers. "She told you about that? Is anything your own in this bloody place?"

"Welcome to village England, Gizzy. What was it about?"

"You obviously know."

"From her side, not yours."

Greene chipped in. "I think this is..."

I flapped a hand and she backed off but I could sense the cogs turning, working out her options. One was the baton over the back of the head and I didn't fancy the headlines as a result of that. Hard nosed ex-copper felled by tap from probationer. Female.

Gizzy said: "It was about Tom running the place for *two fucking years*. Jim came home for a few days and told him he'd done it all wrong."

I turned to Tom. "Well, you haven't. Julie wouldn't have let you." He was nodding. "Where were you last night?"

He looked at Gizzy as if memory had failed him.

"He was up here watching the telly."

"Up here," said Tom, "watching the telly. England v Ireland. D'you see it?"

"Sir, I don't think you should ask any more..."

"Who was in the bar last night, Gizzy? Anyone I know?"

"Well, Jack was there," she said. "Stefan too, and Uncle Elvis."

"What about sober people who might've seen something?"

"Martin Falconer and his wife, table seven. Forty other covers, early on, regulars mostly but not from the village."

An average sort of night, then, for a Friday and for the setting. Busy but not heaving so any strangers might well have stood out.

"You don't know if Jim had any problems, do you? People, giving him grief?"

Gizzy looked at Tom for signs of life. His eyelids were drooping. "I'm not sure what you mean," he mumbled, eventually. "People complain about the food occasionally but they do that..."

"Had he mentioned people at Grendon?"

I was trying to pack in the questions before whatever the quack had given him kicked in for a second time. Grendon seemed to be a place he'd never heard of. He closed his eyes, back went his head on the cushion and sleep overtook him.

A colleague of mine used to say that when you talk to someone for five minutes you learn fifty things about them and a couple of things about yourself. It may be stuff you don't realise till later, sometimes years later, but it goes in and sits there till you need it. I'd learned a few things about Tom and Gizzy that day, sure, and something about myself that I wasn't too keen to know.

Retirement's a bastard of a thing, makes a real monkey out of the people it's forced upon. When I'd woken in the armchair earlier that morning, I wasn't just counting murders, I was thrilling to the latest one that had come my way. It was all systems go, heartbeat thumping, breathing sharp and shallow and the rush I'd felt on hearing that first gunshot had barely subsided. It doesn't take a genius to work it out. The life I'd loved, the life I'd buried six months ago when I put in my papers, had been exhumed up on The Ridge Road. I could've sworn I'd put it all behind me. That's what boozers say. They stay on the wagon for six months and a single drink can throw them off again.

But to think of myself in that light, surely that was pushing it? So why had I woken from a sleep I badly needed, having been at The Radcliffe most of the night while Laura Peterson helped to save Julie's life? Why was my mind now racing with the next phase of an inquiry I'd nothing to do with? Get a team together, argue the toss with the guvnor, get the very best, the smartest. Old coppers who'd plod down a hundred streets, bang on a thousand doors and at the thousand and first sniff out something which pointed the way. Bring it back to the young kids fresh from their computer courses who'd put it all together. Find nothing. Start again. Until one day, as a team, we find *something...*

I stopped. This was bloody mad. This was lack of sleep stuff. I hauled myself back to the simple truth of the matter, the one word I could get a grip on. Habit. I was the victim of pure habit and one I had to break or forever keep wandering off into the past, like a fully paid up old codger. Until one day I'd lose my return ticket.

And God knows, you could hardly call my life at the moment dull! In fact some people would have given their eye teeth for a life like mine, I was always being told. With so many offers lined up, all I had to do was pick one and buckle down to it ... like Head of Security at McSweeney's Spice Factory. Most people don't realise it but in the world of culinary spice there's all manner of villainy: people pinching your recipes, workforce doctoring the products, unscrupulous foreign suppliers pulling a fast one. They really did need a good man to sort it out, preferably one who could stand the smell.

Then there was lecturing at Bramshill, giving young officers the benefit of my experience, handing down the secrets of how it should be done. Knowing they weren't listening. Had I listened, all those years ago?

Then there was the book. Before he took off round the world with his beautiful redhead my eldest boy, Con, introduced me to a book editor he'd been at Cambridge with. Twenty two years old, going on twelve, a guy with real clout, I thought cynically, especially when it comes to the nitty-gritty of money. A month later a contract landed on the doormat, two months after that an advance for: *'The History of the Hamford Crime Squad: a Memoir'*. Catchy title, don't you think?

Con had phoned a couple of weeks ago from Queenstown, New Zealand, at the top of a ski-slope, asking if I'd made a start yet. I said yes. The very next day, Fee called from an onsen in Japan and, in a voice her mother would have used, told me I shouldn't lie to Con. A day or so later, Jaikie phoned from L.A. with a variation on the theme. He recalled that together last Spring we'd bonded, in a spiritual sense, as we built the log writing cabin. Were the disagreements we'd shared over its construction all to be for nothing? Good heavens no, I'd told him.

Then, hard on the heels of Jaikie, Ellie had called from Paris. Youngest of the tribe at eighteen she had a short, superior manner and an eye for the truth.

"Book," she'd said. "You've no intention of writing it, have you."

I said of course I had, it was just a matter of harnessing creative forces.

"Bollocks, Dad!"

I reminded her that she wasn't in Paris to hurl telephonic abuse at me but to practise her French.

"Eh, bien. Testicules, Papa. Tu n'as pas d'intention d'ecriture, n'est ce pas?"

I missed her. I shouldn't say this, and I certainly shouldn't commit it to paper, but of all of them, I missed Ellie the most.

I'd offered many excuses for not having started the book but best among them was Hideki. Hideki Takahashi was a seventeen year old Japanese boy who'd come to stay for three days and a month later showed no signs of moving on. He'd been one of Fee's pupils at the English Language School in Asahikawa, a right sod according to his parents, though I detected Fee's translation in the remark, with as much grasp of English as I had of Kanji. He'd set off on his travels with little more than a note in Fee's handwriting. It said: "In case of emergencies please direct this person to Mr Nathan Hawk, Beech Tree Cottage, Winchendon, Bucks HP27 9JH. Telephone 01296 968954". Hideki duly arrived on the doorstep greeting me with a bow and the words:

"Harrow, Mister Hock".

He turned out to be a most independent young man, polite and unobtrusive, with a twenty fags a day habit and a routine of going into London, or Rondon as he preferred to call it, most days except Sundays when, like every teenager I've ever known, he stayed in bed till lunchtime.

So that's the story of how McSweeney's were still looking for a Head of Security, Bramshill was one lecturer short and the book still hadn't been written.

- 3 -

Next morning, Hideki knocked on my bedroom door at some ungodly hour and said: "Nathan, there are gentlemen to speak of you."

"*To* me, Deki," I corrected, without opening my eyes. "There are gentlemen to speak *to* me."

"Okay," he said. "I tell them to go?"

"No, tell them I'll be down in ten minutes, whoever they are."

"Policemen," he said.

When I struggled into the kitchen at half six, Hideki was talking to DI Ralph Charnley whom I'd met on Saturday night at the hospital and hadn't liked. Heavy accents did for Hideki and Charnley's was right up there with George Formby's so DS Faraday was translating from broad Lancashire to standard English. Hideki was explaining where Hokkaido was, untroubled that both men thought Japan consisted of just two islands - called Nagasaki and Hiroshima.

Charnley rose to greet me. He was in his early forties, six feet tall and powerful. A rugby player, no doubt, given the long, off-centre nose and misshapen ears. No sign of the occupational beer gut, though. The dark hair was close cut, but from choice, not necessity.

"I know we took most of the details, guvnor, but there's one or two bits and pieces. Okay to have a word now?"

I nodded. "Hideki, stick the kettle on." Hideki looked at me, both of us with fleeting images of a kettle glued to something. "Sorry, *put* the kettle on. Put."

He filled it at the sink and started making coffee.

"I like the cottage," said Charnley, strolling the room like a potential buyer. "Plenty of land, nobody breathing down your neck, but help within reach if you need it."

"It looks especially good this time of night," I said.

He smiled. "Yeah, sorry for the early call. Long day ahead."

He went to the window and looked across the green to the tree cottages.

"What's that thing, like half a bloody melon, stuck on your neighbour's wall?"

He was referring to the CCTV high up on the front of the Watermans' cottage. Will had had it installed that summer to the consternation of most of his neighbours. It could both see and hear into our gardens and that, according to the law, was just fine.

"You're kidding," said John Faraday. "You mean it's legal?"

"Unless he sells the tapes of me cutting the grass and doesn't pay me a royalty. Data Protection Act."

"I wouldn't stand for it," said Faraday, bristling with youthful indignation. "I'd have it down one dark night."

"Aye, and his balls up there in place of it," his boss agreed.

I told them I was working on it.

John Faraday was a neat sort of bloke, twenty-six or seven, wearing a pricey jacket and chinos. His aftershave blotted out the smell of damp plaster and warm dog which characterised Beech Tree Cottage. He was tall and athletic, fair haired with a handsome face, his feelings easily read in the gentle features. Right now he was apprehensive about something. Just how far Charnley would go, I imagined, when he got round to scolding me for talking out of turn to Tom and Gizzy.

"Who's in the middle one, then, next to Cecil B de Mille?" asked Charnley, still at the window.

"He's Stefan Merriman, local window cleaner, she's Italian, Annabella Castellone, works for the council. Nice couple. Far end it's a young divorcee, Kate Whitely."

"How nice is she?"

"Well, she's Giselle Whitely's sister so she's tarred with the same brush. Uppity, but I like her."

"And the apple tree in her front garden," said Charnley, "is a Blenheim Orange, in case you're interested."

Put all the coppers in Britain together you could compile an encyclopaedia of utterly useless crap. Charnley's contribution, by the sound of it, would be fruit trees.

"Julie Ryder," he said. "I reckon you saved that poor bitch's life."

"Not me. Dr. Peterson."

"Oh, aye, nice woman," said Charnley. "I forgot to ask you both Saturday. What were you doing out at that time of night? Just for the record."

When he spoke, his bottom lip spooned out as if to sip a possible reply before swallowing it.

"Not that it's any of your business but we'd been to supper with mutual friends. The Mitchells. We didn't know each other before but we do now, by God."

"Yeah, blood and guts break down the old barriers, eh! She's available, I'm told, should the fancy take you. She's just broken up with this ear, nose and throat wallah at Stoke Mandeville. Caught him pumping up one of the interns." He flexed his eyebrows to indicate a move from small talk to serious business. "The shots you heard, take us through 'em again, will you."

"The first one must've been eleven thirty-five or six. We were about a mile away. I knew something was up - gunshot, late at night..." I heard myself thrilling to the idea of it much as I'd done at the time. I jumped on it. "Four, five seconds later a second shot."

Faraday made notes, saying: "That will have been Julie. Jim first, poor bastard, then his missus. She tried to get away, we think."

"I agree," I said. "Then maybe thirty seconds later two more shots, one after the other. Car boot?"

"We found the keys," said Faraday. "Ten yards into the woods. Either Jim or Julie's chucked 'em there sooner than hand 'em over. Matey-boy's tried the boot with a tyre lever first, no prints of course, he's worn gloves but..."

Charnley cut him off. "Yes, well, don't let's carve it all in stone, Johnny."

He turned a chair round, sat down at the table and leaned forward over the back of it.

"Just so you know, we've set up camp at Penman Manor, some old stables there. Phones are in, hardware's there, troops are assembled..."

"Two guns, right?" I said.

Charnley nodded. "No sign of 'em yet but that's no problem. Car they used, we think it was nicked from Wheatley, tea-time."

"Motive?" I asked.

"Money."

He looked up at Hideki who had set a mug of coffee down on the table in front of him, saying discreetly: "Table move. Coffee slop."

Charnley smiled at him, showing capped incisors, the originals having been kicked out in a collapsed scrum, I imagine. Or in the line of duty. "We got Pearl Harbour out, the other night, me and the wife. Ben Affliction and that girl whose dad was in Porridge. There's a bloke in it looks just like you."

It was half joke, half jibe, but Charnley's thick accent had made it whistle over Hideki's head. He looked at me for the simplified version.

"It's okay, Deki," I said. "Two dogs pissing up trees, seeing who takes the territory. By getting at you he gets at me."

Hideki blinked. I'm not sure Faraday understood what was really being said either.

"It's just that my father was in one of the camps," said Charnley. "Place called Matsushima. Six and a half stone and ribs like a washboard." He paused and turned back to me with the flexed eyebrows. "There's no mystery to it. Jim Ryder's been in prison for eighteen months. You meet shite there even at a holiday camp like Grendon, so that's the way I'm heading. Doesn't it make you laugh, guvnor? A prison without gates?" He turned to Hideki. "How much do *you* weigh?"

"Leave him alone," I said.

Charnley drummed his fingers on the table for a moment or two, a dull sound. Bitten fingernails. Then he said:

"There were two blokes in the pub, night of the shooting. Strangers."

Faraday flicked back a page in his notebook and read from it: "Mid-twenties, five eight, built like a brick wotsit with dark hair, the other taller, six feet, curly fair hair. Not much to go on, is it..."

"Any ideas, though?" asked Charnley.

I shook my head. "Who reported them?"

"Mrs Sharon Falconer, J.P.," said Faraday. "She was having dinner there with her husband, saw them on her way out. Rang to tell us first thing."

I grunted. "Forget what Sharon Falconer told you. She may have her nose in everyone's trough but she invariably gets it wrong."

Faraday chuckled.

"Typical magistrate, then." said Charnley. "Even so, some bugger took a chance the other night and it paid off handsomely. They came away with nigh on twenty grand, weekly take at The Plough."

"Well, I say forget the Grendon idea, look closer to home, someone who knew Julie's routine..."

I broke off, hearing my voice rise in pitch and tempo. Charnley's had remained calm, blunt and Up North.

"Early days," he said, eventually. "By the way, did you know any of Jim's friends? I'm talking *lady* friends, I reckon."

"No. Why?"

From his pocket he took an envelope inside which was a small sheet of blue notepaper.

"This was in his mail this morning, we've just picked it up. Post mark Thame, no address and just about as short and sweet as you can get: *'Jim, ring me. S.'* D'you know an S in his life?"

"I only know a J and that's his wife."

He folded away the note and put it back in his pocket. He turned to Faraday.

"Right, well, we'll need a proper statement from you, guvnor, to put through the mangle. John here'll take that, 'less you fancy coming down to the stables. Boys'd like to meet you, I'm sure." He rose, returning his chair to its position at the table. "There aren't many big names in our trade for the kids to look up to but yours is definitely one. Melanie Pike kidnapping, The Canal Barge Murders, Stephanie Black shooting...?"

Faraday was looking apprehensive again. I was also aware that not many details had been checked, the pretext of his visit.

"...all big stuff, in its day, and fair play to you. But they're history. Not current affairs. Leave this one to us, eh, guvnor?"

"Cocking your leg again?" I said. "You should get that looked at, could be prostate."

Suggest to a man that his dick's in trouble and nine times out of ten he'll turn nasty. Just as Charnley did.

"A little bird by the name of WPC Greene says you flew into her nest, bright and early yesterday morning and started asking questions of two witnesses." He placed his hands firmly on the edge of the table and leaned in. It rocked once, the coffee slopped and he fixed me down the barrel of his crooked nose. "I've met old coppers before, all too anxious to be one man crime squads. They get in the way, so keep your fucking nose out of my business."

I looked at him for a moment. His head was perfectly placed for grabbing, pulling down on the table, nose and teeth first... Perhaps this was a good time to call on the services of The Map.

The Map was a device used by an old bank-robber called Roy Arthur Pullman. He was nine feet tall, four feet wide whichever angle you looked at him from, and cursed with an even shorter fuse than mine. When he felt the need to break someone's head he simply reached for this imaginary Map of the World. He'd go through the whole rigmarole, right in front of you. He'd take The Map from his pocket, unfold it, smooth it out and even don a pair of imaginary specs. Then he'd set down his forefinger at "a more agreeable place" as he called it. In some parallel world, safely away from the damage he might otherwise have done.

Charnley watched me go through the motions, taking The Map from an non-existent inside pocket, unfolding it, flattening it, putting on the glasses. I believe he glanced at Faraday when I finally whispered: "Los Angeles." Then he faded from view as down went the forefinger, pulling me into Jaikie's world, via the brief e-mail I'd received three weeks ago.

"Hi, Dad. Everything great, in case you're worried. How's it with you? Please write. J."

Not a great letter writer, our Jaikie. Always leaving me to read between the lines or, just lately, the gossip columns. He'd landed a plum part in an adaptation of a thirties novel, *All Good Men and True*. I'd got the book from the library. It was an old-fashioned romance, top heavy with tall, good-looking young Englishmen thrilling to the prospect of war with Germany. Wept over by beautiful young women with expensive educations and no desire whatsoever to use them.

An actor, then, our Jaikie. An ac-tor with a deep, dark voice and a beautiful face. I recalled the day we'd agreed he should apply to drama school and forget university. Why the sudden change of heart on our part? Because earlier that evening Jaikie had walked onto the stage in a teenage assault on *The Tempest*. He played Adrian the servant, said hardly a word for two hours yet no one could take their eyes off him. Some people are like that...

I heard the front door slam. Charnley and Faraday had left. Hideki was collecting the coffee cups. I refolded The Map and put it back in my pocket.

The trouble was I knew what Charnley meant about keeping old gits at bay. When I was a DS at Witney this hooded man had us buzzing round like blue-arsed flies for six months. His game was to break into houses, middle of the night, entering snake-like through the smallest of windows. Then he'd rape the female inhabitants at gun point. So far so nasty.

Then along came ex-Detective Chief Inspector Brimmer, recently retired from the Met, claiming to know who this charmer was. His sources had confided in him, he said, he'd put two and two together and got forty-one. A forty-one year old plumber from Blenheim.

When I said I'd look into it, having no intention of doing so, Brimmer complained to my boss that I'd been indifferent. The A.C.C. Crime had me in for a bollocking, saying that Brimmer had forgotten more about police work than I'd ever know. Unfortunately, among the bits he'd forgotten were some basic procedural things that two nights later scooped us a thirty year old farm labourer from Faringdon, Clifford Arkley. He was later charged with a dozen rapes and went down for eternity.

Did the A.C.C. apologise to me? Did Brimmer drop in and do likewise? No. So I knew what Charnley meant and with the courtesy afforded one officer by another I decided to keep out of his way. By and large.

- 4 -

For the next three days, Winchendon swarmed with coppers and the villagers were agog. Nothing this exciting had happened since 1743 when, apparently, Simon Fulbright bludgeoned his wife to death in Hermitage Cottage for having dished up a lousy supper.

Mindful of Charnley's request I tried to keep my mind on other things besides Jim Ryder's murder and thought it might help if I tackled some of the odd jobs I'd been putting off. So, I polyfilla'd the hole at the bottom of the stairs. It had been shedding the fabric of the house for about six months and, with the piles of dust I'd swept up nearly every day, I could surely have built two more cottages. Then I planed the edge of the scullery window so that it closed and, while I was there, I replaced a tap washer. Then I made the mistake of getting ambitious. The kitchen table.

I'd bought it in Chinnor from a bloke I thought I'd probably like because he called his business "Jones, Son & Daughters", not that I'd ever seen a woman in the shop and the son always seemed pissed to me. The table, though, was exactly the right size and for a good two weeks it justified the four hundred quid I'd spent on it. Then the warmth of the kitchen started to buckle it and, in doing so, lifted one of the legs. The table rocked with a mocking double beat which I started to cure with folded paper under the offending leg. It worked for a day until the weight of the table pulverised the said paper and the rock returned. I cut a slither of wood to take its place. The slither worked for a fortnight until the weight of the table split it. I gave up. That was nine months ago.

Then, as I lay in bed - it must have been the Thursday and I was really struggling by then not to think of Jim's murder - a really bad idea came to me. Were I to measure the gap between the lifted leg and the floor and cut that amount off the other three legs my problem would be solved.

I duly measured up, laid the table on its side and went to work with Maggie's dad's tenon saw. With a certain sense of pride, a return to the artisan within me, I set the table back on all fours. The rock on the lifted leg remained. And two others had developed elsewhere. I spent all morning, filing, sanding, sawing, hitting and swearing until the obvious dawned on me. There was nothing wrong with the table. It was the floor! With a terrifying forward glimpse of flagstones being lifted and re-laid, I surrendered. The table could rock.

At that point Hideki appeared and looked round the kitchen, covered in tools, sawdust and broken dreams. He laid a sympathetic hand on the table and pressed.

He asked with a frown: "What is this?"

It's a table, I wanted to say. Shorter than yesterday but still a table.

"What is what?" I asked.

He pressed again, the table rocked in several directions.

"Rock," I said. "Verb. I rock, you rock, he rocks, the bleeding table rocks..."

"In Japan we have thing? You put under leg?"

Everything he said these days had a question mark buried in the tone of it, a request to have his English checked. I usually did so with a brief nod.

"I'll bet you have," I said, nodding.

"And then you turn..." He made a screwing up motion with his fingers. "Table go up, table go down. You have them in England?"

"Who knows?" I said.

"I e-mail my mother, she send."

I looked at him, suddenly realising that the daily routine of Beech Tree Cottage had been shot to hell in more ways than one. He had not gone to Rondon.

"No, no, I stay here to see murderer caught?" he explained.

"Might take a few days."

He shrugged. He was a man with all the time in the world.

"How was murder?" he asked.

"How was the murder *committed*, you mean? A shooting. Bang!"

I fired an imaginary shotgun.

"Why?" he asked.

"Why was he murdered? If we knew that we'd be halfway to catching his killer."

Hideki's eyes twinkled. "*You* are going to catch him?"

And there I was, courtesy of my house guest, back thinking about it.

"Not me, no. Others will do that. I am retired."

Hideki nodded. "Ah, so. You had bad sleep."

I hadn't the stomach for an explanation of tired versus retired. It would end, I knew, in us wrestling the English language to the ground and kicking it to death. Instead I told him to be ready in five minutes, we were going to the pub for lunch. He understood that perfectly.

The Crown was our neighbouring village's yuppie pub, with Y registration BMWs on the car park to prove it. It was fuller than usual this Thursday lunchtime, a fact which the landlady, Annie McKay, put down to the temporary closure of The Plough. A Wag at the bar with gelled hair and a small group of admirers said she ought to shoot people more often if this is what it did for business. His friends laughed appreciatively. I heard one of them say it was Jim's old boss who'd pulled the trigger, getting even for the loss of two million pounds.

For the sake of his English I made Hideki order the food and drinks. Bread isn't popular in Japan but as soon as he realised that we put raw fish into some of our sandwiches he became a big fan.

"Two round of smoke salmon, please," he said. "On brown. And orange juice for me. And for Nathan cheese and tomato on brown. And glass of red wine."

I nodded all the way, making a mental note to explain about the indefinite article fairly soon. Then he felt his pockets for money which he knew he hadn't brought with him. I eased him aside and said I'd call him when his expensive raw fish sandwiches were ready. He bowed slightly and went over to a corner table where two girls he'd become pally with were delighted to see him.

Uncle Elvis was at the other side of the bar, sitting with his mother, both seeming to hang from a cloud of cigarette smoke. The old lady pushed her empty glass across the table and without a word Elvis rose and came over.

"Howdo, Nathan," he said. "You're on the same kick as me and Mother, I expect."

"What kick is that?"

"Pastures new, mate. Stands to reason, with Jim a gonner and Julie a cabbage, where we all going to get rat-arsed?"

"I shouldn't write Julie off too soon," I said.

On the edge of my hearing, the Wag and his fan club had moved on. Jim had now been shot by people he'd met in prison and presumably upset.

Elvis said: "Yeah, well I don't like Tommy anyway. I thought he was temp'ry but with Jim gone she'll have to promote him. Won't please Mother, she don't like that arsey tart he's banging. So all in all The Crown is now my local."

"Looks like you've got a new customer, Annie."

"I'll order the new Mercedes," she said and moved away to get Elvis's drinks.

Elvis drew on a roll-up cigarette almost as thin as the match he'd lit it with and closed one eye as smoke drifted towards it. Or was it a deliberate wink, given that he lowered his voice and confided: "You know, me and Julie, we had this thing going. Don't tell anyone, but with Jimbo being inside she had certain ... needs."

I watched his face for signs of self-mockery but there were none. He must have been a good looking man at one time, though. Still was, underneath the purpling skin. The sweep of white hair lapping at his collar gave him an academic bearing and the dark eyes seemed to peer out at the world on behalf of a scholarly mind. But, in spite of appearances, a thirty second conversation with Elvis was enough to convince you that his marbles had left the building long ago.

The Wag and his friends had moved on again. Suppose it had been one of Jim's customers, getting their own back for food poisoning or over-charging? Stranger things have happened.

"Here, you were a copper," said Elvis. "Where've they all gone, then?"

"Who?"

"The tits on birds like Annie and her at the end there."

He jerked his head at a slim, attractive girl standing at the far end of the counter.

"It's not really a police matter," I said.

"Mother says it's all this circuit training they do, bounces it off 'em. One thing you can say for Julie, she's no gym junkie, eh! Hey up Jack, come to join the deserters?"

Jack Langan had entered and came over to us. He was looking worried, but then again he always looked worried. I gestured to the pumps.

"Pint of Morrells, mate," he said. "You ain't seen my niece, have you?"

"Which one?" I asked.

"Kate."

Elvis said we hadn't.

"Typical," said Jack. "Supposed to meet me here, wants her boiler moving. Christ, it's like doing a bloody square dance with that boiler. Here in the corner first, then back in the fireplace, then dozy-do over to the recess. God knows where she wants it now."

"Back to the corner, I should think, if it's a square dance."

He chuckled and settled on the stool next to Elvis.

"What's all this murdering stuff about then?" he asked, once he'd got comfortable. "I mean you can understand it in London or New York, but Winchendon?"

"I'm trying to keep out of it," I said.

Jack thought that was a waste of resources. "Man of your experience? Jesus! They should rope you in. I saw this documentary the other day..."

Jack had seen a documentary on everything, from Archimedes to Zsa-Zsa Gabor. He had a semi-endearing habit of taking you through them, in fine detail, even if you'd seen them as well. I jumped in quickly.

"I saw that too. All of it. They're taking old coppers back to work on burned out cases."

Annie put Elvis's drinks down on the bar.

"And a pint for Jack," I said, reaching for my wallet.

As I dug for a twenty-pound note and Elvis wrongly assumed that I'd pay for his drinks, so Kate arrived and fancied a large vodka and tonic. All in all it had turned into an expensive five minutes but at least we were spared a re-run of the documentary on ex-coppers.

Kate Whitely was tall, like her younger sister Giselle, with the same fair hair and blue eyes. They both had a naturally tanned skin and exuded the lanky sexiness that was fashionable that summer and no doubt beyond. But unlike Gizzy, who could prattle with the best of us, Kate was more measured in what she said. Maybe marriage had knocked the stuffing out of her. Her ex-husband was a teacher from Manchester, twelve years her senior, who had known her as a child in his classroom. Jack hadn't liked that and I can't say I'd have been overjoyed either. They'd married on her twentieth birthday and five months later were divorced.

She pecked Jack on the cheek and set her bag down on the bar.

"Not working today?" he asked.

"Day off," she said.

"Kate's a designer with Turner's, the wallpaper mob. We've got one of her designs in our front room. Branches with berries on."

"Autumn Sprig," she said right at me, in case I should ever re-decorate.

Elvis glanced away at his mother who mouthed fiercely that he should bring her drink to the table. He shouted back that he'd be right there but stayed to hear Jack and his niece discuss her boiler. Basically she wanted it back in the fireplace. Jack said he'd be round tomorrow. He had a key but would she turn the hot water off overnight.

"And what about Jim and Julie, then?" said Kate.

"We were just saying," said Jack. "This killing people, what's it all about..." His voice tailed off and he stared into the pint of Morrell's, seeking the courage to say: "I suppose you haven't got round to seeing Gizzy?"

"Why would I want to do that?"

The two sisters had had a row a couple of months back. About Tom. They hadn't spoken since, much to Jack's distress, and in spite of his constant efforts to reconcile them.

"You don't think this is different?" he said. "You know, like a reason for letting things drop?"

"She knows where I am if she wants me. How's the brain cell, by the way? Bearing up is he? I guess he will be, given that he stands to inherit The Plough."

I looked at her. "You're kidding."

"So Gizzy reckons. She's seen a draft copy of Julie's will, grabby little bitch."

"Please, don't talk about her like that," said Jack, face all screwed up with anxiety. "She's a good kid. Good worker, smart, knows what she wants."

"She wants The Plough," said Kate, insisting on having the last word.

Saving us all from an awkward silence, Elvis's mother called out from the corner:

"Billy! Leave your copper friend and bring me that drink."

There was threat in the words, reaching back into Elvis's boyhood, if the way he suddenly froze was anything to go by. Then he remembered his age and called back to her, defiantly.

"He's ex-copper, Ma. He's an 'as been not an is now."

The pub went suddenly quiet. Every pair of eyes was on me, my status well and truly declared. Has been. I was monumentally pissed off and turned to Elvis. The flowing white hair was right for grabbing, the head would come down onto the bar with a crack they would hear in the next village. But by some miracle I held off. Elvis hadn't meant it the way it came out. He'd meant the truth, that I had been a copper and wasn't one now.

I took the gin and tonic over to his mother. Since I'd paid for it I felt I had every right to throw it in her face. The Wag stood back and gave a low hoot to warn of impending conflict. The old lady looked up from beneath the brim of a frayed straw hat, piercing blue eyes in a wrinkled face, all freckled and whiskery. Lips concertina'd in defiance, not a hint of fear in her demeanour.

I looked at her for a moment, then said: "Your drink. Sorry you've had to wait for it."

I set it down on the table in front of her. Her mouth relaxed, she drew on her cigarette and waved me away with the back of her hand.

As conversations round the bar were picked up again, so the Wag felt impelled to say: "Losing your touch, then?"

One of the girls giggled. She fell silent, indeed the whole place fell silent yet again, when I asked: "You reckon he's funny?"

She turned away. Others of the entourage fell back too, leaving the Wag isolated. I was searching for The Map. I must have left it in my other jacket.

"She reckons you're funny," I said to him. "I don't reckon you're funny."

His eyes were jumping like beans, his neck and face reddened in pure fear. As I grabbed him by the lapels an unmistakable voice next to me said: "Nathan, we go now."

I looked down to find Hideki's hand on my elbow. I relaxed my grip on the Wag's jacket and Hideki steered me safely from The Crown.

Back at Beech Tree Cottage I tried to put lunchtime at The Crown in the box marked "Forget It" but the lid wouldn't close. It's one thing to know the truth about yourself and keep it hidden but to suddenly realise that others can see through the disguise is to be finally dispossessed. Of image. Respect. Status. It is to join the ranks of the 'as beens not the is nows. Earlier that morning I'd been merely retired, as if I had a choice in the matter. By one o'clock I was on the scrap heap. And now I wanted to stick a fist in my mouth and gnaw it down to the bone.

I decided on a long walk beside the river, maybe to reconsider the McSweeney Spice offer. After all, I hadn't yet turned the job down officially. Perhaps I should write to them now, I thought, accept their offer in principle and post the letter at the end of the walk in Nether Winchendon.

I nipped into the cabin and began typing the letter without internal argument. Best do it quickly, I thought, as I'd done most things as a young man. When I was young I wasn't troubled by alternative thinking: I leaped in and if I started going under I swam all the faster. You do when you're young. Funny word, young. If you say it often enough it loses all meaning, if you take it to bits it becomes unpronounceable, but the world still pays homage to it.

"Dear Mr McSweeney," I began. "Thank you for your kind offer of a position with your company as Head of Security..." I paused in a moment of mature reflection and allowed the wisdom and experience of my years to take over. "You can stuff it. Yours sincerely."

I signed it, addressed the envelope and stamped it with a resounding fist and set off.

Down at the river, Dogge set off in pursuit of a bumble bee and surprised a young couple in the long grass at the first bend. They sat up and the girl tried to pretend that her blouse had come unfastened while she'd been reading her book. The boy was equally shamefaced about his pleasure. He too reached for a book and fumbled his way to a central page, feigning total absorption in its contents. I wanted to go over and tell them I'd been their age myself once but it sounded so patronising in my head and when verbalised would doubtless have been cringe-making for all concerned. I made my own pretence, of being deep in thought about the state of the river and called Dogge absent-mindedly to heel. As we rounded the bend I heard the kids giggle and, no doubt, return to their reading.

Ahead of me on the long stretch I could see two fishermen, perched like garden gnomes ready to answer the call of a daft little bell on the end of their rods. As I got nearer, so Dogge tore off to greet Stefan Merriman with her usual delight and, after he'd given her a chunk of whatever sandwich Bella had made him, she settled. The person sitting with Stefan was Tom Templeman.

Stefan was a man in his late thirties, a disturbing figure to some who knew him, refusing as he did to endorse their preconceptions of cleverness. Back in the spring I'd met a man who'd known him at Cambridge. He told me about their graduation photo, re-distributed at five yearly intervals with labels above the smiling faces telling how each had progressed. Such-a-body was now in the Foreign Office, so-and-so was president of a certain company, the blonde haired girl had become a Member of Parliament. Above Stefan's head was a single word. Unknown. I was able to reveal that he had reached dizzy heights, albeit on a real ladder. He was a window cleaner.

He came towards me, tall and angular in his perpetual denim, a fresh cigarette between his lips.

"Long time no see, Nathan," he said, shielding his match as he lit up.

He gestured to Tom who had raised a hand in greeting.

"Tommy and I thought we'd get some air." He lowered his voice to a whisper and added: "He's doing well, better than I expected. Any news?"

"On the murder? Not that I know of. Nice of you to take him under your wing, Stef."

He smiled, slowly, easily and went to heed a call on his line. It was a false alarm. The breeze had ruffled the water here in this becalmed inlet, the float had dipped, the bell had tinkled. I watched him re-bait the hook, wanting to say that it didn't matter to me that he was stoned, that I'd seen him chuck the spliff he was smoking into the river as I approached. But I couldn't bring myself to say it, not just then, because his action meant that he still thought of me as a copper, someone to be reckoned with.

I sat down on the grass beside Tom who was gazing into the water.

"Anything happening?"

"Fishwise?" he said. He shook his head. Then, as if the gesture had reminded him of his head's existence, he tapped his temple. "Plenty going on up here."

"Such as?"

"Aunt Julie," he said. "She don't seem to improve none, Nathan."

"What do the doctors say?"

"I don't ask. Gizzy does, but they don't tell her much. Stable, they say. That's doctor speak for 'we are as much in the dark as you are'."

Stefan handed me a beer from his coolbox and opened one for Tommy who drank from it, mechanically, for a few moments. Then he turned to look at me again with pale blue eyes, so pale one might almost believe a light behind them had been dimmed.

"I didn't like him much," he said. "Jim, I mean."

"You're not alone."

He smiled, faintly. "You reckon that counts? I can say all this to you Nathan, you're a friend but I can't say it to the cops, that Charnley. In fact I thought he was an arsehole."

"Charnley?"

"No Jim, you daft bugger..." He smiled for a split second. "Charnley too, I expect."

"You can say whatever you like, Tommy. To me, Charnley, anyone. Are there other things you want to say?"

"That's about it. I didn't like him. Now I've got to do his funeral. I've never done that before. How does that work?"

"Well, first, you dig a bloody great hole, then you put 'em in it."

Stefan chuckled and Tom wondered why but he didn't question it. He was used to being left behind.

"Have you made arrangements?" I asked.

"Well, I got this bit of paper from the Coroner's Officer bloke."

He shook his head wearily and his mind drifted away on the tail end of whatever the doctor had given him on Saturday night.

"You want me to see to it? The funeral?"

He drifted back to us. "Kind of you, mate. I know I should be able to, at my age I should be able to do these things. I mean death or no death, says Gizzy, life has to go on."

"No 'should' about it."

He nodded. Stefan and I waited. "I'd like to talk to you sometime, Nathan."

"Yeah? What about?"

"Just ... things." His eyes flicked away to Stefan and back again. "Private stuff. Me and Gizzy stuff. Not the obvious but the *not* obvious... Jesus, this has been a bloody week, ain't it. I've to open the pub next Monday and here I am, sitting here by the river, gassing to you blokes."

He made to stand up, I pushed him down again.

"Finish your day. It'll do you good."

He shrugged. "Never catch anything, do we, Stef?"

Stefan was miles away by then, probably wondering about the private stuff Tom wanted to talk to me about. Just as I was.

My letter to McSweeney Spice having been posted I'd reduced my chances of future employment to two: lecturing at Bramshill and the book. It may have been that narrowing of options which sent me up to the cabin early next morning to make a start on *'The History of the Hamford Crime Squad: a Memoir'*. If I was going to tackle this thing like a pro, people had said, I should get myself into a routine, do things in a certain, ritualistic order. Start by turning the computer on.

As it booted up my mind wandered off in other directions without so much as a by your leave. That's the trouble with writing, there are too many distractions and at the flick of a synapse they become reasons for not getting down to the job. The excuses range from the pencil not being sharp enough (not that I use one) through to the deeper, darker problems involving inspiration. Or lack of it.

A beep took me back to the screen and I wondered if the title was absolutely right. Wouldn't *'A* History' be better, less dogmatic than *'The* History?' The latter had an official ring to it, a hint of government approval whereas *'A History'* would be more my own point of view.

I checked my e-mail while I thought about it. There were three. One from the on-line gas company, another from the bank and the third from Con, who was still in New Zealand.

"Dad, hi! E-mailing rather than phoning because it's two in the morning where you are and well, guess you might be asleep. Or something..."

Or something? What did he mean, for God's sake? That I might be up to something nocturnal - burglary perhaps, grave robbing, a passionate foray with a new love? Or was the "or something" merely verbal punctuation? And was there nervous-ness there, almost certainly heralding a request? For money.

"...anyway, having a great time and as much as I could stay here longer well, you know, promised Fee that we'd go and see her next month..."

There it was. He needed the onward fare to Japan.

"...only the old finances. Ouch! Know what I mean?"

Well, yes, mate, I do know. I also know that the classics degree from Cambridge had a purpose. When you finally got into the big world you'd be able to earn a good living doing something really, really interesting. Remember?

"Started the book yet?"

I smiled and wrote a return e-mail.

"Yes I have. How much?"

Was that a kind of admission, as good as saying 'no I haven't written a word but here's the money to keep you quiet'?

I needed a diversion, not too far removed from the police work of my past life but enough to steer my thoughts towards what was essentially an autobiography. Maybe if I wrote my thoughts on Jim's murder down, I could put it out of my mind and really get down to *'A History of the Hamford Crime Squad: a Memoir'*?

Jim and Julie had been shot, they'd been lured out of the car by two people, each with a shotgun. The two strangers in the pub earlier, maybe? Were they operating off their own backs or on behalf of someone else? Gizzy and Tom stood to inherit The Plough, according to Kate. Tom wanted to talk to me about private stuff. Would he soon be telling me that he and Gizzy had hired two professional hit men to...?

"Jesus Christ!" I said out loud, rising from the desk. The harder I try to leave this murder alone the more it keeps tapping me on the shoulder. The noisy heartbeat was there again, drumming away in my ears. There was even a sprouting of sweat, just below where my hair line used to be. I sat down again, unclenching fists, teeth, stomach, toes, shoulders. I took a few deep breaths.

'A History...' mocked me from the screen, blank and white, a vicious little box asking if I'd like to save the non-existent document. 'Yes', I answered, with a jab at the keyboard. It taunted me further. What did I want to save it *as*? I turned and picked up the old flat iron I used as a doorstop, weighed it in my hand like a knuckle-duster and just as I was about to narrow my options even further by punching the computer's lights out, an unexpected visitor came to my rescue.

The knock on the window was from a hand used to getting its own way. It belonged to Petra Wyeth, disguised as a Zulu Queen, in traditional African wrap whose theme was large vegetables, turban and all. The latter was to hide the lank, greasy hair I'd noticed at Angie's last weekend, the frizz at the end betraying an ancient perm.

"Come in, Petty," I said.

She may have got a double first at Somerville but the catch on the cabin door stumped her.

"Lift it," I said.

She lifted it and entered.

"Nathan, wasn't that a super..." She broke off, startled by the surroundings. "Good God, you don't *work* in here, do you?"

"I try to."

"It's like being a woodworm. You're surrounded by timber - ceiling, floors, walls."

"I like it," I said. "You were saying?"

"Yes, super evening up at Angie Mitchell's, don't you think? I agreed that it was.

"And the new doctor. Charming, I thought."

She wanted a response to that but didn't get one.

"Anyway," she went on, "how are the kids?"

There hadn't been much talk of offspring up at Angie's the other night, Laura Peterson and the Mitchells not having any, so I filled her in at length and she gave a pretty good impression of someone listening, even caring. When I'd finished I asked how Daisy and Digby were. There'd been even less mention of them on Friday. Diggers and Daze were fine, she assured me, but in truth she didn't know what they were up to, barring essentials. Daisy worked in advertising and Digby was a ski instructor in St. Moritz.

"They won't be joining you at ... *Eruditio*, then?" I said.

"No, they're not academically inclined, that's the polite way of putting it. All the same, poor old Al and his pals could do with some cranial input right now. Negotiations are at a delicate stage. Wealthy benefactors and institutions are being relieved of their money as we speak."

"And then?"

"Then we start, buying up, re-furbishing, kitting out those big country houses people can't afford to live in anymore! Turning them into proper schools, Nathan, where kids will get a real education, from qualified teachers, not these oiks who leave university unable to spell their own name. And all will be done in an atmosphere of dedication, discernment and dis-cipline."

"I feel as if I've just read the brochure."

"Oh, there's a lot more to it than a few slogans, I can assure you, and market research proves that Mr and Mrs Jones will pay good money to have the little Joneses properly taught."

"And you and Allan will be there to collect?"

"Not as much as you think. Some people still put ideals ahead of material gain. I'm sure you're one of them."

The lesson over, she turned to the main purpose of her visit. She leaned forward on the wicker chair, knees together, hands resting nervously on a cabbage and a head of broccoli respectively.

"Nathan, this murder," she began. "The police have been to see us."

"Nothing unusual about that."

"Yes, but they wanted to know if we'd seen anything on The Ridge Road. Seen what, for Heaven's sake? These people who shot poor Jim and Julie, perchance, strolling along, rifles over their shoulders? Did we stop and take photos of them, maybe?"

"Did you?"

"No!"

"Then there's an end of it," I said. "Coffee?"

She looked at her watch.

"Thanks, no, I'm off to give Sharon Falconer a shoulder to cry on." That'll be either on the turnip or the tomatoes, I thought, depending on which shoulder Sharon chooses. "You heard Martin had left her, I suppose?"

"No, I didn't."

"Been on the cards for years, of course, but he's shillied and shallied. Men can be such thorough going cunts, don't you agree? Well, no, I suppose you'd feel obliged to argue the point. Hardly the language of a teacher, I know, so do forgive my Anglo-Saxon and, more so, the use of a female body part as an expletive, but sometimes it's the only word that'll do." She paused to draw breath. "Detective Chief Inspector Charnley, his name was."

"Speaking of Anglo-Saxon, you mean?"

"I'm sure he didn't believe us. He asked if he could see the car and was most put out when I told him it was in for repair."

"The exhaust?" I asked.

"The dreadful noise coming out of the back. Do you think you could have a word with him? Better still his superiors. You must have left Angie's just after us, you can vouch for us not speaking to any murderers on The Ridge Road. I'd be so grateful."

Grateful or not, she clearly believed that her wish would be my command. She turned, fought briefly with the door and hurried off to enjoy the tragedy of Martin Falconer ditching his awful wife.

It was habit again. The need to check her story, prompted by the fact that she clearly had something to hide or why else had she come to see me? There were thirty-four car body shops in Aylesbury, according to Yellow Pages and I started to ring them in the name of Allan Wyeth, asking when my wife's Volkswagen would be ready. Nine of them, not surprisingly, told me that I must have the wrong garage. The tenth said it was a bigger job than they'd first realised. The front panel was badly buckled, the fender twisted. My missus must've given it a real hammering the other night. I thanked the voice and put the phone down.

So, the African Queen and erudite Al had had a prang last Friday, up on The Ridge Road. Why had Petra just played it down? With the implications of that troubling me I could hardly have been expected to go back to the book. I just wouldn't have been able to give it my best.

- 5 -

I was still puzzling over the lie Petra Wyeth had told me when I took Hideki to the station for the 11.10.

"Have a good day," I said to him, as we pulled onto the forecourt.

He gave his usual response. "I will have *great* day."

He was going to Abbey Road, with the sole purpose of having a photo of himself taken on The Zebra Crossing made famous by The Fab Four. In Asahikawa he would be king.

"You will catch murderer?" he asked.

I laughed. "No, no, as I told you the other day, someone else will do that. Mr Charnley."

As he got out of the car he was smiling. Had we been earlier I would have called him back and asked him why. Instead I put it down to oriental inscrutability.

I arrived home to find John Faraday seated on the garden bench, smoking a cigarette. He rose to greet me and appeared to have grown taller since our last meeting. No doubt because he wasn't with Charnley who had a knack of reducing those around him in order to give himself stature. He stretched out his hand.

"Sergeant Faraday, guvnor."

"Yes. I remember," I said. "You want a beer or something?"

"Be nice, thanks."

We went into the house where Faraday folded his jacket over the back of a chair with feminine precision. He picked a couple of seeds off the sleeve and sprinkled them into the ashtray. He wasn't just taller, he was more himself in other ways: easy, vulnerable, likeable.

"This your mob, then, guvnor?" he asked, referring to the photo of my kids, pinned to the cork notice-board.

"Mob's about right."

"Good looking bunch. I mean in big families you get the odd one or two but rarely the whole gang."

He knew the right things to say.

"You married, Sergeant?"

"Nah! My sister's got a couple of kids, though. I kind of stand in for their old man since he upped and left her."

I took a couple of cans from the fridge and slid one along the table towards him.

"What can I do for you? Statement?"

"No, no, that can wait, if it's okay with you."

His face shifted into an anxious frown as, from a set of rehearsed possibilities, he chose the best way to say what he wanted to.

"The other day..." he began and stalled.

"When you were here with Charnley?"

"Yeah, he shouldn't have said what he did. To you or to the boy. It was well out of order."

"I agree but he does have a point. We often get in the way. Old coppers."

He was still frowning as he pushed in the tab on his beer and sipped the foam.

"What's really on your mind?" I asked.

The frown broke away and his face relaxed into a grin.

"Jesus Christ, old coppers, eh! You can't get anything past 'em."

He went over to the window to gather his thoughts. Eventually he turned and said: "I'm not saying he isn't a good copper. He is, that's why I'm still working for him after two years, but I think he's got this one all wrong. He's up at Grendon Prison every day, slogging through records, interviewing staff and prisoners alike to see who didn't like Jim and, meanwhile, time's passing."

"What's that got to do with me?"

"Well, nothing, but like you said I reckon the answer's closer to home. Those two blokes in The Plough they weren't in prison with him, surely. I mean would they walk into his pub and risk him seeing them?"

"I've got a variation on that," I said. "Why risk *anyone* seeing them? Identifying them later?" He looked at me for an answer. "One, they're stupid. Two, they knew they'd be a long way off by now. Another country."

Faraday slid sideways onto one of the chairs at the table and looked up at me.

"So what are you saying? Charnley's right, wrong, what?"

"Charnley's looking for shortcuts, budget driven, wants to impress the guvnor with a quick solution. The answer isn't at Grendon, though, I'll bet money on it."

"So, where is it?" he asked, eagerly.

I paused. The growing look of satisfaction on his face was that of a man halfway to reaching some target. I wondered if he'd been sent here by Charnley to pick my brains and I was allowing him to do just that.

"I don't know," I said.

Reading his easy features again, I could see he was disappointed.

"Oh, come on, guvnor, you must've given it some thought, old pro like you."

"I was told to keep my nose out," I reminded him. "That's what I've done."

He nodded. "Yeah, well ... pity. You know there was a documentary on last week, how the Met are taking old coppers back to work on burned out cases..."

"I saw it."

"What did you think?"

"I think it would've been smarter not to retire us in the first place. By the way, did you ever find out who S was?"

He flicked his head as if clearing it to cope with my question. I still had to explain it to him.

"The note to Jim in his post, blue paper, the Monday after he died."

"Oh, that. No. Mind you, given that she wanted him to ring her we don't think she killed him first."

"It's definitely a woman, then?"

Faraday shrugged. "The handwriting geezer says it is."

He picked a few more seeds from the bottom of his trousers and rose to leave, taking his beer with him. At the door he turned with a cock-eyed smile:

"So, the boss telling you to mind your own business hasn't done the trick. Hasn't put you off."

Maybe that's why he'd been sent. To check that I didn't have my nose in their business, in spite of the warning.

"I'm a casual observer," I said. "Nothing more."

He tried to make that seem like a shame but the shrug was too contrived.

"Well, if you casually observe any other bits and pieces, let me know, will you. I mean, Charnley reckons by the middle of next week we'll be looking at a double murder. Julie's going to cark it, he reckons."

"Where's he get that from? Doctors?"

"Nah, but it's the one thing we agree on. Cirencester, where I was before, there was this farmer, shot himself by accident. It wasn't the blast that killed him, it was digging the shot out afterwards followed by a nifty bout of M.R.S.A."

From the kitchen window I watched him walk to his car, parked on the verge in Morton Lane. As he drove away I turned to the ashtray and picked out one of the seeds he'd dropped into it. Sticky, the size of lead shot, ironically. I was forever picking them out of Dogge's coat at this time of year. Bindweed. It only grew in one part of my garden. Behind the cabin. It was a small detail but a telling one. John Faraday had been up there, on instructions from Charnley, I imagine. He'd tried the door then gone out of his way, round the back to look through the window. To get a glimpse into my privacy. I was glad I'd locked up before taking Hideki to the station.

The phone rang. I didn't recognise the voice at the other end to begin with.

"You were rude to me," she said.

"Who's this?"

"You mean you're rude to lots of people? I suppose that should be a comfort."

"Laura? How was I rude to you?"

"You were hyper-critical of my driving."

"So I was."

I could sense her smiling.

"If you were to buy me a drink at, say, The Harrow, I'd be prepared to forgive and forget. Shall we say half an hour?"

She'd chosen The Harrow at Long Crendon for three reasons, she told me. First, she could cycle there in comparative safety. And get there a damn sight quicker than by car. Second, with it being a Victorian pub its high ceilings meant she wouldn't have to stoop beneath Elizabethan beams, cherished features of most local pubs. Third, you can get a nasty burn under the Winchendon microscope and in Long Crendon she wasn't known to anyone.

Maggie had been beautiful. That isn't just my opinion, everyone said it. No one will have said it about Laura Peterson. When we'd met at Angie Mitchell's the other night I'd realised that she was a triumph of style over content. Elegant clothes veiled wide hips and broad shoulders, subtle make-up softened the more prominent features of her face. Then I'd got drunk and thought no more about it. Here, in the sober light of a Friday afternoon, in the bay window at The Harrow, the disguise wasn't quite so polished nor the lighting half so kind. The jeans had a deceptive cut to them, the angora sweater reached to her thighs hoping to diminish all beneath it but neither garment could work magic. Under a colourful bandana lay short-cut brown curls, highlighted at the ends, falling with unruly care over a prominent forehead and hugging the back of a boomerang jaw.

There were plus points, however. First among them were the dark, dark eyes, not riveted to mine in some phoney display of self-confidence or trustworthiness, but scanning my face constantly, for signs of humbug and wrinkles, no doubt. Those eyes belonged in a more beautiful face. Then there was the voice. Her appearance prepared you for the boom of a dowager aunt yet out came the husky strains of seduction. Being asked where it hurt by Doctor Peterson must have sounded like an invitation to sleep with her. The voice, like the eyes, belonged in a different being.

"You've bought a bottle," she said when I returned from the bar. "I only wanted a glass."

I poured her some of the Fitou. "We can always finish it later."

I could see her wondering if my getting canned at Angie's had been the exception or the rule.

She said: "You know we were being set up the other night, don't you? Angie Mitchell's the local matchmaker. I've told her time and again not to bother on my account but she still pegs away."

"Are you widowed, divorced?" I asked.

"Just never got round to marriage. I have had a couple of offers, not especially good ones. A surgeon twice my age - I was twenty-six at the time - and a barrister who knocked me off my bike with his Jag. He didn't propose as I lay there in the gutter, of course, he waited till his fourth divorce came through and to this day can't understand my reluctance to jump at the chance of him. Now, at forty, everyone thinks I'm a dyke which is annoying but people are slaves to popular myth." She paused. "Okay, forty-three. You?"

"Age? Fifty. Well, okay, fifty-two."

I went on to explain that I was a widower, that Maggie had died two years three months and seven days ago from a stroke. Laura tutted. Like me, but from a professional angle I guess, she deplored the waste. She waited to see if I had more to say about Maggie. Rather than go on about her like some jilted teenager I topped up my glass and brought us back to Jim Ryder's murder.

"Let me ask you a question," I said. "Would you kill two people for twenty thousand pounds, especially if you had to divvy it up?"

"You'll be pleased to know that I haven't given the matter a great deal of thought. Even though I have the means to kill people at my disposal and plenty of patients I wouldn't miss. Why do you ask?"

"Well, say you're the proud owner of a shotgun. If it's money you want why not rob a post office or a building society, come away with five times as much? What I mean is, I think there's more at stake here than what Julie had in her handbag. I think this is about the two million quid which Jim relieved his boss of and hasn't been seen since..."

She interrupted. "Julie says Jim didn't steal that money."

"I refer you to the time-honoured response of Mandy Rice-Davies – 'she would, wouldn't she?'."

"You and Mandy don't believe anyone, then, on principle?"

"Whether Jim stole that money or not, and I think he did, he was an arrogant bastard. Thought he could handle his own defence. He came up against Georgina Hales, Q.C. and made the mistake of trying to charm her. She had him for breakfast."

For some reason that bothered Laura. "Didn't Julie try to persuade him? To get real help?"

"I don't know and right now it's pretty academic. These two boys up on The Ridge, I'm guessing they were hired help to make it look like a robbery that turned nasty. And they were paid, or at least promised, a damn sight more than twenty grand for their trouble."

She nodded and offered me her glass to refill. "By whom?"

"By someone who was expecting a big pay day."

"And you haven't told the police?" she said.

I shook my head. "They told me to keep my fucking nose out of their business."

We carried on talking for another hour or so, a rambling sort of chat mostly but I know my kids came into it somewhere. How clever they were, how individual, and how proud I was of them. Then, true to form, I apologised for banging on about my family in the hope that Laura would say that it didn't matter and I should tell her more. She did and I did.

At one point, when I must've been winding down, she said:

"So, they're all true citizens of the world, Japan, Los Angeles, Paris, New Zealand."

"That's another way of saying they've all left home, all skipped the country. I took it personally to begin with but then I asked myself what would I do, time over again?"

"And?"

"I'd go. I don't know where, but I'd go."

It turned out that Laura would have gone as well, indeed it was still on the cards that she might. She'd studied medicine with all the usual hopes of making a difference and found herself washed up in Winchendon, attending the side-effects of human indolence and excess, not the problems of need. Africa, she thought. She might be of some use there. It was all to do with being of use.

It broke the conversation. I'd only known her a few days, liked her for only a few hours but the thought of her disappearing to the other side of the world brought me down. Perhaps it was a series of sudden flashbacks that got to me: those last few days with Maggie or the following year saying goodbye to my kids, all of them within the space of a month. Keep in touch, e-mail very soon, phone if you need me. None of it – goodwill, strength, promises – makes up for being left behind.

We put Laura's bike into the Land Rover and drove back to Beech Tree Cottage to finish the bottle. As we turned into Morton Lane I could see Jack Langan loading tools into the back of his pickup. He was a physical man, Jack, with strains of Irish and Welsh running through him in equal measures, madness and pit pony his wife used to say. Reddish hair, not an especially tall man but strong and fit and, at this precise moment, only a fool would've picked a fight with him. Uncharacteristically he was fuming, clattering the ladder down among planks and poles in the truck, slamming shut the tail gate. Maybe he'd finally had a bellyful of indulging his niece, Kate Whitely, in the matter of her boiler.

When he saw the Land Rover coming he stood to one side and raised a hand for me to slow down. He motioned that I should wind down my window.

"Nathan, need a word, mate..." He noticed my passenger and his manner softened. "Sorry, Doc, didn't see you there."

"Hallo, Mr Langan," she said. "How are you? How's Jean?"

"No, no," he said, as if a denial were called for, "we're both fine. Nathan, give us a call will you. Your convenience. Only make it this evening."

"You look fit to kill a rhino, man, bare hands. Why not follow us down, get it off your chest, help us drink the rest of this."

"No, don't want to intrude. It'll keep. But only till this evening, mind."

He raised a hand and turned away, in case I tried again to persuade him to join us. As I drove down to Beech Tree Cottage I glanced in the rear view mirror, saw him get into his truck and drive away too fast for such a narrow lane.

Laura and I took the wine and some coffee into the garden and for another hour sat chatting beneath the silver birches. As the branches dipped in the breeze and the sunlight fluttered across her face, I caught glimpses of a beauty I hadn't noticed earlier. Not fashionable beauty but a more interesting, still waters kind.

Jack Langan came up in conversation again. She knew his wife as a patient and liked her. She asked what I liked about him.

"What makes you think I *do* like him?"

"Your body language, when you spoke to him."

"He was here first," I said. "In this village, I mean. Born in that cottage over there. Will Waterman's. Yet these ponced up marketing consultants we're overrun with, they treat him like a bloody foreigner."

She smiled. "So you treat him as a friend?"

"Not just to buck the trend, no, but because when I tap him he rings true. Men like that should be on every quango, every magistrates' bench, every board of school governors in the land, speaking their good sense. But those jobs get snapped up by village Englanders looking for a hobby. Nobody wants to hear what the likes of Jack Langan have to say..." I stopped. "I'm sorry, I just went off on one. You must stop me. If I do it in the future, you must shoot me down."

She nodded and reached down to stroke Dogge.

"I keep thinking about getting a dog," she said. "You know, for company, letting me know when people are about. Where did you get her?"

"She's a Drugs Squad reject. They were kicking her out so we rescued her. She's been rescuing me ever since."

She smiled and drank the last of the coffee.

At four o'clock, before she left for the evening surgery, she reminded me that I'd promised to phone Jack that evening. I told her it was uppermost in my mind.

As I watched her pedal off down Morton Lane, the word powerful, as a description of her physique, became replaced in my mind with its slightly less derogatory cousin, sturdy.

I was in bed asleep. Dreaming. I was back in the alley behind my father's fish and chip shop in Whetstone, North London, the smell of it overpowering me. Fish heads, old batter, peelings, all rotting quietly in greasy dustbins. But it wasn't the setting that bothered me, it was the people inside waiting to be served. Laura Peterson was one of them, deep in conversation with my mother. Just as I tuned in to what they were talking about, Hideki said: "Nathan, there is phone call."

"What time is it?"

"Three o'clock."

In an instant I was out of bed, hauling on my dressing gown, heading for the door. It could only be one of the kids. Some foreign copper at the end of the line would go through the motions of sympathy...

"Is Mr Langan," said Hideki.

I stopped and my heart came back down out of my gullet.

"What the hell does he want?"

It was a question better directed at Jack, once I reached the kitchen phone.

"Jack, what the hell do you want?"

At the other end of the line was a drunken Jack Langan, apologetic in the extreme, slow beyond belief.

"I'm sorry, mate," he began. "I mean I really am. Three in the morning, you can imagine it must be something pretty big for me to phone you..."

"It's me who should be apologising," I said, softening, remembering the times he'd come to my rescue in the past year over blocked drains and leaking pipes. "I said I'd phone you. I forgot."

I beckoned Hideki to bring me a chair. Not only had it all the signs of being a long haul, the threat of a recently televised documentary was ever present.

"What's on your mind, Jack?"

"You know I moved Kate's boiler? From the corner back to the fireplace. Christ, the number of times I've..."

"Jack!"

"Well, it's not just a simple matter of moving it. The flue-pipe has to be re-connected. Being crafty..." He chuckled in appreciation of his own guile. "Being crafty, I left the old flue pipe up in her loft first time I moved it, just in case she changed her mind. So up I go into the loft, start working and over in the corner, I see this box. Long and narrow, mahogany, brass fittings, and I think "What's that?" I go over. On the front is a brass wotsit, what do they call 'em...?"

"Plate?"

"Plate. With initials on it, J.A.M. Jam tomorrow, jam yesterday but never jam today, I'm thinking." He chuckled again, no doubt at his devastating irony. "So I open it and inside ... inside there are two ... well, have a guess."

"No."

"Shotguns."

I was suddenly awake. "What?"

"Purdeys, mate, all silver chasing and polished up a real treat. And they've been used recently, according to the smell."

"Where are they now?"

"Still up there."

"What does Kate say?"

"I haven't spoken to her. I mean that's where it gets difficult. How would I put it to her? Here's a shooting last Friday night, here's two shotguns on your loft a week later?"

"Have you told the police?" I asked.

"No, should I?"

"Not yet. Listen, Jack, I want to see these guns. What time does Kate leave for work?"

"Half seven."

"Meet me here, quarter to eight. Meantime, cork on the bottle, get some sleep."

"Right, mate," he said. "I feel a lot better for talking to you. Weight off my mind, know what I mean?"

"You did the right thing, Jack. I'll see you tomorrow."

- 6 -

I was woken at six o'clock on Saturday morning by an internal alarm clock which had always known my schedule better than I had. It used to go off usually as dawn broke, to remind me that Maggie had died. It somehow knew that each night I'd close my eyes and forget that she was no longer with me. It didn't need to do that anymore so I lay there in sleep-wake limbo for ten or twelve seconds, waiting to be told of the early call's purpose. Gradually a pair of shotguns drifted into my mind.

I ran through the gist of my night-time conversation with Jack. He'd found shotguns up on Kate's loft. They'd been recently fired. Jam today. What the hell had Kate got to do with Jim Ryder's murder, I asked myself on the way to the bathroom? What would she gain from having him killed? Did she have some grudge against Jim that had yet to be revealed? As for this wretched draft will that Gizzy had seen, according to her sister, surely the hope that The Plough would pass down to Tom was too obvious a motive even for someone as soppy as him.

Speculation, of a fairly low order, then, and I only had Jack's three in the morning, pissed as a rat word to go on but it had given me ... expectations. I put a finger to the vein in my neck in case I needed to curb them. I couldn't tell what speed my pulse was doing but at least it was doing it quietly. And all would be revealed shortly after seven forty-five when Jack was due to pick me up.

I twitched the kitchen curtain and looked across the green to the tree cottages, their facade darkened by a murky sunrise behind them. Stefan and Bella were up. With the aid of bin-oculars I could see Bella at the kitchen table, sipping her coffee over a magazine. Next door I saw Kate pass from the main room to the kitchen where she switched on a light. She leaned to where she kept the bread. Toast for breakfast. A working day for Kate, then, even though it was Saturday. No slackers in the wallpaper business. She'd be gone by half seven.

And so she was. A little earlier than half seven, in fact, which nearly caught me on the hop. I watched her slam shut the boot of her car and walk round to the driver's door. One thing jarred. She wasn't dressed up today, in the long summer frock, close fitting, floral in design with high heels and a businessy jacket. That was her usual style. Today it was jeans and a T-shirt.

I turned and boiled a couple of eggs, toasted a squad of soldiers.

At seven forty-five, and still eating, I started pacing the kitchen. I was early everywhere and expected others to be. If Jack bowled up now he would merely be on time and find me glancing reproachfully at my watch. By eight o'clock he still hadn't arrived. By eight fifteen I was beginning to wonder if I'd dreamed the whole night-time conversation. The answer to that would've been to wake Hideki but there would have been language problems involving verb declensions we hadn't covered yet.

I phoned Jack's cottage and got his wife, Jean, just as she was about to leave for work.

"He's not with you, I take it," she said. "He asked me to say he was called to the yard dead early, someone delivering granite setts."

"But he must still have been pissed?" I said.

"He said he'd be back soon as possible."

"Well, yes. What's dead early, Jeannie?"

"Six o'clock."

"Six? Don't people sleep anymore?"

"That's what I said, or similar." She was anxious to leave. "Anyway..."

"Sorry, Jean. Off you go. He'll turn up, I'm sure."

But by nine o'clock Jack still hadn't shown. I phoned his yard, near Ludgershall. It was engaged. I tried again ten minutes later, then started to worry. I decided to go in search of him.

As I turned out of Morton Lane in the Land Rover, a car coming up from my left flashed me. Sure, I'd sprung out into its path pretty sharply but neither of us was going that fast. As I pulled away it flashed me again, longer pulses this time. I stopped. If there was going to be a punch-up it would have to be a quick one.

The other driver was Sharon Falconer and she was out of her car by now, sailing towards me. I wound down the window.

"Nathan, good morning. I understand you're at a bit of a loose end, professionally."

"They call it retirement," I explained.

"Well, I'm sure Petra told you that my bastard of a husband has left me." She waited for a reaction but didn't get one. "Oh, don't go all strong and silent on me, Nathan. The whole *world* knows. I want him found. I'd be willing to pay, of course."

I smiled at her. "More than he'd be willing to pay to stay lost?"

She looked at me and tried to smile back. She must once have been a beautiful woman with that long, chestnut hair, greying now but not overly so, and a tilt of the head that would surely have held any man's gaze. But as age had set in, so the skin on her face had shrunk back leaving only the eyes, it seemed, in their original place. It made her seem forever affronted by the rest of us which must have served her well on the bench.

"Well?" she snapped, as if talking to a shoplifter, hauled up before her. "What have you got to say?"

"I've an unrelated question. Those two lads in The Plough, the night Jim and Julie were shot. What did they look like?"

"Scruffy."

"That's the J.P. in you, summing up. I asked you what they looked like."

"Can't say I really noticed. Just an impression as I passed by. Of scruffiness. Curly hair, one of them."

"The other?"

"Well, I didn't actually stop and take details. Other things on my mind."

I nodded. "Pity. As to finding Martin, I'll give it some thought."

We both knew I didn't mean that. She smiled and went back to her car. I drove out of Winchendon and took the road to Ludgershall.

Jack's yard was tucked away in a woodland of spindly trees, fronted by chain link gates and a security firm's decidedly unthreatening plate. I knew why Jack had chosen the place to run his business from. It was as quiet as the grave and just far enough away from home to make him unreachable except in an emergency. His nearest neighbour was a charcoal burner called Steggles about half a mile down the lane, a man who had opted for obscurity and, come the rise of the barbecue generation, had found himself making a comfortable living.

The gates to the yard were open. I turned in and pulled up alongside the train carriage Jack used as an office. Great Western, third class, Jack said. It would've been worth a fortune, a passing railway buff had told him, if Jack hadn't ripped its guts out in order to use it.

The buildings beyond were closed. Jack kept such machinery as he possessed there. In the larger, modern one, a small digger, a Kangol hammer, a stone cutter. In the other, older building, once a forge, he'd installed a second hand saw, driven by a belt from an ancient generator. Stacked in the rafters he kept half a dozen pine tree trunks, seasoning in readiness for next year. Cut pine, a smell you couldn't beat, he said.

I got out of the Land Rover and looked round, immediately aware of the silence. I don't mean the peace and quiet Jack had paid good money for but the utter stillness which overhangs a tragedy, like the holding of breath before a gasp of horror. Here, in a builder's yard there should have been recognisable sounds: saws whining over local radio shows, vehicles coming and going, phones ringing. More to the point there should have been a pile of granite setts, delivered by the early morning caller. It was nowhere to be seen. I knocked on the carriage door.

"Jack?! Jack, you about?"

I tapped on one of the windows. Still no answer. I opened the door and peered into the gloom. No sign of life but the curtains had been opened and Jack was meticulous. Every evening, at dusk, he drew the curtains, every morning he opened them as soon as he arrived. I stepped inside and called out again:

"Jack? Jack? It's Nathan."

I glanced round at the homely mess of the place. Nowhere to hide, or fall and be missed. There was a diary on the table, open at today's date. In Jack's scrawl were the words "Richardsons, Corby. Deliver. Setts." The phone was off the hook.

I went back out into the yard and walked across to the forge, inventing workaday excuses to explain it all. Maybe Jack had walked into Ludgershall for some milk or cigarettes or something. Did he smoke? Yes, and he drank more coffee than was good for him...

I pulled back the huge door to the forge and entered, pulling at the light switch.

"Jack? Jack are you...?"

I stopped dead. Before me was Jack Langan sprawled across the big, steel saw bench, motionless, face down in a giant's daubing of his own blood. It had sprayed and spattered everywhere - floors, ceiling, walls - as the blade had sliced through his upper body. Flies were already gathered for the feast. I looked at Jack's face. It had been untouched by the blade and in the way of these things, it had a peaceful look to it. Asleep, though unwakable. I made a mental note to tell his wife that, in the absurd belief that it would make a ha'porth of difference.

What was the safety guard doing off? I wondered. Why was it on the floor, with the old drive belt? That was the key to it, he'd been replacing the belt, tested it, slipped and fallen on the revolving blade. And in a split second had become one with it, flesh and metal welded into some grotesque sculpture.

For some reason I called out again, albeit in a near whisper: "Jack? Jack?"

Again the special silence. Even the birds he used to curse for nesting in his rafters were paying their respects.

I retreated to the doorway and looked round, trying to make sense of what had happened. Within ten seconds the whole thing was my fault. I hadn't kept my promise to phone him last night. That gave him time to get well and truly pissed so that when he got here this morning he was in no shape to mess with bench saws.

And then, as I switched off the light, I was forced to accept the truth of the matter. Jack's death hadn't been an accident. Someone had killed him.

I closed the door on the forge, went to the Land Rover and phoned the incident room at Penman Manor stables.

"Hallo, guvnor," said an upbeat John Faraday. "How's it going?"

"John, your boss wanted a double murder," I said. "He's got one. Only not Julie Ryder but Jack Langan."

"Who?"

"Fucking hell! Surely you know him as a witness. He was in the pub the night the Ryders were shot."

There was a pause.

"We'll be down there in five," he said. I could hear him scrabbling round for a pencil and paper. "Give me the address."

I should have waited for the police to show up at Jack's yard and I knew there'd be repercussions for not having done so. I drove back to Winchendon all the same.

Getting into Kate's loft was no problem. Will Waterman had dropped his key through the letterbox before leaving for Devon. I could go up into the loft via his ceiling trap and walk the length of the connected attics. But before hacking around up there I wanted to be sure that I had the place to myself. Kate was away designing wallpaper, I'd seen her leave and, to my relief, Stefan and Bella were out too. The supermarket run, no doubt.

I let myself into the Watermans' cottage and was freshly amazed by its aspirations to be a stately home. A leather sofa that would seat forty people was matched by a coffee table you could land a B52 on. In the scullery were showers for the goats and, for all I knew, saunas and massage parlours too. Flickering under the stairs was the CCTV command post, the monitor alert to any sign of life that came within fifty yards of Will and Prissy Waterman's castle.

I went up onto the small landing and, standing on a chair, pushed at the trap door. It hinged backwards and I straightened up, head and shoulders going into the loft. I pulled myself up into the roof space, up into the rib cage of this three hundred year old creature.

Jack would have loved it, that was my first thought. He would have seen a documentary on how places like this were built, how elm and oak were taken from Penman Wood, brought here by horse and cart to be cut by craftsmen old before their time; how carts of wheat straw would follow and thatchers teach youngsters urgently, lest they depart this world before handing down their skill. Why did that scenario, three hundred years ago, ring with such good order? Why did the men within it seem so contented with their lot? What had happened between then and now to turn all that around? The documentary never covered that.

Batting aside the drapery of cobwebs, I stooped my way across the beams, past packing cases and cardboard boxes set out on islands of hardboard, to Kate's end. There I swept the torch beam past Christmas decorations, an old computer, worn out rugs, and the odd piece of furniture. No box, no jam today. No guns. In truth, I hadn't expected to find any. I thought it wise, though, to go down and check Kate's rooms.

I found the trap door, a similar one to Will Waterman's, a simple flap hinging upwards to rest against a cross beam. It was bolted on the landing side. There was no way I could gain access.

Down in the Watermans' main room my eye was caught by movement on the CCTV. A cat, a great fat tom who lived at Stefan and Bella's, was strolling down the path, unaware that he was being spied on. For some reason his indifference made me smile and, sooner or later, I thought, we'd all be on someone's CCTV given the current market in fear and the assumed malice of strangers. However, when we ventured out, would we behave as this cat was doing, unashamed of a certain truth revealed in our gait, our expression? Or, in time, would we all put on a performance every time we went to post a letter? Would intrusion into the petty moments of our lives serve only to make us guard our secrets better? Who had been up and down that path, in the cat's footsteps, little knowing they were being watched, I wondered? Postman, milkman, papergirl?

Just as I began to get intense about the Watermans and their high-tech nosiness, I realised that it might have the answer to an important question: who had brought the shotguns to Maple Cottage. Kate's visitors would have been caught on camera and there were half a dozen videos stacked beneath the stairs. I flicked through them, expecting to find dates on the labels but there were none. I picked a tape at random and loaded it into the player. Within moments the blue screen flickered into black and white life and there, on a dishevelled bed, were Stef the Window Cleaner and Bella the Clerk.

For a moment I couldn't make sense of it but finally I had to accept the evidence of my eyes. They were screwing. Did they perhaps sell videos of themselves doing so and Will had bought one? Was there a cottage industry here that I hadn't heard about? Transfixed by the sameness of what I was watching, and notwithstanding my high regard for Bella's physical attributes, surely this was feeble stuff. The most unimaginative of directors would by now have given his audience a change of angle, the odd close-up, an occasional pan? Another two seconds and I realised they were being shot from above, from a camera fixed in the ceiling. And without their knowledge, if the lacklustre performance from Stefan was anything to go by. I loaded another tape, then another, and another, all at random. All had the same subject matter. Stefan and Bella going at it, albeit in a somewhat desultory fashion.

I went back up into the loft, stepped over the beams until I found roughly the centre of Stefan and Bella's bedroom. Five amp cable ran between the joists to feed a light fitting and alongside it ran the sleeker, smoother cable that must surely have powered the mini camera set in the plaster. The cable ran all the way back to a recording device in Will Waterman's CCTV command centre.

- 7 -

I'm not sure what time it was when the phone rang. Hideki answered it and brought it over to where I was sitting in Maggie's dad's old rocker, creaking to and fro like some Mississippi inbreed. All I needed was the banjo. Not that I could've played it, even if I'd been sober.

"Is Doctor Peterson," said Hideki, quietly.

"It is," I corrected him. "It ... *it* is Doctor Peterson. What does she want?"

"She want you, Nathan."

I took the phone, Hideki bowed and retreated.

"Hallo?"

"Hi! I'm just phoning to see if you're okay. I mean I know it's a tall order but ... Jack Langan."

"Right."

She sighed. "Yes, well, you sound much as I'd expected you to. Do you want me to come over?"

"No, thanks. Who told you about it?"

"His wife. I was called to her earlier on. She's okay, shocked of course, but spine of steel and all that. What are you drinking?"

"What are you wearing?"

"No, be serious."

"No, you go first. Start with what you're wearing on the outside, work your way in..."

"Oh, for God's sake! I'm coming over."

"No, please..."

But by then I was talking to the dialling tone.

She arrived on her bike about ten minutes later by which time it was dark. From where I was sitting I watched her front lamp light-sabre its way down Morton Lane as she wove between the potholes. She was getting to know them.

"You must be Hideki," she said when he greeted her at the front door.

He bowed and took the offered hand and she towered her way past him to the kitchen. She paused at the archway and a look I thought I knew crossed her face. It asked if the notion she'd entertained of a long term friendship between us would ever amount to anything.

"Denim," I said, referring to our phone conversation. "You're wearing denim."

"And you're drinking..." She lifted the bottle, got the general gist of the label and glared at me. "Port? Clare College port? You're a copper. Aren't you supposed to drink whisky?"

"It's Con. Every time he couldn't think of a present for me, or if I needed softening up, he gave me a bottle of that stuff. There's about thirty in the garage."

"I could tell you stories about port that would make your hair stand on end."

Her eyes drifted to the top of my head.

"Go on, say it. If you had any."

She shook her head, denying that such a pathetic joke had even crossed her mind.

"You're not going to believe this," I said. "I don't actually drink a great deal." She raised an eyebrow, like Dirk Bogarde used to do. "No, really. Hideki'll tell you 'cos he's nothing if not honest. Deki, I don't drink much, do I?"

"No..." he said.

I knew how he'd answer, of course. Being Japanese, and unerringly literal, he would respond to the question itself, not to the subject matter within it. "No, that isn't true," he would have gone on to say, if I'd let him, "you drink like a fish."

"See?"

Laura wasn't fooled. She screwed the cap back on the bottle until it squeaked.

"As your doctor..." she began.

"You're my doctor?"

"You're registered at the Health Centre so, as your doctor, stop drinking this stuff every time there's a hiccup in your life. It will kill you."

"Now just a minute. Didn't we have this conversation once before? I'm fifty not fifteen..."

"I thought we'd settled on fifty-two not that age has anything to do with it."

I looked at Hideki for support but he busied himself emptying a new packet of biscuits into the tin. He was embarrassed but damned if he was going to miss out on a good English row.

"Hiccup?" I said. "Hiccup? Yeah, well it's true that I've just eaten something indigestible because my friend here has yet to discover fire and it's ability to cook things, thereby making them edible. Supper tonight was raw swordfish. The bloody thing is still splashing around inside me. But of course, you're talking metaphorically." I swung round to Hideki. "And here's a challenge for you, Doc. Explain the concept, first of a hiccup, then its metaphorical equivalent and then teach the bastard to cook!"

I brought my fist down on the table and looked up at them both. There was a pause before Hideki stepped towards me.

He pushed coffee cups, biscuits and sugar to one side then took an imaginary map from his inside pocket. He unfolded it and, with meticulous care, laid it out on the table.

It was characteristic of him. Wise beyond his years, forgiving where others would take umbrage and as courteous a human being as you could wish to meet. Earlier I'd seen him talking to his two girlfriends from the village. They'd called at the cottage, all giggles. He'd met them at the gate and told them, I like to think, that he had a duty to look after me. They departed.

I reached out to put a hand on his shoulder but he stepped back quickly.

"Map," he said.

Full of the emotion which only a gut full of port can bring I said: "Yes, I can see that. Thanks, Deki. Kind of you."

"Map not for you," he said. "Map for me."

He sat down at the table, closed his eyes and brought his forefinger down on a coffee ring, somewhere in Japan, I imagine.

Laura said, with a touch of the school marm rising: "Would somebody care to enlighten me?"

"It's a long story," I said.

"Yes, well, if you blow your top too often, like you just did, you won't live long enough to recount it. Any second now you're going to tell me you smoke forty cigarettes a day, eat fry-ups for breakfast and can't pee without the aid of a pump."

I took a deep breath. "My friend Jack Langan, you referred to him as a hiccup. Have I told you how Charnley warned me off poking my nose into Jim Ryder's death?"

"You have."

"Yes, well, like a fool I did what I was told. I backed off and let them get on with it, regardless of John Faraday coming here to pick my brains. If I'd followed my instinct and started poking around, if I'd made Jack follow us down here yesterday and tell me what was biting him, maybe he'd still be alive."

There was a pause while Laura thought of something positive to say in my favour. What she came up with wasn't spectacular.

"Well, I don't see what else you were expected to do..."

"Laura, you don't get it, do you."

She bridled and rose a good two inches, looking down at me, slouched at a narrow angle in the rocker.

"If I don't 'get' something it's invariably because it has not been explained properly. In keeping with most drunks, Nathan, you're half as lucid, a third as funny and one sixteenth as attractive as you think you are. Forgive the assessment being in fractions, I'm something of an old-fashioned gal."

"He was murdered."

That shut her up. For all of five seconds.

"Murdered? As in ... killed?"

"No, murdered as in bouncing round the room on his fucking head!"

"I meant ... I'm not sure what I meant ... I meant has it got anything to do with Jim's death?"

"Two murders in a backwater like this? I'd say they were linked if they'd happened in the same century, never mind the same week. Hideki, I'm sorry, really I am ... pour me some more coffee, there's a good chap."

He refolded the map carefully before feeling the coffee pot and deciding to make fresh. Laura sat down at the table in his place and reached across to take my hand.

Eventually I said: "I've got a reason for drinking today, wouldn't you say? Jack Langan is number thirty-five in my catalogue of corpses, only no junkie's buzz in my head, no thrill, not this time. This time it was a friend, a man I'd grown to admire for his downright decency..."

"Just a second," she said. "How do you *know* he was murdered. Jean says it was an accident."

"Because that's what the police will have told her. And if

that's what they really believe it means they've ignored a real humdinger." I turned to Hideki, mindful that a new word had just foxed him. "Humdinger. Big, important thing. I nearly missed it myself. There was the yard, quiet as the grave, and there was Jack, spread across the saw bench, sliced in two. So, after he supposedly fell on it, who turned off the saw?"

She puzzled over that for a moment and came up with a reasonable suggestion, one I'd thought of myself and rejected.

"Maybe it had a safety device built in. Gets too hot, clogs up, cuts out."

"Yes, well, not to put too fine a point on it I didn't smell any chargrilled flesh, or see bits of him bunging up the system. It was all a lot cleaner than that. Apart from the blood, of course, everywhere. No, poor old Jack was on the saw just long enough to die then someone switched it off. And they did so, not from the bench, or there'd be footprints in the blood. They did it from the fuse box by the door. And there were no granite setts there, either"

"What difference does that make?"

"Someone phoned him at the house, got him to the yard on a pretext. Early delivery, granite setts. Like a fool he went."

To my way of thinking it was all the proof we needed but instead of Laura's face clearing it was clouding over even more.

"I still can't imagine why anyone would want to ... do such a terrible thing."

Hideki, who never spoke until spoken to, must have thought it crucial to butt in at that point.

"Nathan," he said. "You leave out another humdinger. Guns."

"Guns?" asked Laura.

I nodded. "That's what he phoned me about. He found shotguns up in Kate's loft but they ain't there anymore. I've checked."

I rose from the chair, taxing my sense of balance, and led

her across to the window. Over at Kate's cottage there were no signs of life. Usually I could see her making supper at this time of day, to the background flicker of the evening news.

I said: "Knowing Jack he's done something stupid like asked her to explain their presence, thinking she's still a kid and he could send her to her room if she got lippy. Well, I think she got more than lippy. She got lethal."

"But they were so close," said Laura, halfway between laughing at what I'd said and being horrified by its implications.

"Two million quid?" I said. "Drives a big wedge."

"The money Jim Ryder took? You're sure these things are all of a piece?"

"Line 'em all up, Laura, never mind the order. Jim gets shot for twenty grand? No. Much more. Shot with pucker weapons, two of them. Two were found on Kate's loft…"

"By Jack. He said."

"Well, he knew a fucking shotgun when he saw one! Now they're not there and he's been killed. Of course it's all of a piece."

Eventually she asked: "So what are you going to do?"

"What I should've done a week ago, when Jim was shot. Find the bastard who killed him because whoever it is went on to kill my friend Jack Langan, right under my nose. The same fucking nose Charnley told me to keep out of his business. Well, from now on he'd better keep his out of mine…"

That was the point, Laura told me later, at which I passed out, turning awkwardly from the window, closing my eyes and crumpling to the floor. They tried to bring me round, they said. Believe it if you will. All I know is I came to about four hours later, in the spot where I'd fallen, body re-arranged into the recovery position, with a travel rug thrown over me and a cushion under my head. Hideki had gone to bed, Laura had gone home. A bacon slicer was carving thin rashers off my brain at every heartbeat.

- 8 -

I sat at the kitchen table, in virtual darkness for some reason, with a notepad and pencil and made a list. Maggie had often tried to persuade me of a list's cathartic properties. Faced with an Everest of tasks she would put them down on paper and thereby, in her mind, lay waste to half of them. Jobs that were written down to do were as good as done, bills that needed paying were all but settled, obligations nearly fulfilled.

This would not be the case with Jack Langan's murder, nor that of Jim Ryder. My list was a head straightener, an agenda, and right at the top of it was Kate. How to tackle her? Head on collision or with a sympathetic line? The latter would be more productive, given that the guns were essentially hearsay. Sorry to hear about your uncle would be the line then, how are you coping, anything I can do?

Right below Kate I put Tom and Gizzy. True or false, this business about Julie leaving Tom The Plough in a will? And where the hell were they when Jim was shot?

Julie. Keep an eye on her. After all, if someone had tried to kill her up on The Ridge and she pulled through, wouldn't they try again? Charnley had a couple of men posted at her bedside, waiting for signs of life.

The two blokes at the pub. Someone could surely give better descriptions than the police had got from Sharon Falconer. Go see her. Tricky with her husband having done a runner but I was pretty sure I could get more out of her than John Faraday's "Mid-twenties, five eight, built like a brick wotsit with curly dark hair, the other taller, six feet, fair hair."

Petra and Allan Wyeth. They were the light relief. In dealing with them I'd be harking back to my days as a young detective when, rarely, we'd find ourselves with nothing to do. No trouble to sort out so we'd go and find some. Make some. Great days, not all of them to be proud of.

The Wyeths had taken no part in Jim's murder, I knew that, but something had happened to them up on The Ridge and they didn't want the rest of the world to know about it. So, straight to it and minimise their embarrassment? Or let them dig a bloody great hole, bury themselves in the exhaust story, at which point I'd reveal that I knew they were lying?

Funeral. Check arrangements with vicar, then undertakers.

Stef and Bella, the tapes, ask about guns on loft.

Jean. Visit. Sympathy.

By seven o'clock the next morning, Sunday, I was at the kitchen window, concealed behind the drawn curtain, binoculars levelled. There was no sign of Kate, though Stefan and Bella were shuffling into life.

At seven fifteen I rang Kate's number and there was no answer, not even a message minder. I wondered if she'd be round at Jean's offering tea and sympathy. I could strike two items off my list with one visit. Jean, sympathy and Kate, guns in loft.

A chill had descended on the village, not courtesy the Grim Reaper so much as the onset of autumn. It had brought with it a clarity of air and light, the better to show us the passing of summer, I suppose. Leaves were turning reddish-gold in its glow, a V formation of geese flew overhead, their choral squawking carried to the Chiltern scarp and back. And the police vehicles had gone. For the past few days they'd been buzzing back and forth, more in a show of strength that out of necessity. In the way of these things, life was returning to normal ... at least for those who weren't involved in the murders.

I tapped on the door of the Langans' cottage and through the diamond of glass saw Jean emerge from the kitchen and glance at herself in the hall mirror. She was about to primp herself then clearly decided that she had every right to look a wreck, under the circumstances, and opened the door to me. She was grief-marked in every respect. Her eyes were red and swollen with tears, her hair lay lank and flat, make-up awry. If she had slept at all it was badly and she had probably done so in the clothes she wore now.

"I know it's a daft question, Jean, but ... how are you?"

She nodded, presumably at the daft question bit, and stood aside for me to enter.

It was a curious place, the Langans' cottage, two up, two down, beamed to excess and in every way, from the absence of a doorknocker to the bare plaster in the living room, a typical builder's house. Unfinished. It was also cluttered with furniture, all in Jack and Jean's particular taste. Hardest to take were the cast-iron kitchen stools, far from their natural home in a Burger King.

"Bloody old fool," said Jean, once we'd settled on them. "The times I've said to him, get proper tools for the job, don't buy someone else's clapped out rubbish just to save a few quid."

"Police told you it was an accident?" I said.

She nodded.

When you tell somebody that a loved one has been murdered you tread on rapidly breaking ground that at any moment might shift, plunging the listener God knows where. They're the bleakest words ever spoken and it's usually some young copper who has to say them, delegated to do so by a reluctant boss. I had no one to give the job to.

"Jean, there's something you should know..."

A sudden thump from one of the upstairs rooms made me stop.

"Gizzy," she explained. "There's a bedside table there and because of the sloping floor things fall off it."

"Where's Tommy?" I asked.

"He's there too. They came over to be with me, insisted on staying."

"And Kate?"

There was the faintest hint of resentment in her reply. "At home, I suppose."

Gizzy came down the stairs, in dangerously unsuitable shoes, tying a dressing gown at her hip. She gave me an arctic glance, went over to Jean and slipped an arm round her.

"You okay?" she whispered.

Jean nodded and Gizzy started on me.

"You're like one of them bloody vultures," she said. "Not enough that your police mates keep pestering us, their cars buzzing in and out of the village like blue-arsed flies, we've got you, first on the scene whenever there's trouble..."

Jean was about to reprimand her but wasn't quick enough. Gizzy rumbled on in a loose tirade about people's feelings and nosy neighbours and arrived at her belief that in a village like this you couldn't do a bloody thing, especially die, without it becoming everyone's business. As the invective petered out, Jean picked up our conversation.

"You were saying, Nathan?"

"I've something to tell you, not welcome I'm sure, but here it is. I don't think Jack's death was an accident."

Gizzy spun round from the sink, kettle in hand. The tap ran hard against the stone sink, sending a spray into the air. I expected another drubbing but she was stunned into gawping silence. Jean stepped over and turned off the tap, then said:

"What was it then?"

"I think he was murdered. In fact I'm sure he was."

She thought about it for a moment or two then shook her head. "Then you didn't know him half as well as you think, Nathan. He may not have had many friends, but he didn't have a single enemy."

"You don't have to be killed out of hate, Jean. Mistakes, wrong time wrong place, lunatics on the loose…"

"Nathan, he's dead," she said. "Let's leave it at that."

"What makes you say … what you said?" asked Gizzy, in a smallish voice. She wasn't meeting my eyes anymore.

I explained how I'd found him, how I believed he'd been lured to the yard with news of an imminent delivery of setts. I told them about the safety switch on the saw, how someone must've turned it off from the door. I mentioned also, for Jean's benefit, how peaceful he'd looked. Unafraid. Unsuspecting.

"That's Jack," she said, faintly. "Never knew what was coming next."

She dipped into a box of tissues and dabbed her eyes. I asked again if they knew where Kate might be. Gizzy professed no interest in the matter, Jean had no suggestion to make but was vaguely concerned at this being my second time of asking after her niece.

"You think something's happened to her?" she said.

"I don't know. I rang her this morning, no answer."

"You don't think…?" Gizzy started. Her fingers went to her

mouth, she began to pace in a small square, held there by growing apprehension. "I mean if Jack was killed..."

"Best thing we can do," I said, "is go round to Maple Cottage and check."

They agreed. Gizzy went upstairs again, roused Tom, threw some clothes on both of them and Jean took a final look in the hall mirror. She decided against repairing the recent damage.

As we walked, all four of us, the distance to Maple Cottage I ran through what I knew of the Langan family which was more than Jean would be comfortable with, I imagined. One night about six months ago, after a row she'd had with Jack, Jean and I fell into boozy conversation at The Plough. Her old man, she'd told me, had been complaining about them not spending enough time together. What did he expect? Aside from her sales job in Aylesbury, she'd run a home, brought up three kids and somehow managed to be a school governor at Lord Bill's as well as on the Parish Council and a Committee Member of the W.I. She had also devised the car lift scheme for elderly Winchendon residents. She'd won a prize for it, Central Television's Good Friend and Neighbour Award.

I remember commenting that she was indeed a busy lady. She paused for a moment, like many a good villain before the moment of truth, and out it came. Seven years previously, she said, when Megan, her youngest, went off to Cambridge, Jean had felt bereft of a like mind to converse with. The prospect of another thirty years with nothing but Jack, dancing attendance to her every need, terrified her.

Then Jean's sister and brother-in-law were killed in a motorway pile-up and Jean was reprieved. Kate and Giselle Whitely moved in with the Langans and provided Jean with a fresh challenge. She rose to it admirably even though certain aspects of the girls' behaviour tested her patience. Gizzy, for example, railed at fate by shoplifting Oxford bone dry and Kate by sleeping with every man she could get her hands on.

One of those men was teacher Mike whom Kate married and moved into Maple Cottage with. Jean held her breath until their divorce, five months later, after which there was talk of Gizzy moving in with her sister to help with the rent. The idea foundered last Christmas, when Julie Ryder offered Gizzy a job at The Plough and, shortly after that, Gizzy moved into the attic flat with Tom.

Jean and Julie both disapproved of the two kids living together, albeit for different reasons. In Jean's case it wasn't simply that she'd miss Gizzy's company and have to fall back on Jack's, or that she objected to the kids playing at grown-ups. Far more seriously, Jean believed, Giselle would end up making exactly the same mistake that she herself had made. She would marry the wrong man.

I paused at the front door of Maple Cottage and gestured for Jean to unlock it. As I watched her bony, bloodless hands strain at the simple task I recalled the sight of Jack severed by his own bench saw and accepted that I'd found something to disturb me. By her own admission, Jack had been dull to the point of screaming pitch. And now he was dead.

Inside Maple Cottage, Jean, Gizzy and Tom stood in close formation by the front door while I checked the rooms.

Kate clearly had artistic pretensions, even though they hadn't carried her beyond Turner's the wallpaper people. She had painted almost every wall in the house with a derivative mural. The living room was after Van Gogh, tall sunflowers dwarfing what was already a small enough room. The kitchen paid homage to Cézanne, with apples and oranges spattered everywhere. The bathroom gave Monet and his water a run for their money and lost. There was no sign of Kate herself, however, dead or alive.

"It's okay!" I called down to the others from the upstairs bedroom. "Nothing to worry about."

It was Gizzy who came to the foot of the tiny stairs and railed at me.

"So, thanks for getting our day off to such a good start!"

"You're welcome," I yelled back, opening a pine wardrobe in the bedroom. It was empty. I checked the bedside table. It was clear of all the usual knick-knacks.

"You should really get yourself a proper job, Nathan," Gizzy went on, ignoring the stumbling pleas from Tom to zip it. "We'll be taking staff on at the pub next week, why don't you write in?"

I hurried down the top few steps, ducked under the beam and glared at her.

"Does Julie know that you're taking over?"

"How can she? She's unconscious. Besides, I'm not taking over, but if I don't do something the place'll grind to a halt." She added, with a touch of pure Gizzy: "So, do you know how to wash up?"

I went back to the bedroom, yanked open a drawer. It was empty, as was the entire chest. The dressing table was bare too, so were the shelves and the window sill. I went downstairs again, checked once more in the bathroom, and then faced them.

"She's left," I said.

"I think we'd realised that," said Jean. "Let's go home, shall we?"

She gathered up Gizzy and Tom, both of whom dwarfed her in stature, and ushered them to the door.

"I don't just mean she isn't here. All her clothes are gone, top clothes, underwear, make-up, toilet stuff. She's gone for good."

And, assuming that Jack hadn't imagined them, she'd taken the shotguns with her.

- 9 -

I had an appointment with Reg Balfour, the vicar of Winchendon-with-Dorton, scheduled for ten o'clock Monday at the church. Jim's will had asked for burial. A curious wish for a man who boasted that he'd never been inside a church in his life.

I sat on the bench at the west door and tried not to care that I was surrounded by dead people. The view across the valley helped, as did thinking about Kate's disappearance. First reason for it, she was guilty. Of something. There was a link, though I couldn't see it, between Jim Ryder, the guns in her loft and Jack's death and Kate was right there at the heart of it. Stretch it a bit for a second reason. Fear. Say a third party had hidden the guns in the attic, with or without Kate's permission, and Jack was killed for finding them. Maybe she thought she'd be next in line and had run for it. Maybe she'd already *been* killed. Mind you, you don't normally take your underwear and make-up to the grave with you and their disappearance pointed to a third reason. It was just possible she knew nothing about all this, not even her uncle's death. I'd watched her the other morning, leave for work, dressed casually, jeans and T-shirt. Maybe she'd simply been dressed for running away...

Reg appeared on his moped at around ten fifteen, cassocked and collared, with a touch of rouge in his cheeks and two make-up pencil lines where his eyebrows had once been. He was excited. It was going to be difficult to get much sense out of him. A party of local school kids was due at eleven and after a brief chat about God, Jesus and The Virgin Mary the fun would begin. Teddy bears would be strapped into parachutes and launched from the top of the tower, the highest in Bucks, by two of the church wardens. Teachers and loving mothers would take photos. In Reg's view it was far more evangelical than threatening them with the wrath of God.

He knew what I wanted to see him about, I'd broached the matter with his wife on the phone.

He said: "Thousand years, that's what we're talking about, Nathan..." He always began in the middle of a sentence. It was a trick he'd learned from Jesus, he'd told me, and it always got the crowd's attention. "If I put Jim Ryder into the ground here, what about the other souls, doomed to converse with him for a thousand years?"

"Where do you get this thousand years from, Reg?"

"Random figure, sounds less churchy than eternity but that's what we're talking about. Jim Ryder wasn't the sort of bloke I'd want my parishioners to spend *any* time with. He served a lousy glass of beer and overcharged for the grub."

"Forgiveness?" I said, feebly.

"Don't change the subject."

I looked across to the yew trees, dipping their branches in the long grass and stingers at the outer edge of the graveyard. "Well ... couldn't you stick him in a corner, out of harm's way?"

"Corners are full," he said, unhelpfully.

He took a teddy bear from a Tesco's carrier bag and straightened its fur. He offered me a stroke of it and I declined.

"Man had no family," I said, as pathetically as I could, "wife's hanging on by a thread."

"I won't be taking her, either. I don't do heathens. If I were you I'd get onto the District Council, they're obliged to take all comers. I'll do the service if you get stuck. Usual fee."

He took a set of keys from the carrier bag and went into the church to prepare.

Back at Beech Tree Cottage, John Faraday was waiting for me in his car. He had come to do his boss's dirty work again and I invited him in.

Hideki had left a note under the kettle saying: "Oxford. Go with Liza and Nicky. H." I offered Faraday a coffee and he refused with a curt shake of the head.

"Oh, for Christ's sake..." I began.

"What the hell were you playing at?" he said. "Jesus, how long were you in the job? You report the man's death by phone and piss off?"

I shrugged. "Your boss told me to keep clear."

"He didn't say make fools of us, break the law."

"The making fools of you, John, is an inside job. I hear you reckon Jack Langan's death was an accident?"

"Charnley does. I've got an open mind."

He signalled that he wouldn't mind a coffee after all. He went over to the biscuit tin, looked in, but there was no shortbread there. He replaced the lid and said, eventually, "So go on, then. What do you know that we don't?"

I explained about the switch at the door, the supposed call bringing forward the delivery of granite setts. He shook his head all the way, just as Jean Langan had done. It irritated me.

"Look, you asked me to let you know if I 'casually observed

any bits and pieces'. Well, here's one. Jack Langan phoned me, early hours last Saturday. He'd been working on his niece's loft where he'd seen a couple of shooters, in their case, recently fired."

Anger took hold of his every feature, every gesture, but he managed to keep a lid on it as he strode the room.

"So, of course, you phoned us immediately," he said.

"It was three in the morning when he called me. He was pissed. When I found him dead, I came back here to check his story, instead of waiting around at the yard for you guys to show up. I went up in the loft. Nothing there."

He stopped pacing and opened his hands to me, pleading to be further enlightened.

"You've got two choices," I said. "Believe they *were* there, and were shifted during the night and Jack Langan killed as a result. Or he dreamed 'em up and then fell on his saw."

He slumped into a chair and looked at me, calming rapidly.

"If I throw this in the pot," he said at last, "this shotgun in the loft stuff, Charnley will go ape-shit."

"Why? Because it comes from me? Or is it just an easy life he wants, not the truth?"

"He still reckons the answer's up there in Grendon Prison," said Faraday, with a hint of despair. "He's got a list, a dozen possibles, all with a grudge against Jim."

"And of this dozen are any really dirty? Any big players?"

"Not really, but Jesus Christ, we all have to start somewhere."

"John, this isn't some over the cell wall squabble. There's two million quid floating around out there."

He didn't have a snap back answer to that.

"Jim Ryder's ill-gotten gains, you mean. Yeah, well, makes no difference you and me agreeing on that, Charnley reckons it went to ground two years ago."

"Then he's a fool! Money doesn't go to ground. It goes into bank accounts, property, paintings. It stays visible."

He raised both hands in surrender and then, like a teenager whose attention span had reached its limit, he flopped forward onto the table, chin on the back of his hands.

"I was sent here to give you a bollocking," he said, eventually. "Can I consider that done?"

I nodded.

"Great. Now tell me more about these sodding guns."

"They were in a case. Mahogany, with a brass plate. J.A.M."

He was digging for a notebook and pen and wrote it down.

"Juliet, Alpha, November?" he said.

"No, M for Mike, jam today. If they're licensed, they can be traced."

"They sound posh. Like they've been nicked."

"Purdeys, according to Jack. Twelve grand apiece."

He smiled. "Any other ... bits and pieces?"

"No."

He was unconvinced, but untroubled as well. The less he took back to Charnley from me the easier his life would be, I guessed.

"I'll have the guns checked out," he said. "Get back to you."

"Thanks."

I could've checked them out myself, I suppose, gone through a horde of old contacts and suffered news of death, retirement and domestic warfare. God knows how long it would've taken me. Faraday could go back to Penman Stables and get an answer that afternoon.

I spent the next hour trying to persuade the Council to bury

Jim Ryder and hit a classic brick wall of disaffected humanity. They were always going to oblige me in the end, we all knew that, otherwise there'd be a pile of bodies on the town hall doorstep humming away like a Welsh choir. But the bloke dealing wanted me to acknowledge that he was important, overworked and unloved. By two o'clock I'd secured Jim plot 47B and rang the undertaker to give him a green light. I told him not to bother with the hand-wringing tone, Jim wasn't a relative, I didn't even like him that much. Then I telephoned an advert to The Bucks Herald, and after negotiating several people's lunch breaks and a host of 'she's in a meeting' brush-offs, I told the world, via a quarter page ad costing seventy-four pounds and eighty pence, that Jim would be buried next Tuesday at ten in the morning, Aylesbury Cemetery. It had been like climbing a mountain of treacle.

I put the phone down, only for it to ring immediately. I grabbed the receiver and barked:

"Yep?"

"I've been ringing you for ages," said Laura Peterson, as if I'd sat on the phone merely to annoy her. "I'm in Oxford for a conference. Lunchtime, I popped round to The Radcliffe. Guess what! Julie Ryder's regained consciousness."

I don't know why the news set me on edge. I was pleased to hear that she'd pulled through, I just knew that it wasn't the end of her troubles.

"How is she?"

"Slow but talking. Can't remember too much but that's fairly typical. It'll come back."

"Wouldn't mind seeing her, pretty soon. Like today. When does your conference finish?"

"Five thirty, allegedly. Why?"

"Well, let's meet for dinner somewhere. I mean, if you've got other plans, that's fine by me."

"I should hope so too," she said. "You know Brown's?"

"Sure."

"Why don't we meet there, seven o'clock?"

I was showered and re-shaved long before I needed to leave for Oxford and decided to take the bull by the horns. Since finding the tapes of Stef and Bella I'd been debating with myself, should I, or shouldn't I? Should I let them know about this nasty intrusion into their privacy and risk all hell breaking loose? Or should I keep it a secret and let Will off the hook. In the end I decided Stef and Bella had a right to know.

I slipped a tape into my pocket and set off across the green to Hawthorn Cottage. Bella was pulling up, just as I got there.

"Blimey, Nathan, you're looking sprauncy. You off out somewhere?"

"Dinner. Oxford."

"Oh, I say!"

"Is Stef in, do you know?"

He called from an upstairs window. "Course he is. This dinner date, she wouldn't be a certain lady doctor, would she?"

"Honestly," said Bella, nudging me with embarrassment. "He's like an old woman, everyone's business."

"I'm a window cleaner," said Stef, laughing. "It's part of the job."

He slammed the window shut and a piece of putty fell to the ground at my feet. If life is a series of straws on camels backs, I thought, how long would it be before I was woken one morning by the sound of Hawthorn Cottage collapsing into rubble, just as had happened to a place in Cuddington. Central heating, they said. Everything that goes wrong in an old house these days you can safely blame on the central heating.

Not that Hawthorn Cottage had central heating but still the outside rendering was falling away in huge patches, taking some of the wychert with it, wychert being the local mud and rubbish most houses in the village were made of. The window frames were flaking and spongy, the stench pipe was leaning at a provocative angle and in one particular spot on the roof, the thatch had fallen in completely and the gap had been tarpaulined.

The front garden was a mess as well, with grass two feet high, thistles and poppies plotting a take-over. Maybe that's why Dogge loved the place so much, it called to her from some wild place in her genetic memory. If we walked past the cottage her tail would go nineteen to the dozen, she'd yap until Bella brought her out a biscuit. I never discouraged her, not with Bella being so good to look at.

The inside of Hawthorn Cottage wasn't much of an improvement on the outside. The furniture was dented and scarred, the rugs clawed feathery by two enormous cats and the place reeked of tobacco, marijuana and old food. Its one salvation was the books, literally thousands of them, lining nearly every wall.

Stef came down the narrow stairs to greet me.

"Hi, Nathan. This'll be about poor old Jacko, right? I dropped in on Jean today. I mean there's not a lot you can do, but..."

He shrugged the subject away and pecked Bella on the cheek.

"Good day, hon?" he said.

"Reasonable. Charlie Travis was up to his old tricks again, speaking to some, ignoring others just cos he's had a bad..."

He wasn't really listening so she didn't waste any more breath on the subject. She turned to me instead.

"Can I get you a cup of tea, Nathan?"

"No, thanks."

She went through to the kitchen and filled the kettle for herself. Stef and I followed.

I'd learned something during the past few days. Nothing useful, or even interesting, just ... new. When you've had the dubious pleasure of watching two people you know have sex together, you never look at them in quite the same way again. In certain cases that fresh regard will be one of admiration or excitement, I'm sure, even a touch of envy. But in Stefan's case, and for all his cleverness, my new impression was of a man lacking in imagination, semi-detached from his forlorn, disheartened and beautiful partner.

"It's Kate I wanted to see you about, actually. You don't know where she's gone, do you?"

They exchanged a glance before Bella said: "Didn't know she'd gone anywhere."

"I just wondered if you knew of a boyfriend, or any friends at all, come to that. When I think about her I see ... just her."

Stef agreed. "Loner. People to ask would be Will and Prissy when they get back."

"Heh, ain't it nice without 'em," said Bella. "You don't feel that that every move you make is being watched."

"Every move indeed," I said.

Stef was gesturing at the fridge, asking if I wanted a beer. I said no with my hands. I was anxious to say what I needed to and leave.

"Night before last, Jack phoned me. He'd been working there, Kate's cottage, during the day..."

Stef looked at me, frowning. "Doing what?"

"Moving the boiler."

Bella giggled, an Essex giggle. I couldn't have lived with a giggle like that for longer than a week.

"Honestly, the number of times that boiler ..."

"Lots, I know. Jack said that up on the loft he saw a pair of shotguns."

They both stared at me for a moment, then Stef said, in a puzzled whisper: "Kate Whitely? Shotguns?"

Once over his initial surprise he took another sip of his beer, eyes still on me.

"That's Jack talkin' rubbish," Bella suggested. "Been on the piss. Made a mistake."

"I don't think so. And I think seeing the guns cost him his life. Police disagree, of course."

Stef was still eyeing me, worried now. "Is this for real, Nathan? I mean bad enough that he dies. Now you say someone killed him?"

"Blimey, what's happening to this village?" said Bella, like a woman twice her age. "It used to be such a nice, quiet place to live."

Stef shook his head. "Nowhere's really like that. Never was, right Nathan?"

I nodded and took Will Waterman's tape from my pocket.

"Since you're both in a philosophical mood, take a look at this."

"What is it?"

"What you do about it is up to you but I suggest you do it through a solicitor. It's a tape of you two. Making love. I found it in Will's house."

Stef took the cassette from me. He wasn't angry, as I would have been. In fact he was faintly amused.

"How's the cheeky sod done that?"

"Miniature camera, size of a ball-bearing, up in the ceiling, near the light. I cut the cable."

"Blimey!" said Bella. "Some people."

They went through to their tiny living room to briefly watch the tape while I stayed in the kitchen. They joined me after ten minutes or so, even more amused than before but trying not to show it. Unsuccessfully.

I couldn't understand it. I told myself it must be a generation thing.

- 10 -

I parked up at St. Anthony's College and walked down the Woodstock Road to St. Giles. At Brown's, the front windows were closed but the smell of coffee still drifted out into the evening air. Passers-by paused to savour the aroma and, more often than not, were drawn by it to the menu in the glass-fronted box by the door.

I liked Brown's for being a packed and lively place but never in your face, never marking your age. It had a colonial feel to it with its huge fans in the ceiling, feathered palms and leather seats. Above the clinking glass and posh-accented hubbub, the planked floor sprung back like a drumbeat with every footfall. The tall mirrors always took me by surprise but had a welcome knack of making me look better than I felt.

I looked around the lobby for Laura. She was drinking coffee at the bar and rose from her stool to air kiss me, her soft skin brushing against my cheek. When we stood back, I half expected to see an angry graze where we'd touched but I'd left no mark. She nodded at the flashing number cruncher on one of the pillars.

"That's us. Number seventeen. You came in the nick of time."

As we studied the menu a burst of laughter from the next table made us turn. A girl in her early twenties with long blond hair, once brown according to the roots, had recalled a funny moment in their recent lives. It involved a young man at the end of the table who blushed and acknowledged his part in the story. A trousers down story, I thought, one of mistaken identity or rudeness to a member of the faculty.

They were distracted from it by the arrival of a young man in a dinner jacket who took his place at the grand piano in the centre of the room. He acknowledged his audience and began to play, something vaguely romantic and mercifully quiet.

"So how about old Julie, then?" I said.

Laura seemed pleased but not overly so. "Marvellous news, yes."

"Police reckoned she'd be a gonner. Gave her a week."

She smiled. "Where did Charnley do medicine? Hendon Police College? I'm going to have the butterfly prawns, twice, and no main course."

"Any idea when she'll be coming home?"

She shrugged. "Shotgun wounds can be tricky. It's the depth of the lesion, needs plenty of time."

I ordered gigot of lamb and suggested a bottle of Cahors Red which, without discussion, Laura changed to two glasses.

I said: "So ... conference, visit to Julie. Anything else?"

"Bit of retail therapy. Some women buy shoes, I buy books, they don't ruin your feet. Guess who I saw in the coffee bar of Blackwells?"

"Er ... Jim Ryder?"

She laughed and looked round, presumably to check that my irreverence hadn't been overheard. "That is a dreadful thing to say! Well, it isn't really, I suppose, but anyway... Tom Templeman."

"I didn't think he could read."

"Come to think of it, he did look a bit sheepish when he saw me. How about your day?"

I began telling her and her eyes lit up at news of Kate's disappearance. She leaned forward and lowered her voice.

"Gone off with a chap? Do we know who?"

"I don't think it's quite that simple."

The second button on her blouse came adrift, revealing the tops of her breasts, not tanned like her face but soft and white, pushing upwards at a black lace bra. Wherever she'd been on holiday that year, and it was certainly in the sun, she'd played the Englishwoman abroad and kept her top on. She saw my eyes hovering at the parted blouse. With a discreet smile she fastened the button.

We clinked the glasses the waiter had brought us and agreed, in the conventional way of such toasts, that it was good to see each other, especially in a place like this. We should do it more often. And as prawns and lamb gave way to bread and butter pudding for me, and guilt-free black coffee for Laura, so the kids at the next table provided a mild diversion.

Their bill had arrived and they'd begun to dissect it. A calculator criss-crossed the table, the addition was checked twice and deemed to be correct. However, there were a couple of rogue vodka's itemised and no one was prepared to own up to them whereupon two factions emerged: those who drank spirits, those who didn't. In the subtle shifts from denial to accusation, I studied the faces, trying to pinpoint the guilty party. I settled on the dark-haired, thoughtful girl beside the pillar. The head waitress was summoned, an exotic creature from North African climes. Was she absolutely sure that these drinks were ordered by someone at this table? North Africa could not have been more certain. I turned to smile at Laura who was deep in thoughts of her own.

"You okay?" I asked.

"I'm sorry, I was miles away." She paused before adding: "I should have told you this the other day, up at The Harrow. In fact it was the reason I asked you to meet me there but I never got round..."

I expected at the very least to be told of an old flame who had appeared out of nowhere and re-kindled their dormant love affair. He would be younger than me, no doubt, with more hair and he'd probably have more money. He would leave my growing admiration for Laura stranded at the second button down.

"And you're not sure whether to tell me now?" I offered.

She grimaced, still searching for the right verbal route to take and finally chose the long way round.

"Something's been worrying me. It's a matter of principles, I suppose. Hippocratic oath versus, well, my conscience. Sounds ever so grand, I know, but..."

She stalled for a moment. The dark, thoughtful girl by the pillar had suddenly recalled the two vodka tonics she'd had when she first arrived.

"Julie came to see me a couple of months ago," said Laura, quietly. "High as a kite with worry. Blood pressure up, chest pains, dizzy spells, panic attacks, the works. It was all to do with Jim coming home, she said. She was dreading it. We talked it over. What could she do? I usually try to put people off chemical help but I suggested a course of Prozac. I mean she spoke with such vehemence I had to do something. She said she wished he wasn't coming back home at all. If she could possibly stop him doing so, she would."

Relieved at there being no mention of an old flame I'd entirely missed the point of her telling me all this.

"I know what she meant about Jim," I said. "Did you ever meet him?"

"Of course I met him," she said, slightly puzzled that I wasn't aghast at her story. "Man was an utter creep. You said the other day that Julie persuading him to get a proper defence lawyer was academic. Suppose she persuaded him *not* to."

"She wanted him to go down, you mean?"

"Well, yes. Suppose after eighteen months on her own she'd grown to so enjoy life without him and would've gone to any lengths to keep it that way. Suppose somehow she was ... involved in his murder and up there on The Ridge it all went horribly wrong?"

I thought about it for a moment, reaching out for my wine glass. It was empty. Laura offered me hers.

"Well, one thing's for sure," I said, drinking from it. "I can't ask her straight out, given that she spoke to you in confidence."

"No, you're right, you mustn't," said Laura, urgently. "I mean I wasn't going to say anything because, well, to be quite honest ... I didn't expect her to pull through either."

I smiled. "And it's your fault that she has. Let's go see how she's doing."

The church in St Giles struck nine as we left Brown's and strolled, arm in arm, down The Woodstock Road to The Radcliffe Infirmary. The chill I'd noticed that morning had persisted throughout the day. It had brought out sweaters and jackets on the wary but the autumn refuseniks, still in their single layers of summer, were toughing it out.

The Radcliffe had always struck me as being more than a hospital. Built in 1770 with money left by its namesake, himself a physician, it had the bearing of a great institute, a museum or library, with its orange stonework, wrought iron gates and statued fountain on the forecourt. For all that it was a working hospital, it smacked of quadrangled privilege and sat neatly in the midst of second-hand bookshops, river-bridges and posh-frock outfitters. It belonged to the Old Oxford of my alternative youth, the Oxford I would have come to had my ambitions been greater, my parents richer.

Inside The Radcliffe it was a different story, one of vinyl floors, disinfectant and harsh strip lights. As for the working of the place, something just short of chaos seemed to be driving it. Perhaps visiting time, though nearly over, made it seem overcrowded, made the skeleton staff look weary and defeated. At the reception desk two manager types were speaking to the receptionist, trying to muffle their conversation. I picked up a simple yet urgent exchange.

"How many? Two?"

"One. But that isn't the point..."

"I know the bloody point! Where is he now?"

I was usually good at snippets, taking them to bits and finding a larger meaning within the component parts. This was workaday stressful chat, a pair of admin wallahs at odds. About numbers, two or one. And if one, then his whereabouts.

Laura guided me to the lifts. Both were stuck at a higher floor. A nurse with a bundle of x-rays in her arms was jabbing at the up button. She was looking to a Rastafarian porter, at the helm of a laundry basket, for explanations. He couldn't help her. Nor could a young Asian doctor who decided to take the stairs. We followed him.

The click and shuffle of feet descending from above echoed in the stairwell. People came into view. Some spoke of the friends or relatives they'd visited, others were complaining about the lifts and high taxation.

Between the first and second floors a man in a boiler suit, carrying a toolbox, overtook us, taking the stairs two at a time on the upward side. We ourselves passed a couple of security guards, ramrod straight but well into their seventies. They had paused to get their breath.

At the next landing there was another crowd, a more voluble one. They were demanding of each other why these lifts broke down with such monotonous regularity, offering reasons that made little sense. The lifts were foreign, old and over-used. Beyond them a young woman doctor was speaking on a wall phone. She hung up and ran past us, up the stairs. A few of the patients, there in dressing gowns to see off their relatives, knew her and said so. There was an odd sort of kudos in that.

At the next landing, the third floor, another gathering of people had more to worry about, it seemed, than the state of the lifts. They turned to me and Laura as we crested the flight of stairs. Who were we, the glances asked. What was our business here? The woman doctor who'd passed us on the stairs was breaking through them, trying to reach the staff nurse waiting for her down one of the corridors.

"Where's Doctor Rickson?" the staff nurse asked.

"Operating. You'll have to make do with me."

The nurse bundled the young doctor into a side-ward.

"What's going on?" I asked an elderly woman with a clear, bright face.

She didn't know but nodded to where two other nurses were coming down the opposite corridor, opening cupboards as they went.

"Where's security?" one asked the other.

They're on the stairs, I thought. They'll be here by Christmas.

"Phone them again?"

"No."

"Can I help?" I asked but the offer was swallowed up in the cross-talk.

The man in the boiler suit took a screwdriver from his toolbox and undid a small panel beside the lift door. He began to mutter under his breath, insults of a technical nature aimed at the manufacturer.

"Did anyone see them?" asked a man in a dressing gown.

The reply, of sorts, came from a porter. "Depends what you mean."

"Were there two?"

"The lifts. They must have jammed the lifts."

"Pillow," said a frightened voice. "They say they put a pillow over..."

I looked at Laura. "Julie," she said and without a pause ran to the side-ward the young doctor had entered. I turned to the two nurses.

"Is it Mrs Ryder?" I snapped. "Is Mrs Ryder in trouble?"

The answer was in the frightened glance the two girls exchanged. The crowd fell back as I set off down the corridor they had yet to check, opening doors, leaving my two companions to close them. Boxes fell out at me, empty syringes, cups and packets of wadding. Another cupboard. Lights were flickering into life all around us. A third cupboard, a fourth, a fifth, all crammed with medical stuff. No place for an assailant, let alone two, to hide.

We'd reached the main ward. News had broken through. Someone had assaulted one of the patients. It was touch and go. There were high pitched exchanges as I walked through, demands to know who I was.

"It's okay," said one of the nurses, "there's nothing to worry..."

I dropped to the floor, scanned under the beds. Nothing. Up on my feet again, out of the ward, posse behind me.

At the lifts, I heard questions with beginnings but no ends. "What's the...? Have you...? Will it...?"

The ageing security guards had reached us, one of them wheezing badly. I snapped at his companion:

"Get these people away from the lift."

"Now just a second, what's going on?"

"Do it, George," said the nurse.

The security guards began to shepherd the crowd to safety. I turned to the man in the boiler suit.

"Can you open the doors? Just enough to look in?"

At a nod from the nurse, he took a dog-leg key from his pocket, reached up and placed one end of it in a socket in the overhang. He unwound the mechanism and the rubber edges of the doors parted with the stretching sound of a cartoon kiss. When the gap was four inches wide I raised my hand. The man in the boiler suit stopped. I peered in. Nothing.

"Open them all the way."

He wound the key like mad and as the doors slid back so I caught my reflection in the lift mirror. It gave me a second's pause in which to ask myself what the hell I was doing here, taking charge, taking over... In the lift mirror I saw a louvered door open behind me, a cupboard, a fire reel inside, wound tight on a red drum and, emerging from beside it a dark figure. He saw me turn to him and he took off like a sprinter, down the stairs. I stooped to the toolbox, picked out a claw hammer, and followed.

He was taking the stairs with athletic ease, stepping the first three or four of each flight then leaping to the flat before the turn. He was losing me, even over the short distance to the first floor landing, where he pushed aside people in his way, some to the wall, some to the floor. I followed the startled gazes, pointing me to my quarry. Dark clothes. Tracksuit. Balaclava. He turned left at the end of the corridor and I followed.

He reached the narrow back stairs leading to the ground floor way ahead of me. As I began to take them, three at a time now, I heard the crash of a powerful physique against the fire exit. When I reached it myself, the door had swung back, juddering on its hinges. I pushed it and stepped out into the night.

There were floodlights overhead, blazing down on the side alley which ran the length of the ground floor clinics. Cars were parked there, people were getting into them.

"Which way did he go?" I yelled.

In their own, extended time, people answered. Arms floated, fingers uncurled and pointed towards a low building with a tall, grey chimney, billowing smoke.

"That way," said a voice I'd already left behind.

Ahead of me, the dark tracksuit leaped a wooden fence and dropped down the other side of it. The fence grew taller as I approached it. I upended a dustbin, went up, up and then down onto a patch of grass beside the main boiler house. A door in the side of it opened and a silhouette in the frame, holding a mug of tea, peered out.

"Here, what's going on..." it began and withdrew, seeing the hammer.

As I ran in the only direction my quarry could have taken, I saw that the mug of tea had been exchanged for a phone and the silhouette was dialling a number. I rounded a corner and there was the tracksuit again, clearer now in the light spilling over the wall which ran along Walton Street, the main road through Jericho. The heavy door in the wall was locked. He stood back from it, kicked it with the heel of his foot, to no avail. He turned to me. He may have been considering his options as he came towards me - I was certainly considering mine - but his didn't involve physical confrontation. When far enough away from the wall, he turned and ran back at it with tremendous power, jumped and scrambled onto the top course of stone and dropped down the other side. I heard a girl scream, then footsteps running off down the pavement. I went to the door in the wall, ripped off the lock with the hammer and stepped out into the street.

The group of kids I'd surprised stood welded to the pavement in fear. I yelled at them:

"Which way did the bastard go?"

A girl in the group raised a trembling hand towards the city centre. As I turned to set off I heard the kick start of a motorbike thirty yards ahead of me, followed by a burst of acceleration, saw the streaming of a headlight as the bike came straight towards me. I stepped back, aimed the hammer, and threw it. The biker swerved, the hammer skidded across the tarmac, sparking against the opposite kerb.

I would have killed the first person who spoke to me.

The Map. I went over to a nearby Fiesta, sat back against the bonnet, took The Map from my inside pocket and unfolded it. If they'd had trouble, those kids, with me bursting through a wall with a hammer, what did they make of me throwing it at a motorbike, then consulting an imaginary map of the world? I wasn't able to ask them. They'd moved quietly away.

I'm not sure where my finger would've come down on The Map. Paris, probably, to check the disturbing e-mail I'd had yesterday morning from Fee. "I hear Ellie has a boyfriend. Enrique. Spanish. Should we thank God or worry?" Worry, every time. But right now I couldn't wrench my mind away from Laura, probably saving Julie's life for the second time in ten days. I screwed up The Map, dropped it in the gutter and hurried back to The Radcliffe.

Back at the side-ward, tribal warfare had broken out. Hospital management, in the shape of the two blokes I'd seen at reception and backed up by the ageing security guards, were blaming two coppers in plain clothes for having deserted their post. The coppers were denying it with blunt aggression. The medical crew, the young woman doctor and nurses, had fallen in behind Laura who was suggesting that the row took place somewhere else, not outside Julie's side-ward. That was good to hear. It meant that Julie was alive.

"He grabbed her by the shoulders," Laura said to me, breaking away from the argument. "Shook her, slapped her face. God knows why. Being Julie, she's fought back. She's going down for an x-ray, just in case there's any internal bleeding, but fingers crossed."

I turned to go into the side-ward and one of the coppers, a man in his thirties with crinkly, auburn hair and a Glasgow accent, placed a hand on my shoulder.

"Who the hell are you?"

I looked at the hand, looked at him.

"He's with me," said Laura.

"I'll give you two minutes," said the copper, slowly releasing his grip.

Julie was face down on the bed when I entered, the nurses were checking the stitches which had held together the gunshot wounds, mostly healed now. She was still badly bruised, though, yellow and purple, the colours of a beaten wife or child. I turned away with a mumbled apology but Julie had seen me.

"Nathan, please ... don't go."

I went over to her and she stretched out her hand. It was cold and spindly, her face white as the sheets around her.

"Who was it?" she asked.

"I didn't catch him. Went after him, but..."

"Youngster?" she suggested.

I shook my head. "Balaclava. Couldn't tell his age. Did he say anything?"

"Yeah. 'Tell me where the money is. Where've you put it?' What's he talking about, Nathan?"

"His accent? Irish?"

"No. English, but kind of ... dressed up."

"And he didn't try to kill you?"

"Well, no, but if these girls hadn't come in when they did..."

I stood back as the nurses pulled the bed gown around her and helped her to a sitting position. She winced a few times, reaching out with an angled arm for support. They arranged the pillows to support her, checked her oxygen cylinder and left. Julie said, almost immediately: "You know about Jim?" I nodded. "They told me this morning." Her head fell to one side, she closed her eyes in despair. "He's been dead to me for ... for a couple of ..."

She looked at me for understanding. I took the bony hand in both of mine and tried to warm it.

"Is Tommy alright?" she asked.

"He's fine, fine," I said. "Can you remember what happened, up there on The Ridge?"

She smiled. "You're as bad as those two coppers. Every five minutes they're in, saying: 'Has it come back to you yet? Do the photos ring a bell?'"

"Photos?"

"Two blokes Jim was inside with."

She withdrew her hand and gestured to the bedside cabinet. I opened the drawer, took out an A4 sheet with two sets of prison mug shots on it. Young faces, one set in a sneer of defiance, the other clearly terrified behind the blank wall of his pose.

"I've been thinking about what we might have that other people would want off us."

"Money," I said, meaning the two million her old man had made off with.

She looked at me. "Well, money's one thing, certainly. I mean everyone thinks everyone else is rich these days. But does that explain it, I wonder."

"Explain what?"

"When Jim was inside, I'd go back to the cottage some nights and get this feeling. Like someone had been in there, turned it over and put everything back, extra neatly."

"Did you tell the police?"

She smiled and winced at the effort of it. "Yeah, like 'Hi, I'm the mad woman who lives in the woods and thinks she's been burgled. What makes you say that, madam? A feeling, officer'."

I nodded.

"Things too precisely arranged," she went on, more seriously. "Drawers closed flush, lids back on things perfectly, great patches of furniture with no dust on."

"Maybe you've got a ghost who does your housework when you're not looking."

"Ghost! That's all I bloody need."

A porter entered, wielding a trolley. The two nurses were right behind him and one asked if I'd mind leaving. I folded the sheet of mug shots and pocketed it.

Outside in the corridor hostilities had ceased. The young doctor had been called to incoming wounded, management and the security guards had retreated to their separate bunkers. I said to the Glaswegian accent:

"Why did you leave her alone in the first place?"

He looked at me with stone grey eyes. "You've had your two minutes, pal. Fun's over. Nothing more to see."

"You mean I don't get to see you having your balls chopped off?"

He looked away and started to chew at his bottom lip. His partner recognised the danger signs and stepped in.

"DC Bailey," he said, in a local accent. "My colleague is DC McKinnon. What he means is that we're as upset as you are. But no one's been hurt, Mrs Ryder's off to be checked over..."

He turned and opened the door for the trolley to pass. It swerved out into the corridor, powered by the porter, guided by the two nurses. Bailey put an arm on McKinnon's sleeve and they followed. I waited until there was distance between us, so that what I had to say became public.

"What will you be telling Charnley?" I called after them.

It was certainly a name they didn't want to hear. They stopped and turned to me.

"You know him?" asked Bailey.

I crossed my fingers and held them up. "Like that we are.

What will you be telling him? That you cocked it up?"

"Nathan..." whispered Laura, the start of an urgent request to keep my temper. I eased her aside as Bailey ambled back to me.

"Well, we'll be making a report, of course..."

"Pair of bloody comics! You left her alone, unguarded, and some bastard walked right in off the street and tried to kill her. Now you're hoping the problem'll go away."

Bailey smiled again. "Things happen. You can't always be in control."

"To hell with justifying it," said McKinnon. "Who the fuck *are* you?"

"Ex DCI Hawk."

"Oh, well, in that case I apologise," he said, with exaggerated sarcasm. "I hereby acknowledge your superior rank and wisdom and humbly suggest that you fuck off!"

I slipped a hand into the inside pocket of my jacket only to remember that The Map wasn't there. It was in the gutter in Walton Street. I took a pace towards McKinnon, he towards me, and Bailey was there between us in a flash, sideways on, arms raised to brace against a sudden collision.

"This is not going to happen!" he said, forcefully. "This is a hospital, for Christ's sake! It is *not* going to happen."

McKinnon and I looked at each other for a moment or two longer. He nodded. I took that to be capitulation. He set off in pursuit of Julie and the nurses and Bailey took Laura and me to the Friends of the Radcliffe Kiosk where he bought us stewed, expensive tea.

Seated on a ripped corridor bench, in the disturbing glare of a flickering strip light, I gave him chapter and verse on the man I'd chased. Bailey then told us the story from his side. He and MacKinnon had been sat in the corridor outside Julie's ward, playing cards, when the staff nurse called them to her office.

Urgently. On the phone was a manager type saying there was a commotion in orthopaedics. Three men were attacking one of the girls there. Bailey could hear the rumpus in the background, then a girl screaming. The manager type pleading, pleading, pleading. Without a second thought the cavalry was on its way.

The orthopaedics department was right at the other side of the hospital complex which, Bailey admitted, should have rung a warning bell and, having declined a nurse's offer to guide them there, they were soon lost in the labyrinthine nightmare of the Sheldonian Annexe. Eventually they found the place they'd been called to. No one there. All closed up. Only then did the penny drop. They'd been screwed over. They phoned reception, told them to get in touch with the ward and hurried back.

Laura took up the story from there. The two nurses went down to check on Julie and there he was, the man I'd chased to Jericho, shaking Julie like a rat, slapping her in between. When the nurses entered, he ran. From then on it's guesswork. He got to the lift, only to find they'd broken down. The stairs were beginning to heave with people going down them slowly. He hid in the fire-point cupboard.

I sat thinking for a moment or two, swilling the anti-tea round in its paper chalice, contemplating its destructive power. Then I asked Bailey: "The rumpus you heard over the phone, the girl screaming?"

He replied, sheepishly: "Any night of the week, on the telly, I guess. Tape-recording."

I agreed. "How long between you leaving the ward and reaching orthopaedics?"

He shrugged with his face. "Ten minutes."

"Time enough to kill someone. So why didn't he manage it?"

"I can tell you that," said Laura. "She wasn't where he'd expected her to be. In intensive care. She was moved up to the ward this morning."

Bailey nodded. "So he's made the phonecall and located her, by which time he's cutting it fine."

"And that saved her life," I said. "I hesitate to say she's a lucky lady but she does seem to scrape through. Did she have any other visitors, d'you know?"

"No," said Bailey. "Not even the usual, Tom and what's her name?"

"Giselle," I said. "Are you sure they haven't been in today, only…"

I was about to say that Laura had seen Tom in Blackwells but, if it turned out to be an important detail, I'd have kicked myself for sharing it.

"Somebody popped in," said Bailey. "Round about dinner time. Didn't want to see Julie, left a big bunch of flowers."

"Who was that?"

"Japanese lad. Didn't leave a name."

As Laura and I walked along the Woodstock Road the mood between us wasn't quite as it had been earlier, in Brown's. The safety factor had gone. She'd seen me lose my rag with McKinnon. I tried to make small talk. What I came out with was so small as to be inaudible to the naked ear.

"Do you always use the Park and Ride?" I asked, feebly.

For some reason she took it as mockery.

"I do," she said. "I'm one of those boring people who do as they've been asked."

"Who asks you?" I struggled.

"The big sign at the roadside."

"I'll drop you off."

We fell silent as we approached St. Anthony's and on reaching the Land Rover, Laura stood by the passenger door and asked, as if it were a precondition of travelling with me: "What will you do about Bailey and McKinnon?"

"I shall drop them in it."

"It was a genuine mistake."

"And if Julie had still been in intensive care, she might be genuinely dead."

There was a glimmer there, under that ghastly halogen lamp, a definite orange hint of a smile. Followed by another question.

"Don't you think you're a bit too old to pick fights with men half your age?"

"Certainly not. More questions or shall we go?"

"One more. Who tried to kill Julie this time, do you have any idea?"

"No, but he or she thinks Julie knows where two million pounds is buried. And I'm really pissed off that he outran me."

We climbed into the Land Rover and I headed back to the city centre.

"Has the ring road upset you too?" she asked. "It's in the opposite direction."

"I know."

She pursed her lips and sat back to weather the detour I was clearly going to make. As we waited at the traffic lights beside St Giles church, I said, "Look ... I'm sorry. I've got a mild case of A.M.D. but I'm getting on top of it..."

"What is A.M.D?" she asked, half knowing, I suspect, that it would be something to deride.

"Anger Management Disorder," I said. "A police shrink diagnosed it ten years ago."

She looked away and took a deep breath.

"It can flare up at the daftest things," I went on, in spite of her obvious scepticism. "But I have this imaginary Map. It's a little trick an old bank robber taught me..."

The lights changed to green, the bloke behind me hooted. I glanced in the mirror, reached out to switch off the engine.

"No!" she said, severely.

I turned and smiled at her. "Just kidding."

I turned into Walton Street which, in essence, lay somewhere between the Oxford of television drama and the Oxford of reality. Jericho hadn't quite surrendered to up-town trashy stores, milling crowds and buses going nowhere. Nevertheless, an army of bollards had advanced and cut off easy retreat down handy side-roads. On its flanks had come the contradictions of the age, hordes of whispering beggars within firing range of a hundred cash dispensers.

"This is where I lost him," I said, parking up on the kerb, opposite the door in the back wall of The Radcliffe.

"Have we come to mourn?" she asked.

"He jumped the wall and ran down there to a motorbike. By the time I was out on the street he was kick starting it and heading towards me."

Now she was really smiling. "I'm surprised you didn't run after him." I opened my door. "I see, you're going to run after him now."

"Won't be a sec."

I got out and walked along the kerb till I reached the Fiesta. I bent down to the gutter and picked up The Map. I laid it on the bonnet, smoothed out the wrinkles, folded it, and put it back in my inside pocket.

On the way to the Park and Ride I explained to Laura about The Map and she listened. Without comment.

- 11 -

The following day, Tuesday, I said to Hideki over breakfast, "You went to see Julie Ryder yesterday."

"No. Didn't go to see, I go to take flowers."

"Went," I said. "Verb. Past tense of go. I went, you went, etcetera."

Almost inevitably he said: "Okay, I didn't went to see, I went to take flowers."

I looked at him for a moment and decided against fine tuning.

"Good," I said. "Why?"

He wasn't keen on being questioned. "I like Julie. She treats me like grown-up."

"You mean she serves you beer and you're under eighteen." He pretended not to understand what I was talking about, so I moved on. "Julie has regained consciousness. Last night, though, someone assaulted her, in hospital."

He flicked his head, like a startled bird. "She hurt?"

"No, just livid. Angry. But did you see anyone at the hospital, suspicious people, near her room?"

"Two policemen. I speak to them, leave flowers to them."

"*With* them. You didn't see ... Tom Templeman, in the hospital, near the hospital?"

"No. But I see Gizzy in HMV."
"When? What time?"
He shrugged. "Four o'clock."
"Did she speak to you?"
"Sure. She buy CD. Eva Cassidy."
I nodded and began clearing the table.

At about ten o'clock I drove over to Penman Manor where Charnley had set up his inquiry room.

The main house was a seventeenth century pile that boasted one of Oliver Cromwell's boots and very little else. It was all front and no back, Jack once told me. The facade was magnificent, the other three sides serving merely to prop it up. Inside, evidently, the rooms were large, tall, freezing in the winter, stifling in the summer. Neither central heating nor air conditioning had been installed mainly because the owner was skint.

I parked on the main drive and walked up to the stables, set above the house in a sloping woodland of pines, most of them as tall and bare as telegraph poles. Hanging from a large hook in one of the porch rafters, was a small deer. Tied by the back legs, in unnatural length, the white fur of its belly was dappled with blood from the fatal wound received when a car ploughed into it, by the look of things. The head hung small, the antlers neat but unimpressive. The vein at its neck had been severed and blood was dripping into a bucket below. Police humour prevailed. Someone had stuck a note on it saying: "Remember the Green Cross Code."

Inside the stables the atmosphere was casual and off guard, feet were on desks, cookery was being discussed. A young woman detective was berating her colleagues, good naturedly. Most could hardly boil an egg, she said, but here they were with every last detail on how to cook venison. John Faraday looked up from a fresh cup of coffee and hollered:

"Guvnor! You're down on my list to call. Guys, this is DCI. Hawk."

Of the ten people in the room, six rose to their feet. The others did so only when Faraday glared at them.

"How's it going?" I asked one of the late responders.

He smiled and offered me a cigarette which I declined.

"If you've come to give us the benefit of your experience," he said, "you've had a wasted journey."

"Two blokes were picked up early this morning," Faraday explained. "They've been held at Banbury. The boss has gone with a couple of blokes to collect them." He smiled. "And we know about last night at The Radcliffe, by the way. Bailey and McKinnon confessed all."

"So these two Charnley's gone to fetch," I said. "He's bringing them here?"

"They've been on the cards for a few days now." He tapped the side of his nose. "Boss wants a quiet word with 'em before he does the interview at Aylesbury."

"You have facilities for a 'quiet word'?" I asked, looking round.

"There's a room out back like a nuclear bunker. In fact I think it *was* a nuclear bunker."

He gestured to the coffee pot and led me over to it. As the others went back to swapping cookery tips, he said confidentially: "I told Charnley about the shotguns, by the way. He had Terry Quilter run 'em through the system. No jam today, no jam tomorrow, I'm afraid. No licence has ever been issued to anyone with those initials."

I shrugged my acceptance of the fact. "Which one is Terry Quilter?"

Faraday nodded at the studious looking bloke, broad face and steel-rimmed glasses. Twelve years old. He hadn't stood up when I'd been introduced. He was also responsible for killing the deer.

"Who's the girl?" I asked, referring to the only woman in the squad.

"That's Jenny Drew," he said, quietly. "Worth all the others put together."

"And Jack's death is still an accident?"

Faraday rocked a hand in mid air. "Inquest was adjourned, as per normal. You'll be called when whoever's dealing has dealt, but meantime, yeah. Langan was pissed, pathologist says he'd drunk enough Irish whisky to fuel an Easter Rising."

The sound of a vehicle pulling up brought a tension to the room. To a man, and woman, they rose to their feet, cleared desks of cups and rubbish, all of them exuding a body language not so much respectful as fearful. Faraday nodded for a couple of them to go outside and help their colleagues bring in the prisoners.

When Charnley entered, ahead of the arrivals, he stopped and considered the attitude he'd take towards me. He raised a hand, part greeting, part truce.

I said: "All over bar the shouting, I hear."

"Quietly confident, put it that way."

"Congratulations."

And at that he visibly relaxed.

"Aye, well, you know what they say. If you don't catch the fuckers in the first week, you'll spend another six months at it."

I smiled. "And you've got better things to do?"

"Too bloody right! I've got a life out there and I'll not have two half-arsed cowboys get in the way of it."

The cowboys he'd referred to were pitched into the room by Charnley's men and stood, handcuffed, where they came to rest. Charnley turned to the squad.

"Right, lads, and for your information too Mr Hawk, these two little fuckers are..."

"Malcolm Edward Jackson," I said, "and Christopher John Evans."

Charnley looked at me. "You know 'em?"

I showed him the page of mug shots I'd found in the bedside cabinet at The Radcliffe.

"Who gave you that?"

"Nicked it."

"Aye, well, what it doesn't say there is that these two fell out with Jim Ryder four weeks ago, just before their release from Grendon." He turned to the taller, curly headed one. "Jackson here admits to saying he'd call in at The Plough one day and kill the bastard."

"Does he admit to following through?"

Charnley laughed. "Surprisingly, no. Fits the description, though, doesn't he. Tall, spindly sod. Mind you, he can go smaller."

He swung round and punched Jackson in the stomach. Jackson gasped and bent to a right angle, head on a desk. Charnley leaned on his neck and turned to the now terrified Evans.

"This is how we do things here, lad, deep in the woods, all dark and spooky, miles from anywhere. Jesus Christ, we've even got a Hawk ready to stoop. Guvnor, is either of these the man you chased through the hospital?"

He pulled Jackson to an upright position by his hair.

"The bloke wore a balaclava," I said. "Hard to say."

"Well, be that as it may, guess what he's the proud owner of. A new Kawasaki, bought three days ago, cash. Julie Ryder's cash, I reckon."

"No!" said Jackson, as forcefully as he dared.

"Take 'em to The Box Room, John. So called because...?"

He cupped a hand to his ear and the expected reply came back from several members of the squad:

"Because that's where we do the boxing, guvnor!"

Jackson and Evans were hauled away; Charnley reached down to a cupboard.

"Fancy a drink?" he said.

"No, thanks."

He poured himself a large whisky, knocked it back in one.

"So ... you *have* had your nose in my business, I hear. Now's a good time to admit it with me being in such a cheerful mood."

"I've stayed clear, just like you asked."

He smiled, not believing a word of it.

"But I have done some checking," I added. "I've a couple of contacts up at Grendon, I phoned one of them this morning. He says your man Jackson, he'll beat the shit out of a credit card soon as look at it. But people? No."

He smiled. "Oh, aye? What's he say about Evans?"

"The same. He reckons you've panicked, lifted these two for a quick result. And to cover up the fracas last night. You've just nicked a couple of petty thieves for two murders."

Still smiling, Charnley raised a finger, his middle finger. "Only one murder. Your friend Jack Langan got careless."

"That's the other mistake you've made."

He flapped the back of his hand at the door to dismiss me and I left.

The Wyeths lived in a cottage which looked as if it had parachuted in and landed neatly between a converted primary school and the old post office. The reason for its appearance was a large, blue tarpaulin, some thirty metres square, draped over the rotting roof by a thatcher in far off Witney who'd been commissioned to renew it.

What had happened, the village believed, was that Allan had over-indulged his favourite pastime of haggling and had reduced the thatcher's quote to a bare minimum. The young man had gone home to his wife who had objected and had visited the Wyeths to argue her case. Allan had, no doubt, woven his flawless charm over the girl and she had agreed to his knockdown price. A few days later the tarpaulin was put in place, pegged down on all sides, and the re-thatch promised within four months. That was ten months ago, but having toyed with other thatchers' quotes and found them to be astronomical, Allan was deter-mined that the Witney firm should fulfil its promise.

The inside of the cottage was a homage to chaos and low standards of hygiene. I'm not saying that my own should be thought of as a bench mark but I'd been for supper at the Wyeths once and we'd eaten off plates that bore evidence of half a dozen previous meals. The knife I was given clearly doubled as a screwdriver, the prongs on my fork were webbed with hardened tomato. I was pretty sure the salmon Petra dished up had been standing about doing nothing but decompose long before cooking.

As for the chaos, it arose from Petra's aversion to the dustbin. It wasn't that she horded rubbish, she merely horded her past, mainly her children's past. The walls and shelves bore witness to Daisy and Digby's educational progress from the year dot. Drawings, paintings, woodwork, pottery, essays, certificates, photos, anything that vaguely celebrated their development, hung from the walls of Victoria Cottage. I've one or two bits and pieces myself that ring pleasant bells, but to have kept Jaikie's portrait of me, done when he was three years old, would have raised many an eyebrow. I'm simply not built like that. Ellie's playschool model of her mother was, frankly, obscene.

The Wyeths' Beetle was parked outside the cottage. The repair work had been done but the fresh paintwork betrayed where the damage had occurred, the night of Jim's murder. Off-side wing. I went up the front path and knocked on the door.

Petra was delighted to see me. She clearly thought I'd come with news about Charnley and his faded interest in them. Allan appeared from the depths of the house, combing the thin, reddish hair to be presentable for a visitor. He was having a well-earned day off, he said, and in order to take full benefit from it was dressed in a baggy sweater which hung down over the brown corduroys, worn smooth in countless patches. He shook my hand and suggested a drink. I could hardly refuse twice in the same day. He opened a bottle of wine.

"How goes the world with you, Nathan?" he asked. "Settling in?"

"Allan, we did all this last Friday, up at Angie's."

"Ah, yes, but one of us was pissed then, if not all six, so it doesn't count."

"He means he can't remember a word," said his wife.

"In that case I'm settling in fine. How go the plans to change the face of education?"

"Extremely well, thank you for asking. In fact, just yesterday we learned that *Eruditio* will receive a substantial - I say again substantial - government grant. What do you say to *that*?"

"You'd think they'd spend it on schools they've already got, rather than ones you haven't bought yet."

"There's method in their madness, dear boy," he said. "If government is seen to cast bread on the water, then big business will do the same, if only to curry favour."

"How much is *Eruditio* after, then?" I asked.

"Are you belted firmly into your seat? One hundred million quid and, by God, we're on track to get it!"

Two million pounds seemed pretty small beer by comparison. Allan tilted the bottle into the glass he'd set before me. I was pretty sure it was a clean one.

"Darling?" he said, raising the bottle to his wife.

"A tiddler."

He poured his wife the smallest drink I'd ever seen and I raised my own.

"To *Eruditio*, then. May your only problem be that everyone will want to put an N on the end of it."

Allan chuckled. "In a way that will be a mark of our success. It'll mean they know what the word means and how to spell it."

We drank, and then Petra turned to me.

"Nathan, did you ever manage to speak...?"

I raised a hand. "All done and dusted, Petty. In fact Charnley told me only this morning that he's arrested two people for the murder. Keep it under your hat."

"Maybe they'll leave poor Tommy alone now," said Petra. "And Giselle, come to that. I mean one can see their point, of course, nearest and dearest, but the one they call Drew, the woman, is down at The Plough daily."

"It'll be routine stuff," I said.

Allan nodded. "And this business with dear Jack?"

"Inquest adjourned," I said. "Accident, say the police."

"But he was such a careful chap," said Petra, shaking her head.

"Poor, poor man," said Allan. "Poor Jean and the girls, as if they haven't had enough to cope with in their lives."

It was said, I believed, not so much out of compassion but relief that they'd got away with having lied to me about the Beetle.

"Let's change the subject," I said brightly.

"Yes, yes," Allan agreed. "Splendid idea. Name it and off we go."

"How about car crashes?"

He tried to hide his immediate shock but, unable to do so, gave me his usually winning smile.

"What do you mean?" said Petra with only a tenth of her husband's charm.

"You pranged your car up there on The Ridge the night Jim Ryder was killed."

"Who told you?" asked Petra.

"I'm a policeman, we find things out. Listen, I know you didn't play any part in Jim's death but something ... something happened up there and I'd like to know what."

They looked at each other for a moment, then Allan nodded and Petra explained:

"Allan shouldn't have been driving. I mean given the current dealings with ... ludicrously wealthy and over-sensitive people, you don't need me to write the headlines, do you? *Eruditio* Big Wig Pissed as a Fart Behind Wheel?"

Allan was clearly uncomfortable with Petra's journalistic pretensions and tried to moderate them.

"When all we did was just ... come off the road."

"Where?"

His wife jumped in as he was about to answer. "The crossroads at the observatory. Allan took the turn too quickly, wretched car skidded."

"And hit what?"

"Whatever was there ... at the time. Rubbish, I think, someone had..."

"Who or what did you hit?" I insisted.

"I've just said..."

Allan laid a hand on the table to calm the proceedings and, hopefully, follow that up with a truthful account. He set his wine glass down in front of him, gazed into it as if glimpsing an uncertain future.

"I turned onto The Ridge without a second thought. God knows, I could see the other car but for some drunken reason I thought it was my right of way." He shook his head at his own stupidity. "Crunch! It rammed us on the off-side. I stopped, he stopped, the whole bloody *world* seemed to stop. Then I saw there were two of them in the car and to my horror they were hooded. Balaclavas."

"You didn't see a face? Is that the truth?"

"We didn't see a face and as I was composing my resignation letter to Lord Shellaby, the Chairman of *Eruditio*, the car sped off."

"Number plate? Make?"

"I'm sorry, Nathan, no, and that's the truth as well. A dark car, though. Saloon."

"And that's it?"

"Yes."

"I think you mean no, Allan. I drove past that crossroads no more than five minutes later. How come I didn't see you?"

They exchanged another glance. They'd obviously prepared a serialised account of what had happened, in case of trouble, and I'd insisted on hearing the final instalment. Finally, Allan said: "Behind the car, their car, was a chap on a motorbike."

"Marlon Brando? Jack Nicholson?"

"He didn't introduce himself," said Petra, moodily. "Not in the conventional sense, anyway. He got off the bike, came over and stuck a gun in through Allan's window. We were terrified."

"I'll bet you were. Shotgun?"

"No," said Allan. "A handgun."

"He wore a helmet, I take it?"

"Oh, yes, couldn't see his face. Black helmet, black visor, black bike. Talk about creature of the night."

"What did he say?"

"Nothing. Held his free hand out, palm upwards. I thought he wanted money so I handed over my wallet, like a fool. But he didn't want money, of course."

"He wanted to know who you were and where you lived. And now he does."

Allan nodded, took a swig from his erstwhile crystal ball.

"Took my driving licence."

"Then what?"

"He pointed down the Pollicott Road, made it clear that that was the way I should go. So I did. He followed, for about a mile then ... all of a sudden he turned and hared off back the way we'd come." He shrugged with his hands. "I've been expecting the worst ever since."

I leaned back in the chair and reached out for my wine, swirled it round.

"What next, then?" asked Petra. "I mean you say the police have arrested two people."

"The wrong people, but that's their business. The right people wouldn't be hanging around, waiting to be picked up by Charnley. They'll have been well paid for what they did. Well enough to leave the country. Tell you what I find ... strange, though, apart from your behaviour."

Petra flared up. "It is not your place to pass judgement!"

"You think so? Well, not to put too fine a point on it, there's every chance Jim would be alive if you'd acted properly..."

Her hands broke away to her face, trying to fashion a large enough screen to hide behind. She turned from me but couldn't avoid listening.

"...but you chose to save your husband's neck. You had a phone with you. You didn't call the police. Why not? Because the phone was traceable, right back to the man who pays the bill."

There was silence until Allan chose to break it.

"What else do you find strange?" he asked. "Something else, apart from our behaviour, you said."

"The man never said a word to you."

"Not a peep."

"Two things follow, then. He either knew you, in which case he wouldn't have needed to take your details..."

"Unless that was just to scare us," he said.

I nodded. "Or, alternatively he didn't want to blow his cover by revealing that he was a she."

Heading home, I found Prissy Waterman tethering the goats out on the green.

"When did you get back, Prissy?" I asked.

"Half an hour ago."

"Good holiday, good weather?" I asked.

"Excellent," she said. "The girls really enjoyed it, didn't you, Tilly?"

I looked down at the goat she'd spoken to. "But you can't beat the green, green grass of home, eh Tilly?"

Prissy laughed, even though nothing funny had been said. Her mouth opened wide but instead of a throaty roar there came the merest squeak of air passing over her vocal chords. When she closed her mouth again I said: "Give Will a message for me, will you. Nathan says *Emanuelle* it ain't."

"I'll tell him," she said, cheerfully.

Once home I collapsed into Maggie's dad's rocker and Hideki came clattering down the stairs, in a dressing gown, still towelling his hair from the shower.

"Good day?" I asked him.

"Great day," he said. "You want coffee?"

"No thanks. Any ideas about supper?"

"The Crown, I say. Tonight is curry night."

"Good one."

"Tea?"

"No, I'm fine."

"I make some anyway."

"I've just said I..."

The kid was trying to be helpful. Why stop him? In fact why not take a photo for posterity of this rare species, a seventeen year old helping round the house? I closed my eyes and drifted around in the day, winding up at my interview with the Wyeths. This third person, the biker Allan and Petra had told me about: who was it? Kate Whitely, up there on The Ridge, directing operations? It wasn't beyond the realms... And the couple in the car? Hired help or Tom and Gizzy? A family affair, to cash in big time. Inherit The Plough, walk off with the two million? As I dozed off the idea fell away into the darkness...

"I make tea," said the unmistakable voice.

"I have *made* tea," I corrected him, without opening my eyes. "I have made, he has made, you have made."

"Is on table," he added.

I opened my eyes and there they were, the teapot and two mugs of tea. But there was no clue as to why he was so gee'd up about them.

"You and I sit at table. We have..." He wagged a forefinger, beckoning the word, then said triumphantly: "Chinwag!"

I had misgivings, born of four children and a whole heap of chinwags. Since when do kids of seventeen sit down for a good old natter with their elders, unless they're in big trouble?

I took my usual place at the table, Hideki took his directly opposite me.

"Okay, then, what's up?" I said.

He smiled as broadly as he'd ever done.

"You don't notice?"

"Notice what?"

"No, no, first you look."

What the hell was he up to? Had he grown another head overnight, was he wearing something new, had he dyed his hair orange?

"Sorry," I said, eventually. "You've beaten me."

He beamed. "Rock gone!"

He laid a hand on the table and pressed down. The table stayed. I looked down at the feet to see that each sat in an ingenious cup with a small knob at the side for raising and lowering. His mother had come up with the goods. It was my turn to beam.

"You little beauty!" I said, getting to my feet.

In my delight I reached out with both hands to pat his face, both cheeks...

I saw it in his eyes a split second before he moved. I don't know what he did, something with his hands so slight that I can't even re-picture it, but my arms flew out either side of me, paralysed, and Hideki was on his feet, crouching like a cat. A second later he didn't know where to put himself. He had misread the signs, reacted instinctively to an imagined attack and had done so with a speed that was breathtaking. It was a good ten seconds before I said: "It's okay, Deki. No problem."

He wouldn't have it. He came round the table, covered in confusion. He took my hands in his and patted his face with them, just as I'd intended. He tried to explain his sudden outburst.

"Sorry, sorry. In Japan we don't do this. Pat face."

"We don't do a great deal of it in England but..."

"What means?"

"It means well done. Humdinger."

"Sorry, sorry."

There was a ring at the doorbell and Dogge went berserk, just in case we hadn't heard. It broke the tension.

"That'll be Will Waterman," I said. "Anymore tea in the pot?"

Will declined the tea and, before he left us to ourselves, I gave Hideki instructions to book a table for two at The Crown, seven thirty.

Will sat at the table, arms folded across the golfing sweater, head slightly bowed. It struck me that I'd never been this close to him before, so anxious was I not to be hauled through his life story.

He was the type of man who thought his talents had been vastly underrated and, but for a twist of fate, he could have been an Albert Einstein or a Bertrand Russell. A twist in the drama direction, Gregory Peck or George Clooney; a twist towards the musical, Placido Domingo or Jose Carreras. What he'd done instead was teach information technology at a local comprehensive and, according to some of his students, he was lousy at it.

He was in good physical shape, though, for his forty odd years, with a full head of soft, dark hair and a pampered complexion. The eyes were slightly dull, however, on account of their stillness. A schemer's eyes. A liar's eyes.

"...you can imagine my disappointment, Will. There I was thinking if these guns did exist, if someone had walked, or driven down with them to Kate's cottage, they'll be on old Will's security tapes. Down I go to the living room, whack in a tape and what do I see? Our neighbour, heaving away like Michael Douglas in one of his films."

He was gazing at a knot in the wood and, as I spoke, he turned his head slightly as if trying to figure out what it reminded him of. I could have told him, having noticed the similarity myself when the table first came to live at Beech Tree. Map of Australia. In spite of his apparent disinterest in what I was saying, however, he'd been listening to me.

"I mean I know this isn't your fault: your photographic style is fly on the wall, or in this case bug on the ceiling, and you could hardly give them direction, but I could've done with Bella being more - how shall I put it? - pro-active."

With his chin still on his chest he looked up at me defiantly, a dirty old man at bay.

"Have you quite finished?" he said.

"Not really. What I was after clearly isn't on the tapes so I wondered if you or your sister had seen..."

"No!"

"I wondered if you or Prissy had seen any strangers visiting Kate, during the week before the murder?"

"Why would we have done?"

"Because if a leaf drops in this village you're out there before it reaches the ground, checking its credentials."

"No. No strangers."

"Did you see Kate herself, maybe? Carrying the guns, a box, so big?"

I described the size of the mahogany case with my hands.

"No."

"I do wish you'd give my questions time to settle, before you answer..."

"It would still be no."

I nodded. "Sure you won't have tea?"

"No tea."

"There you go again..."

He leaned forward, looked square on at me and stressed every word: "I have not seen any guns!"

"Fair enough. Prissy..."

He was in there like a shot again. "If I haven't seen any, Prissy hasn't seen any."

"You share eyes, then, do you? I was going to say: Prissy, does she know about your hobby?"

"No."

"Who's going to tell her? You or me?"

He looked at me with something almost akin to dignity. "If you'd enjoy doing that, Nathan, go ahead."

"Better coming from you," I said. "Then there's Stefan and Bella. Bit of a problem there, of course. I mean how do you tell a man, without giving offence, that his next door neighbour's got hours of him on tape, screwing?"

I hadn't had much trouble at all, to be honest, but I didn't want Will to know that. He reached down to stroke Dogge's head while he thought.

"I won't say it doesn't bother me, Nathan, because it does. I say that because the rest of the village may think Stef's a bit of a joke, stoned out of his mind half the time, but I live next door to the man. I've heard him when he doesn't get his own way and it isn't a pretty sound. If he were ever to find out about this I'm pretty sure he'd take ... commensurate action."

"If you thought that, why rig up the camera in the first place?"

"We all have our weak spots, our ... compulsions. Yours is an easy one, of course, you drink too much."

I rustled The Map in my inside pocket. Will rose and went over to the window, looked across at Stefan and Bella's cottage. He stood there, quite still for a moment, that smidgen of dignity there in his manner again. Then he said: "I may be a bachelor, Nathan, and no doubt some people in this cruel village think I'm a closet poof. But my weakness is for Annabella Castellone. I'm not saying that a halfway decent tabloid couldn't make me out to be the devil incarnate. I'm sure they'd have a field day."

"Given that you keep goats, I'd say you were playing right into their hands."

"The truth is they simply wouldn't understand."

I slapped the table. No rock.

"If you're going to say the tapes are some kind of homage to her, don't waste your breath."

"The tapes are what they are. But while they're the nearest I'll ever get to Annabella, they also serve to remind me that her husband doesn't deserve her either." He turned into the room, grabbed the air in a passionate fist. "To me she is as beautiful as she's mysterious." He voiced the name, slowly with a flourish of his hand and the best Italian accent he could muster. "Annabella Castellone! The romance of all Italy is in that name! Can't you hear it, see it … feel it?"

"For Christ's sake, it's Bella we're talking about." I imitated her Essex girl accent. "Blimey, Nafan, that dog of yours don't 'alf go nuts for our leftovers."

He smiled, sadly. "That's what England has done to her. Next time she says anything to you, ask her to repeat it in Italian."

"Just so that I understand, you mean?"

He was clutching the air again, both hands this time. "You'll see an instant transformation, from the woman you've just parodied into exotic Neapolitan beauty. Is it any wonder that the great singers have all been Italian? Voices projecting a language the rest of the world could listen to forever!"

His performance was so good I was beginning to wonder if he believed it himself.

"Tell me, does she fuck in English or Italian?"

"Trust you to bring us back down to earth again, Nathan. That's the law for you. No wings."

He jabbed at a particular spot on his head, presumably the focal point of my flightless imagination. He resumed his place at the table and leaned forward, saying, "By the way, if you should feel the need to mention the tapes to Stefan, be sure to tell him that I know what *else* goes on in the bedroom."

He raised his eyebrows, as if to say what do you think of that, then?

"Sounds interesting," I said.

"Not so much interesting as useful. I have a tape of it and, if the need arises, if he threatens me with violence, I shall use it against him. I won't bother you with details, Nathan, it might compromise your position as an ex-police officer. You should also know that the tape is not kept, I repeat, *not* kept in Willow Cottage."

"He will know what I'm talking about?"

"Most definitely." He patted Dogge once more and rose. "Now, could I have the tapes you stole from me back, please?"

The man I thought I had at full squirm had put on a pretty good show.

"I've placed one of them with my bank," I lied. "You can have the other two."

I went through to the living room to get them.

Every second thought I had throughout dinner at The Crown involved Stefan and the 'what else' that went on in the bedroom. Had Will conjured it up in desperation? Or was it real, something he could use as leverage, if need be? I was such bad company throughout the curry that Hideki ate quickly and left me chatting at the bar to a jeroboam of pennies labelled 'Comic Relief'. He went through to the snug where his two girlfriends, Liza and Nicky, welcomed him with a squeal or two.

It came to me in the middle of the night, not with any great force because, as far as I could see, it didn't have a bearing on who killed Jim and Jack. I'd been dreaming, rather casually, that I was strolling down Morton Lane and Dogge had heard Bella's voice. She hared off towards Hawthorn Cottage, leaped over the bottom half of the front door and disappeared. I called several times but she wouldn't come. Bloody dog, I muttered, if I'd had her from a puppy she'd be a lot more biddable than…

Then, as I surfaced, I remembered who *did* have her as a puppy. Drugs Squad. She may have been a reject but that didn't mean she hadn't learned anything. She tried to get into Stef and Bella's house every time she passed it because she'd got a whiff of something she'd been taught to recognise.

So what were we talking about in Hawthorn Cottage? Or rather what were Will Waterman and Dogge talking about? Half a million poundsworth of Burmese heroin or a few quidsworth of local weed?

It could wait, at least until after Jim's funeral.

- 12 -

Aylesbury Cemetery was an average council graveyard, a petrified forest of stone stumps as far as the eye could see, everything below ground, and most things above, long dead. The plot I'd secured for Jim was on the eastern boundary and there was only one wrinkle in the otherwise smooth operation of laying him to rest. I didn't tell Julie, I wasn't sure how she'd take it, but in accordance with a new council ruling, Jim was being dumped on top of somebody who'd died in 1893. His name was Alfred David Fryer, he was thirty when he keeled over, and my heart went out to him at having Jim Ryder dumped on top of him. The headstone had been temporarily removed as a courtesy to the newcomer.

There was quite a turnout to see off James Anthony Michael Ryder. More than I'd expected, but then Julie had become something of a local celebrity and that will have pulled in the riff-raff. She'd been covered extensively by Central News and had appeared on the front page of the local paper three times in a row. First, when the shooting happened, again when she regained consciousness and just this morning, albeit in a bottom paragraph, saying that she'd be attending the funeral. That may have been why Charnley had a police officer poking out from behind every headstone.

Julie was brought to the cemetery from The Radcliffe by the two coppers guarding her that day, who just happened to be Bailey and McKinnon. The latter pushed her to the graveside in a wheelchair. She looked well, considering what she'd been through. Mind you, perhaps two million quid to do as I pleased with would have put the colour back in my cheeks.

She thanked me for arranging the burial and for persuading Reg Balfour to conduct the service. I told her Reg had insisted on doing it. That made up, in some measure, for the poor show he put on. I won't say his manner was offhand but it was clear that he hadn't liked the man he was burying. He kicked off with John, chapter eleven: "I am the resurrection, and the life, he that believeth in me, though he were dead, yet shall he live..."

No chance, I thought, looking round. Live on in the minds of this lot? Jim had no brothers and sisters, his parents were dead. There wasn't one person here today who was going to miss him, not even his wife.

At Julie's side, Gizzy clung to Tom, both kids looking suddenly grown up in their borrowed black. At one point Gizzy turned to Tom and began to sob into the lapel of his overcoat. Given her feelings about Jim, it could only have been for public consumption, an attempt to give credence to the nice girl image she occasionally tried to project. Tom stood resolute, as bewildered as ever, then reached out for his Aunt Julie's hand.

Reg did a quick hop-scotch, skipping a couple of chapters. I'd had the bible knocked into me so hard as a kid I thought it had fallen out the other side, but evidently the names and numbers had stuck. John fourteen: "In my Father's house are many mansions: if it were not so, I would have told you. I go to prepare a place for you..."

Yes, well, we did have a bit of a do lined up for afterwards, back at The Plough.

A proper funeral caught my eye, not fifty yards away from us. A large family was burying a cherished relative, someone who mattered to them. You could tell by the way they stood, propping each other up, bent towards each other in a hive of distress over the grave, white handkerchiefs rising to faces from the pockets of dark clothes. Real tears. Real grief. Folk there because it was important.

A well-cared for woman in her fifties stood apart from them. She wore a black scarf over her head tied under her chin, like a peasant. Only peasants don't carry Gucci handbags. A late arrival, perhaps, unwilling to break the mood at the graveside. She turned and caught my eye. I looked away, back at our cha-rade.

Behind Julie stood Stefan and Bella, she with her arm through his. Stef had found a dark suit from somewhere which was pinching him in the groin and round the stomach. But then so was mine. I tried to see Bella in the way Will Waterman had described her yesterday, made easier now by the long black coat, the black veiled hat. All very Donna Corleone, very Mafiosa, but I could still only see ... Bella. Beautiful, yes. Until she opened her mouth.

As for the thing Will had seen, apart from snippets of their sex life, it was still on my mind. Big drugs or little drugs? You couldn't tell with Stefan. He smiled a lot, spoke softly and cleaned a decent window but that was really all I knew about him. Except that he was clever. When clever men conspire to do evil, an old boss of mine used to say, the rest of us are in trouble.

Talking of clever, Allan and Petra had also turned up which didn't surprise me. They had guilt written all over their clever faces. They stood at the back of the proceedings, beside Charnley and Faraday. They in turn stood convivially with three or four old lags from Grendon.

I must have missed Reg's switch to Revelations but caught up with him at: "And God shall wipe away all tears from their eyes; and there shall be no more death, neither sorrow, nor crying, neither shall there be any more pain..."

I thought yes mate, okay for you to talk, you didn't have a wife like mine. There was a pause in the ceremony, a silence. I thought Reg, in his hurry to get off home, had lost his place. All eyes had turned to me, forcing me to realise that I hadn't just thought the thought, I'd voiced it. I stepped back with a mumbled apology, Laura stepped back with me.

Odd how your mind can roam over things like who killed Jim Ryder, is Stefan Merriman a drug dealer and who's the well-cared for woman in the neighbouring party, all to suppress what's really on your mind. In my case the funeral I'd been to two years, three months and sixteen days ago...

She had moved. The well-cared for lady had come to within ten yards of us. She was either a funeral groupie or had turned up late and, asking for directions at the gate, had been directed to the neighbouring ceremony, not ours. Ours was the one she clearly wanted. She hovered close to us, trying not to be part of the proceedings while at the same time anxious to witness them. She had a hankie up to her face and was dabbing her eyes. I nudged Laura.

"Who's that woman?" I asked, in a whisper. "Do you know her?"

Laura looked at her, narrowed her eyes. "Left my glasses in the car."

"I didn't know you wore them."

"I try not to."

"This puts an entirely different perspective on our relationship."

"What relationship is that?" she mouthed.

"The one you could easily see, if only you'd brought your glasses."

She pinched my arm. John Faraday must have seen me ask Laura who the well-cared for lady was.

"That's Stella Taplin, guvnor," he said, as we walked away from the graveside, five minutes later. "Wife of Jim Ryder's old boss, Freddie. I expect she's come with a load of readymix concrete to bed Jim down with. You coming back to The Plough?"

"Yes," I said.

From the way he nodded, slow and away from me, I got the feeling that he wished I wasn't.

At the traffic lights on the Aylesbury Road, next to the Technical College, I pulled up at a red light and Laura put a hand on my arm.

"You alright?" she asked. "Maggie and all that?"

I nodded. "Guilt, I suppose. She was buried too. I've never been back."

"Maybe you have better ways of remembering her."

A car pulled up beside us, signalling right. The lady driver's hair, halfway between blond and brown, caught my eye. Mouse, they used to call it, but not the way this lady wore it. A tight mass of ringlets falling in expensive disarray. Too much of a nose, I thought, but the rest of the profile worked a treat.

"The woman at the funeral?" asked Laura.

"Stella Taplin," I said. "Not only does her name begin with S, she was crying, back there in the graveyard."

"Nice car, though."

She was referring to the brand new, powder blue Jaguar Stella Taplin was driving. Her light went green, she purred off towards Pollicott and all points north. If Jim had stolen two million from Stella's husband, it clearly hadn't left him penniless.

You could hardly have called it a wake since there wasn't really a party atmosphere, no celebration of the man's life. There were drinks and canapés, sure, but more as a warm up to the re-opening of The Plough that evening. Normal business would be resuming at six o'clock, according to Gizzy, and there were twenty-three tables booked to prove it.

"I can see I needn't have worried," said Julie. We were sitting at the window table, watching Gizzy organise the other girls into serving the drinks and food. "Or do you think I haven't worried enough?"

"Can't have it both ways," I said. "If she'd let the place go, you'd be spitting feathers. She's made a fist of it, you don't like that either."

She raised her eyebrows at Laura. "Men," she said, with a Julie smile. "They'll believe anything if the arse is cute enough."

If the remark had come from somebody who hadn't been shot in the back two weeks earlier, and her husband murdered, I'd have taken exception to it. Tom and Gizzy hadn't exactly restyled the entire pub in Julie's absence, Jesus Christ they hadn't had time. The place had always had a nice mixture of the traditional and the minimal and Gizzy had just beefed that impression up a little. Plenty of tat on the walls - pictures, prints, horse brasses - bare minimum on the tables. In the restaurant she'd hung a series of black and white photos from the 1920s, urchins standing outside local factories, looking forlorn and historical. She'd given the tables unity, she claimed, by the addition of austere vases, each with a single rose in them. Hardly a thorough makeover.

"I like it," said Laura, the peacemaker. "But then I always liked it."

Julie frowned. "Then tell me this. She's twice as bright as our Tommy, so what's her game if it isn't gold mining?"

She beckoned to one of the girls and took a glass of wine from her tray.

"Nice to see you, Mrs Ryder," said the girl, timidly.

"Thank you, Marcia. You too."

Laura and I took drinks and the girl moved on. Laura tried to neutralise the conversation.

"When are you coming home, Julie?" she asked.

"Friday, Doctor Rickson says. I've never been one for the NHS but they've done me proud. I'm even down for free trauma counselling..."

"What's that when it's at home?" asked Elvis, barging into the conversation with his usual finesse. He collapsed heavily into a nearby chair and sledged it up to our table.

"It means I need help to stop jumping six feet in the air every time I hear a bang," she told him. "Or when I think of Jack Langan. What was all that about?"

"Accident," said Elvis, before I could open my mouth. "Silly bugger, changing the drive belt on his saw, slipped and fell on it. Hey presto! A double dose, as they say." He added an ill-considered prophesy: "Carry on at this rate, we'll soon have a village full of widows. You and I'll be laughing, Nathan."

He chuckled and slurped the head off his beer.

"Elvis, you're wanted," I said.

He looked round. "Where, mate?"

"Anywhere but here. Fuck off!"

He looked at me, baffled, expecting an explanation as to how he'd offended. I gave him a fixed glare that said refer to my last instruction. He rose and departed, shaking his head.

"Same old Uncle Elvis," said Julie.

"Is that really his name?" asked Laura.

Julie shook her head. "So called because of the hair-style. It used to be jet black."

"His name's Billy," I said. "Billy Leonard. And he should've been shot years ago."

We looked round the bar. People were congratulating Tom on the food he'd prepared. He'd changed into his chef's whites when he got back from the cemetery and looked like the Tom I knew. The beanpole kid who, in a strong enough breeze, might fold in half. Gizzy was still in her black, looking ten years his senior and bossing him and the girls in fine style. Maybe Julie had a point. Why had Gizzy latched onto Tom? Thinking about it brought back his words to me, the day I'd seen him by the river with Stef. He'd said there were things he wanted to talk to me about. Private stuff. Him and Gizzy stuff. Not the obvious but the *not* obvious...

"I guess it's why she hasn't shown up today," said Julie. We looked at her. "Jean Langan, I mean."

"Understandable," I said.

"Oh, no criticism of her. Poor cow's got enough on her plate."

"Nathan doesn't think Jack's death was an accident," Laura said and, at Julie's request, she went on to explain why.

When she'd finished I said: "How's your memory, Julie?"

She smiled, the polite smile I'd seen her give customers she wasn't sure of. "It's better than the last time you saw me."

"How many people, up there on The Ridge?"

"Two."

"I know you didn't see faces but did you recognise voices, smells, clothes?"

She smiled. "You're beginning to sound like a policeman, Nathan. Voices? Well, I'm not sure one of them wasn't Irish. Belfast as opposed to nice Irish."

"Did you tell the police that?"

"Of course."

"And did you and Jim have any ... outstanding problems?"

"Have we upset anyone recently, you mean? I certainly haven't, I can't speak for Jim. Anyway, Charnley reckons these two young men he's holding..."

"How about things between yourselves?"

Julie smiled at Laura, laying a safe bet in her mind that

she'd told me about the Prozac. "You mean people still keep secrets?"

In case Laura responded, I said quickly, "I just want to catch whoever tried to kill you, Julie."

"I thought that was the police's job."

"Have they asked you where the two million pounds went to?"

I watched her face for signs of uneasiness. There weren't any.

"They have and I told them I don't know. I know you don't believe it but Jim wasn't capable of stealing it in the first place."

She beckoned me to lean towards her, as if she had a confidence to impart, but a gust of laughter over by the bar distracted us. It was the first break in an otherwise sombre morning and came from Charnley and two of the Grendon lags: Charnley had told the joke, they had over-responded to it. Faraday looked as if he'd heard it a million times before.

One of the girls put a tray of canapés under our noses and we chose from it. She moved on. I reached behind for another glass of the red from Marcia and told myself that Laura hadn't seen.

Gradually, as the wine ran freer, so the gathering loosened up. Some friends from way back came over to speak to Julie, Laura and I turned away to give them space.

The black outfit suited her, made her look slimmer for a start. Jacket over a classy top with bunches of silver at her neck and wrists. Huge earrings, like Maggie used to wear. And since an element of comparison had crept in, I wondered how the face looked in the mornings, just after waking up. Better than mine, I reckoned, by about six ravines on the forehead and a couple of gouges down the side of the nose...

"You look great," I said, quietly.

"Thank you." She obviously couldn't bring herself to lie about my appearance. "How long have you had that suit?"

"If I were to say twenty years, almost to the day, what would you say?"

She giggled. "I'd say happy birthday, suit. Is that why you've been knocking back the vino? Celebration?"

I reached out for her hand and didn't care who saw me.

"You weren't supposed to notice."

I was momentarily distracted by the arrival of a couple I'd seen up at Penman Stables, the twelve year old DC Terry Quilter and WDC Jenny Drew. Worth all the others put together, Faraday had said. The pair of them made no approach to Gizzy or Tom, nor to Julie for that matter, but headed straight for their boss, still holding court at the bar. I found that strange. I turned back to Laura and said what I'd been trying to find a moment for all day:

"I take it you and me are ... alright?"

"I'm very well, thanks."

"You know what I mean. Oxford the other day. Losing my rag with Black and Decker over there."

I nodded towards Bailey and McKinnon who were talking to Faraday at the bar. McKinnon had half an eye on me, I knew that. Laura said: "My father had anger management disorder, as you call it. We just called it a filthy temper. He could've drunk you under the table any day. I hated him. I hated him as a child and I..."

She stopped, feeling that she'd spoken disloyally, maybe.

"At least I've got The Map," I said.

"On you?"

I laughed. "Do you think I'll need it?"

"You can never tell with A.M.D," she said, and giggled again. It was a giggle you could live with.

"You've had quite a bit to drink yourself," I said. "That's why you haven't been rationing me. How many?"

"Put it this way. If I try to stand up, it may not happen."

The old friends Julie had been speaking to did some watch checking and the bloke mentioned something about a dog being left alone for too long. They promised to keep in touch with Julie, now that this awful business had brought them together again. They kissed her and took their leave. It was the move most people had been waiting for.

The Wyeths left shortly thereafter and then Bella and Stefan came over to Julie. She thanked him for having propped Tom up over the past fortnight with fishing expeditions and a couple of late night chats. Stefan said it was the least he could have done.

I smiled at Bella. "Hi! How goes it?"

She appeared unwilling to admit, in front of a theoretically grieving Julie, that things were okay.

"Fine," she whispered.

There hardly seemed any point in asking her to repeat that in Italian. I beckoned her closer and said: "Say something in Italian."

She rolled her eyes heavenwards. "Blimey, Nathan, you're as bad as old Will. He's always asking that. What you want me to say?"

"Anything. Say: 'The man over there is a policeman and I don't trust him'."

She glanced round. "Why not?"

"Just say it. Please."

"*L'uomo là è un poliziotto e non se lo fido di.* Fair enough?"

Whatever Neapolitan magic there might've been in the Italian bit, the 'fair enough' killed it.

Once Stefan and Bella had gone, I went over to John Faraday and managed to separate him from his colleagues. A whole host of things were making him anxious, according to his face. He wouldn't say what they were. He was embarrassed. I didn't need to ask the reason for that. His colleagues. He was sober. I said he should get a few drinks down his neck. He refused.

"You staying?" he asked, about as casually as a judge passing sentence.

"Party? I'm first in, last out mate."

He nodded, looking away at Tom. Somebody was complimenting him on the food.

"I wanted to ask you something, John. It's nothing to do with all this. It's my neighbour."

"Which one?"

"Stefan Merriman. This'd all have to be off the record, right?"

He smiled, relaxing for the first time. "Whatever you say, unless he's killed someone."

"Is anything known about him?"

Faraday shrugged. "Couple of things, I believe, both pretty minor. Credit card fraud as a kid and possession, five or six years ago. Cocaine."

"No dealing?"

I knew the look on his face. I'd seen it on coppers a thousand time. Had he overlooked something? Was Stefan the missing link to ... whatever was missing? I tried to make it sound run of the mill.

"Listen, I'm not saying there's a problem but I wouldn't mind you checking, to see if there's more. If you get a free moment."

He turned to where two more coppers had arrived. It seemed odd, the party being nearly over, but they turned out to be Bailey and McKinnon's reliefs. They went over to Julie and asked how the funeral had gone. Like a funeral, she said. Did they want a quick drink before they headed back to The Radcliffe?

While they knocked back a couple of scotches apiece Julie gathered her stuff together and thanked me again for arranging the funeral. She rose and addressed the hangers on, specifically the police faction, telling them to make the most of the free booze. Next week they'd be paying for it. It was said as much for Gizzy's benefit as anyone else's; she was letting her know that her short reign was about to end. With a pause to look at a few of the black and white urchin photos, and turning her nose up at them, Julie left with her escorts.

I wasn't happy that Bailey and McKinnon stayed on. It meant that, including them, there were six coppers in the place now. Everyone knows what happens when coppers get glued to a bar. Nothing. For three days. Ten minutes later, when the Grendon faction and a few stragglers had departed, the coppers outnumbered the rest of us. I could see Gizzy anxious to clear the place ready for the evening. Elvis was at the bar and Tom was trying to shift him. I went over to help.

"Elvis, home to Mother, mate. Give her my disregards."

I'd always thought of him as easy going but he shrugged my hand from his shoulder and pointed at Charnley and his people.

"They're still here," he said in a strop. "Why shouldn't I..."

"They're just going," I told him. I turned to the coppers. "Gentlemen, Mrs Ryder asked me to convey her special thanks to you but Gizzy and Tom have a busy evening ahead, I think we should call it a day."

Charnley looked at me down the broken nose, as if taking aim with a fairground rifle.

"Got yourself a nice little job, then, guvnor? Bouncer in this place?"

His people laughed. They knew better than to do otherwise.

"Not at all," I said, "but unless you've got other business..."

"We have." He set down his glass, leaned back on the bar and said to Faraday: "See to our other business, John."

Faraday looked at me, a mite sheepishly I thought, then walked over to Tom and stood in front of him. "Thomas Malcolm Templeman," he began. "I'm arresting you in connection with the murder of James Anthony Michael Ryder..."

Tom frowned, as if he'd been told a joke he didn't understand. Charnley turned to the WDC. "Jenny, do the girl..."

Drew went over to Gizzy but she wasn't the pushover Tommy had been. She started to back away, planning to make for the door and run like hell but Quilter was there before her, slamming it shut, leaning back on it. Gizzy looked round, picked up the nearest weapon, one of the vases on a table. Rose and water slid out as she raised her arm only for it to be held aloft by Bailey. He took the vase from her and set it down. Drew led off over a stream of Gizzy invective: "Giselle Anne Whitely..."

Any plans I'd had to stay calm must have nipped out through the door before Quilter got to it.

"What the bloody hell is this?" I asked Charnley.

"What's it look like? We're arresting them."

"What happened to the two jokers I saw the other day, Evans and Jackson?"

"They were just the muscle."

Out of the corner of my eye I could see Laura, coming towards me. If she'd had trouble getting to her feet, it didn't show.

"Keep out of this, guvnor," said John Faraday, handcuffing Tom. "We tried to do the right thing today, get Jim buried and his missus on her way back to Oxford."

Quilter and Drew had cuffs on Gizzy by now and were dragging her closer to the main action, where she carried on effing and blinding. Laura reached for my arm. I shrugged her off.

"So what's your case against these two?" I wanted to know. "Two lines in a fucking Will?"

As I took a step towards Charnley, McKinnon was there in a flash, right between us.

"I'm talking to your boss," I said. "You're in my way."

Bailey caught me by the left arm and, as I reached out to grab his head, McKinnon delivered the punch he'd wanted to throw at The Radcliffe the other night. Laura was yelling at them to stop. As McKinnon went to have a second dig at my stomach Faraday caught him by the shoulder, turned him and grabbed him by the lapels. He shouted in his face. "Enough! You too, Bailey!"

Charnley slapped the bar a couple of times and a kind of order descended.

"When you're all quite done," he said, "there's work to do. Get this place locked up and the kids down to The Box Room."

Five minutes later, with Tom gazing at me out of the back window of Faraday's car, like a calf going to slaughter, and Giselle in Drew's car, yelling and spitting at her captors, Charnley and his mob sped away.

It had started to drizzle, that fine misty rain you get in the first weeks of autumn, letting you know there'll be worse to come. Laura and I stood in it. Half a minute must have gone by before I asked, "What happened to Elvis?"

I'd no memory of seeing him leave.

"He high-tailed it through the back door as soon as the trouble started. Are you alright?" I nodded. "That was quite a blow he struck you. Do you want me to take a look?"

"Not right now. Not here." She understood completely. "But I'll have that bastard McKinnon if it's the last thing I do."

- 13 -

Laura came back to Beech Tree with me and while I made sandwiches she sat in Maggie's dad's rocker and dropped off to sleep, courtesy the wine she'd had down at The Plough. Head down on her chest, lips not puckered, mouth closed, no snoring. All of them plus points. I left a note by her sandwich, saying: "Cabin".

I hadn't checked my e-mail for days and needed to touch base with my own kids before I tried to rescue somebody else's. There were thirty nine messages from people I'd never heard of, most of them offering me mortgages and viagra, and four from people I had: Fee, Con, Ellie, Jaikie. They were all well and, from what they'd written, each was reassuringly the son or daughter I knew.

"Dad," said Fee, clearly hysterical. "Bad news about Enrique, Ellie's new bloke. He's in his second year at bloody bull-fighting school, for God's sake! This family does not sanction cruelty to animals of any kind, Ellie knows that, and has put two fingers up at it. Write to her. Tell her to stop seeing him..."

Yes, my darling, and while I'm about it I'll tell the rain not to fall.

"...Glad to hear the book's going well. Love, Fee."

Who told you the book was going well? Ah, yes, that was probably me.

"Dear Dad," said Ellie. "Can you tell Fee to get off my back about Enrique. Love yer loads. Ellie."

Yes, I'm fine, thanks, Ellie. Bit of a sore gut at the moment but that'll pass.

"Dad, Hi!" said Jaikie. "Weirdest thing. Remember Sophie Jenkins, went to Central with me? Well, she's Sophie Kent now, changed her name so as not to be cast as a Taffy all the time. She's out here in L.A. and she's got a part in *All Good Men And True*. We've been seeing quite a bit of each other, lately..."

Say no more. But he did, of course. Screeds about himself, the film, himself again, then Sophie Kent, once Jenkins, and finally about himself, just in case I hadn't got it the ten other times.

The message from Con was, predictably, about money.

"Dad, wouldn't do this to you if you weren't my father..."

Oh, no? Somewhere down the lengthy explanation about a deposit being needed for a car, which he and redhead Rosie could sell before they left New Zealand, were the words: "A hundred quid should cover it."

I should hope so too. A hundred quid covers most things in my life.

"And don't worry about how we're keeping body and soul together. We've got jobs. You want me to repeat that? Jobs! We're pruning apple trees, in an orchard. Rosie wants to be an orchardist now, not a lawyer. Women, eh!"

As if on cue, one tapped on the cabin door and Laura entered.

"Sorry, fell asleep," she said. "This is good."

She was referring to the sandwich which she'd brought with her. She stooped down and kissed me on the cheek. She must've forgotten, what with the wine and the sleep, that we'd never kissed before.

"Kids?" she asked, glancing at the screen.

"Yes, I've got a bit of calming down, praising up and forking out to do, then I'll be with you. Have a seat."

When I'd finished with my children I switched off the computer and turned back to Laura.

"So what now?" she asked.

I tried a full body stretch, in so far as you can in a computer chair. My stomach muscles weren't too keen on the idea.

"I'm going to see Jean Langan. Last time I was round there I never got to ask her what I wanted to. It all went a bit pear-shaped. Tom and Gizzy were there, then we found that Kate had done a bunk. Maybe Charnley's right. The whole thing is a family affair, though I don't know where that leaves old Jack." I gestured vaguely in the direction of Maple Cottage. "Kate's still not back and it was her loft the guns were in."

Laura nodded, reached out and patted my knee. The wine had really loosened her up. Worth bearing in mind.

"And that bloody Stella Taplin is bugging me."

"Because she came to the funeral?"

I nodded. "Why was she there? Why was she crying? Why was she on her own?"

Laura didn't know, anymore than I did.

The unofficial guide to being a copper tells you that bereavement loosens the tongue. Catch someone on the raw, after a personal tragedy, they'll tell you everything you need to know. Unless the bereaved is Jean Langan.

When she opened the door to me it was clear she'd expected to see someone else standing there. She immediately checked her watch. I did the same. It was half-seven and Jean was definitely dressed up for something and it wasn't mourning her husband. The grief damage to her face had been repaired. The freshly streaked blond hair, the smart shoes, the crisp outfit and protective bubble of Calvin Klein's Eternity had assignation written all over them. And why not, I immediately started saying to myself. Why shouldn't she make up for lost time? Good looks like hers, there'd be plenty of men willing to set her clock running again.

She beckoned me in, not because she wanted my company, but because she didn't want the neighbours to see her dressed for a new life.

We stood in the main room, me cramped by the low central beam, Jean near the front door as if inviting me to leave as soon as possible.

"You were just off out," I said.

"Yes ... yes."

"To see Gizzy? I take it you've been informed. Have you heard from Kate?"

She hesitated, wondering which question to answer first. "I've seen neither hide nor hair of Kate. Gizzy's being held at Chesham, I'm going over to see her later."

"Well, I won't keep you but there is something I need to know. Did Kate ever own a motor-bike?"

She frowned, wondering where the question had come from. "Yes, she had one for a while, terrified us all to death, but..."

"What about Tom? Does he ride one?"

"I've no idea."

And with that she clearly expected me to leave.

"Where are your other kids, Jean? I'd want mine here, time like this."

"Well, I didn't. I'd rather cope on my own."

I looked her up and down. "Not *all* on your own, though."

"Nathan I don't know what gives you the right to question me like I'm some shoplifter you've dragged in..."

"You mean my curiosity puzzles you? Well, your behaviour does the same to me. Your old man was killed five days ago, one niece has been arrested for murder, the other's nowhere to be found and you're off out on the razzle."

She looked at me, scared of where I might go next. The phone rang and she gestured for me to go through to the kitchen and I obliged. I eavesdropped on the conversation. Make what you will of her side of it:

"No, yes ... Yes ... Five minutes? ... No, village hall, yes ... Right."

"Sorry about that," she said, coming to join me in the kitchen.

I'd settled on one of the wrought iron stools.

"You should've seen him," I said. "Jack, I mean, lying across that saw. I've seen bodies chopped up before but none was a patch on your old man." She shuddered, closing her eyes. "How long were you married, I forget?"

She held her hands together, pleading. A bit too melo-dramatic to be convincing. "Nathan, you have to let me deal with this business in my own way."

"But I can help, Jean. I've been through the sudden death thing. Different to you, of course, but then I was never married to the wrong person."

With that low blow I conceded the moral high ground, always assuming I'd held it in the first place. She looked at me with steady, intelligent eyes.

"Yes, I'm sorry I confided in you that evening at The Plough. Jack and I were badly matched, certainly, but it doesn't mean I'm happy that he's dead. And it certainly doesn't mean I have to account to a sanctimonious old copper for my actions."

"You will, if I find out you're in any way connected to his death."

"That is a terrible thing to say, Nathan!"

"Till you've done my job, Jean, you don't know what people are capable of. They'll do anything if the price is right, the urge compelling enough."

She cocked her head, facetiously. "Well, I'm glad we've such an authority on evil, living in the village. Makes me feel a whole lot safer." She stared at me for a moment. "I have to go now."

I made to leave, turned back at the door.

"I like the hair, by the way. And the new outfit. Anyone I know?"

"Different league," she said.

I didn't go straight home, of course, I took a detour up Backwater Lane to the village hall. It was dusk and a few kids were skate-boarding in the road. Learners. One of them fell off and was up on his feet in a flash, back on the board.

A car was parked outside the village hall. It was a powder blue Jaguar, same registration as the one Stella Taplin had driven to Jim's funeral in. The bloke at the wheel was fifty-ish with dubious fair hair, the colour almost certainly out of a bottle. He also had a sun-tan like nobody ever gets, so presumably that was out of a bottle too. He was talking on a mobile and tried not to look at me as I walked past. I tapped on the window, he finished the call and the window slid down.

"Who are you?" I asked.

"Freddie Taplin. And you?"

"Nathan Hawk. We must have a chat sometime. Jim Ryder and all things deriving therefrom."

He smiled and reached into the glove compartment for a business card, handed it to me.

"Drop in, any time you're passing."

"I'll do that." I nodded back the way I'd come. "She won't be a minute."

I didn't bother going to bed, I sat up watching a film instead, one I'd seen so many times before I was virtually singing along. As a little kid Jaikie used to do a lot of that and it annoyed the beJesus out of the rest of us. Not only would he say the lines, he'd tell you what was going to happen ten seconds before it did. Throw what we could at him, cushions, food, soft toys, we never stopped him. I'm not sure if we really wanted to.

The film ended in the same way that it had every other time I'd seen it. It was two-thirty, time to set off for Chesham. The police station there had the only provision for women within twenty miles, that's why Gizzy had been taken to it.

Am I kidding myself, or was there a time, not so long ago, when night was night? Most people went indoors when it got dark, by midnight most of them were in bed. Those still walking about a town like Aylesbury at two-thirty in the morning were either coppers or up to no good. Nowadays there's a whole civilisation strutting its stuff all through the night. Hundreds of people walking about, kids gathered under the perpetual daylight of street lamps, adults moving from all-night shop, to bar, to party. I read somewhere that we sleep two hours less a night than we did in 1950. That's an awful lot of time in which to break the law. And not a copper to be seen.

The road to Chesham was off the dual carriageway out of

Aylesbury. You took a left and climbed up the scarp, the countrified road lit only by security lights on the front of people's houses, tripped as you passed by. In the rear view mirror I could see cars below me, making the same twists and turns as I had, headlights sweeping the side of the hill as if looking for me.

That was another thing. Cars at night. It wasn't that long ago that someone driving after midnight was either a long-distance lorry driver or a villain. Or maybe I'm remembering it all wrong.

I turned right, by the Old Priory at Lee Haven, a short-cut Jack Langan had once shown me. The road takes you through beech woods for about three miles and lands you on the outskirts of Chesham. I took it carefully, mindful of the deer Terry Quilter had killed. It would've been on a road like this, unfenced with the trees skeletal against the moonlit sky. Roots ran the length of the high banks, like pipe work through some ancient building, twisted and of many sizes, but somehow doing the job.

I'm not sure what it was that alerted me. I think it must've been the contradiction of a motor-bike, keeping its distance behind any car, especially one going at no more than thirty-five miles an hour. But there he was, two hundred yards behind me. At first I thought it was a car with a duff headlight. I wound down the window and accelerated. I heard the bike accelerate too. He, or she, was following me.

If it was the same bike I'd tussled with at The Radcliffe, then the rider wasn't here for the good of his health. Or mine. I tried not to put myself centre stage, I didn't like the role I'd been offered, but on past performance this bastard had come to kill me. That begged a simple question. Why? The answer was another question. Two in fact. What had I found out that was so crucial? What did I know that I didn't know I knew?

I drove on for another mile. The biker kept his distance, two hundred yards. And then I realised I was being paranoid.

The guy behind me was one of a million bikers, taking it easy on a winding road. If he'd been after me I'd have seen him earlier, right back at Winchendon. He'd have seen me leave, I'd have heard him, noticed him, especially on the dark stretch out of the village, by the church.

It was a good argument but that was no reason to believe it.

There was a row of cottages round the next bend, seven or eight in all. Sixties farm cottages, now owner occupied. I remember seeing one for sale last year and choking at the price. I signalled left, pulled into the lay-by behind a row of parked cars.

The motor-cycle slowed down. When the rider drew level he stopped, turned and looked at me, through black visor in black helmet. The creature of the night Allan Wyeth had described. He was five feet away from me and whichever way I'd argued it before his intentions were now clear. He'd been following me and now he'd caught up with me. We must have gazed at each other for another ten seconds, which is a long time when you think the other bloke's got a handgun somewhere. All the time I was thinking: I know one thing about you, much good it'll do me. You aren't Beanpole Tommy. He's in a police cell in Aylesbury. The thought made me feel better. In fact it spurred me into action. I put my foot right down to the floor, turned the wheel towards the biker and the Land Rover leaped the distance between us. It caught the bike on the back wheel. The bike almost came away from beneath the rider. He held it, just, revved the engine and screeched off towards Chesham. I took a deep breath.

A light came on in one of the cottages. Then another and then a third. I spent the next ten minutes explaining how some maniac had tried to overtake me. I was offered tea and sympathy and use of the phone. Someone suggested I call the police. I said I'd drop in at the station when I got to Chesham.

I thought they'd done away with nicks like Chesham but it must have slipped through the net. It was a dead ringer for the first police station I ever worked in. Seppleton, North London. That too was shamelessly Edwardian, with a curved hard wood counter, parquet floors and radiators like organ pipes. From the front door you could see the stone steps down to the cells. They were tellingly well worn and the cells themselves, not visible, were iron barred, dark and forbidding with high grilled windows, open to the elements. When it rained the prisoners got wet and called up the stairs to the duty room. The duty officer would call back, usually with unhelpful suggestions.

The Duty Officer at Chesham was a Sergeant who looked as though he'd been sat behind the counter for twenty years without moving. He was close to my age with off-piste white hair either side of a glacial slope running down to a smooth, shiny forehead. Set in the bumpy slush of an overweight face, the eyes were alpine sky blue. They grew alarmingly large, as he looked up at me through powerful reading glasses. He lowered his head slightly, peered over them and they shrank again. I put a slight tremble of exhaustion in my voice.

"Morning," I said. "My name is Whitely, I believe you're holding my niece, Giselle."

"Among others," he said, looking me up and down.

"I left home the moment I got the call. Been driving ever since."

"Where from?"

"Keswick. The Lakes."

"Nice place to live, I shouldn't wonder, before the tourists got to it."

I nodded. "I wondered if there was any chance of me being able to see her."

He still hadn't risen from the chair. He leaned forward, looked me up and down again, then yelled: "Becky! In here, please!"

A WPC came to an adjoining doorway, plastic cup in hand. "Sarge?"

"Go up and ask Miss Whitely if she'd like a visit from her uncle..." He looked at me.

"Nathan," I said. "Nathan Whitely."

"From her Uncle Nathan. Take a good look at the gentleman, describe him to her first."

"But she knows what I look like, Sergeant."

I thought it was a nice touch. Innocent. Naive. And it gave him the chance to patronise me.

"Security from our end, sir. For all I know you could be anyone."

I could hardly fail to see his point. When the WPC returned to say that Gizzy would love to see me I was taken to the back entrance of the building and led across the car park to a modern development, the secure female units. The Custody Officer there spoke of them like bed-sits she was trying to let.

"They were only built last year," she said. "E.C. specifications, proper facilities, all nicely decorated. Wouldn't mind spending the odd night in one myself. D'you mind if I just check you, Mr Whitely?"

I raised my arms and she whisked her hands over me and neither of us felt a thing.

"Right," she said. "Your niece is in number five, I'll give you, say, quarter of an hour. Enough?"

"Plenty. Thanks."

Gizzy played the role as written for her. When the Custody Officer showed me into unit number five, she hurried over and flung her arms round me.

"Uncle Nathan!"

I held her and shushed her gently. She began to sob. Gizzy making a meal of it, I thought, until I held her at arms length. The tears weren't an act, they were relief, anger and fear rolled into one. I drew her close to me again and winked my thanks at the Custody Officer which gave her an edge of confidence to leave us on our own. She closed the door to within six inches, holding it ajar with a shoe. I saw her shadow on the wall, hunched and monstrous, as she took a chair and planted herself within easy reach.

I let go of Gizzy and gestured for her to sit at the small table opposite me. I put a finger to my lips.

"Just the words," I said, nodding at the shadow. "Soft and low, no temper, no swearing, no Gizzy-isms. Otherwise she'll be in here like a shot."

I pushed the box of tissues across the table to her, she took a couple and blew her nose.

"Why come at three in the morning?" she asked, with a sniffy smile. "Couldn't you sleep?"

I lowered my voice to a whisper and felt the shadow beyond the door move closer. "No one's going to ring Charnley at this time of day, to check if a man answering my description can visit you. Have you been questioned?"

She nodded. "Down at Penman Stables. DC Drew. She is a real cunning bitch! Tommy was in the other room, I could hear him getting upset and them really winding him up..." I calmed her again, finger on lips. "Where've they taken him, do you know?"

"Aylesbury. Listen, Gizzy, I don't know if you're mixed up in these killings or not." She was about to protest, I stopped her. "That's the truth, I don't. But on a scale of probability, you're up at the innocent end and that's mainly my nose at work. I like you, Gizzy. Always have done and we both know that. But I also know the police must've had a reason to pull you in."

She put her forearms on the table, rocked back and forth on them in a classic show of distress. "The will. Julie's bloody will, naming Tommy as her sole beneficiary, or whatever it's called. Do they really think we'd be dumb enough to kill her, two weeks after she signed it?"

"What other reasons did they have?"

"Tom's fingerprints. They're all over the boot of Julie's car, inside and out. Did I know how they got there? Drew asked me. Of course I bloody knew! He fetches and carries the kitchen stuff, I said, uses Julie's car." She looked up at me. "Why's it so important?"

"One of the killers blew the lock off with a shotgun, to get at Julie's bag."

That seemed to alarm her, but she kept her voice down.

"Shotgun? That'll be why they asked me about Tommy and his shooting."

"Does he own a gun?"

"Yes, they took it away days ago."

"You mean they came round to the flat and he just handed it over?"

"Yes, why not?"

"No, that's good. Nothing to hide. Who asked for it? Who came to the flat?"

"There were two of them. Terry Quilter was one, he used to go to the same gym as me. The other was called Bailey, I think. Young, dark haired, bit spotty. We told 'em, he's into clay shoots and rabbits and stuff, but not bloody people. Specially not his own flesh and blood!"

The shadow in the corridor shifted a little. It was a diplomatic warning for us to keep it cool. Gizzy added, sheepishly, "Drew, she tried to tie it in with Tom's police record."

I took a deep breath and sighed accordingly, sinking down in the chair. Uncomfortable. I think better like that.

"I'm learning stuff tonight. I didn't know he had a record"

"Nor did I." She pursed her lips. If they ever got out of this situation in one piece it would be a sore point between them. "Four years ago, he stole a CD player from Comet's, the stupid sod. He took it down off the shelf, according to Drew, ran for the door and legged it across the car park, followed by half a dozen customers. He got to the Fire Station and his asthma caught up with him, he had to stop. So there he was, player in one hand, inhaler in the other, threatening to use it on them. I mean that's his level, right?"

"I didn't know he had asthma either."

But it was a comforting thing to learn. It meant he could hardly have been the person I chased through The Radcliffe. Nevertheless, I said, "You were in Oxford, the day someone had a second go at Julie." She nodded. "Why didn't you go to see her? You'd been every other day?"

She shrugged. "We had ticket for Jongleurs, the comedy club."

I nodded. "Friend of mine saw Tom in Blackwells, looking ... out of place."

She smiled at that. "Looking guilty, you mean. When we're in Oxford, he goes there for a flick through the cookery books, pinches a recipe or two. Cheaper than buying the book."

I laughed gently, partly to keep the shadow happy. "Tell me something, Gizzy, and I'm not the only one who'd like to know this ... Jean, for example. Why go for a bloke like Tommy?"

She drummed her fingers on the table for a moment, crisp, sharp and fast.

"Jean went for a bloke like it. So did my mum. Maybe it runs in the family." She looked at me, fiercely loyal. "Not that it's anyone's business."

"It means the police'll think you're the brains of the outfit."

"We're not a bleeding outfit!" she said, too loud.

I heard the metal chair in the corridor scrape along the floor. I turned to see the bulbous shadow rise and loom towards us. The door opened and the Custody Officer put her head and shoulders round.

"Everything okay?"

I was patting Gizzy's hand by now and she'd started to sob. Phoney, this time. I pushed the tissues across to her all the same.

"We're okay," I said, with another wink. "You know what it is. Time to reflect and all that..."

She nodded but didn't go.

"Five more minutes?" I asked.

She answered by withdrawing her head, replacing the shoe in its door wedge position.

"So, police have been round to the flat in the past week?" I asked.

"They came first of all to tell us that two blokes had been arrested. They kept coming back."

"Ah!"

"What does that mean?"

"It means Charnley's a bit sharper than I gave him credit for. There were certainly two blokes in The Plough, the night of the murder, but the lads they arrested, Jackson and Evans, it wasn't them. They were hauled in as decoys, if you like, to make you drop your guard."

Gizzy looked up at me, like a boxer with both hands tied behind her back.

"It worked?" I said.

"It was that WPC Greene. Remember her?"

I nodded. "She was with you, the night it happened, baby-sitting."

"She came back again, several times. One time - I must have been in the shower or something - she and Tom started talking about the football match that had been on, night of the shooting. I mean it's straight out of Columbo this and being Tom he fell for it. Did he remember that goal dispute, some bloke being off-side? Tom said he did..."

She started rocking on her forearms again.

"And there wasn't a dispute?"

She shook her head. "We hadn't been watching the match. I mean we'd left the telly on, but..."

"Where were you?"

"Round at Kate's."

"I thought you two weren't speaking."

"Well, that's the point. It was time to make up." She paused, picked at one of her fingernails. "And things."

"What things?"

"Private. The solicitor said I didn't have to answer."

Regardless of the shadow on the wall, I said sharply, "Fuck the solicitor! It's a murder they're investigating, Gizzy. Private has gone public, and you lied to them. Why?"

She took a moment to think, searching her fingernails for inspiration.

"It was daft, I know, but I thought it would look so bad for us. We wanted to quit working for Julie. We were sick of the arguments, Tom being told he was useless, me being groped by Jim on his weekend leave. We thought Kate might be able to help."

"By doing what? Killing Jim?"

"Don't be so daft!" she protested. "We wanted to borrow money, to buy our own place. We thought she might know people we could ask, without it getting back to Julie."

"What time did you get to Kate's?"

"Tennish. Tom had the evening off, Julie said I could finish early. She didn't like me hanging around if Jim was in the kitchen."

"And he was shot at eleven thirty-five."

"I know. They kept asking, over and over, where was I..."

"Over and over? You mean you haven't told them yet?"

She looked at me. The eyes said she hadn't.

"Kate's your one alibi, Gizzy!"

She was still looking at me, waiting for something to dawn.

"Okay," I said, "so Kate's disappeared but..."

That wasn't it. She was still looking, not a flicker, not a twitch on her face.

"Oh, Christ," I said, when the penny finally dropped. "You think maybe she *did* go after Jim. You're trying to protect her."

She nodded. "We left her cottage at eleven," she whispered. "That gave her thirty-five minutes..."

For the first time since I'd entered the room my neck muscles let go of my head which flopped a little out of sheer relief.

"Thirty-five minutes?" I said. "In which to rally two trigger happy friends and get up to The Ridge? Either one of those things would've taken half an hour. Then there's the motorbike, where did she magic that from?"

"Stefan has a bike. He's just done it up. Him and Tommy are always messing about with..."

With spanners, I thought. Somebody had just used one to tighten up my neck again .

"Right," I said, as heavily handed as I could in a whisper. "Tomorrow morning, if it ever comes, you tell Rosa Kleb out there you want to see one of Charnley's mob. Whoever comes – it'll be one of the girls - you tell them exactly what happened that Friday night."

I rose from the table and so did she.

"Where are you going?"

"To find your sister."

I made it sound like a job almost done but part of me still wasn't sure I'd find Kate alive. All very well for us to see her as an avenger, albeit one who had overstepped the mark and done away with Jim Ryder. But what if she turned out to be a victim, just like her uncle?

- 14 -

The girl on the switchboard where Kate Whitely worked was too chirpy by half, but then I'd only had three hours sleep.

"Good morning, this is Turner Wallpaper, my name is Siobhan, how may I help you?"

"Kate Whitely, please."

There was a flicking of pages at the other end, right through the alphabet to W, presumably.

"I'm afraid I've no one of that name on the list," said Siobhan.

"Sorry, that's her maiden name. Try Kate Jamieson."

More flicking. No luck. And a measure of suspicion in Siobhan's voice.

"I don't appear to have that name either."

"Right, can you put me through to the Personnel Officer?"

Siobhan countered: "I think you mean the Human Resources Director."

"I know what I mean, but if the Human Resources guy wants a chat, I'll be happy to oblige."

"It's a girl," she said.

"I'll be even happier."

"May I ask who's calling?"

"Mr Carter," I said.

"Won't keep you a moment."

That was a lie, born out by most of Beethoven's Pastoral being pumped down the line while I waited. It was meant to sooth my nerves but didn't. I was thinking about Kate and why Siobhan had never heard of her. Eventually a perky voice said, "Good morning. Human Resources, Deirdre McKay speaking."

"My name is Carter, I'm a solicitor working on behalf of the Accident Compensation Board. I've been trying to get hold of one of your employees at home, Mrs Kate Jamieson, or Miss Kate Whitely, as her claim form puts it."

"Kate? Yes, I know Kate. She hasn't worked for Turner's for nearly a year."

I asked if she was certain about that. She couldn't have been more so. Ever hopeful, I asked, "Where does she work now? Do you know?"

"I have an address. Studio 5, Blenheim Stalk, Foley Bridge, Oxford."

"Thank you."

I put the phone down and made breakfast.

Over a second cup of coffee I opened the road atlas and found Stadhampton where the Taplins lived. Most people I know live on the edge of a page, which makes finding their houses difficult enough. The Taplins lived dead centre, right in the fold, underneath a staple. At Ashenham Place, according to the business card Freddie had given me, the day of his assignation with Jean Langan. It was on the way to Oxford. I could nip in to see Stella *en route* to Kate's new business address.

It must've been ten o'clock as I drove out of Winchendon and, passing Victoria Cottage, saw John Faraday and Quilter emerging from it, walking towards the former's car. Petra was standing at the front door, watching them go, her face as hard as the meaning of her forename. I slowed down and said to Faraday, "How's it going?"

He turned and pointed at me, lips tight, eyes narrowed.

"Word," he said, angrily. "Not here, though."

"Pub?" I suggested.

"It's not that kind of a word. Village hall, the lay-by."

I drove round to Backwater Lane and waited for them to join me.

The first thing Quilter did, when they pulled up, was to light two Gauloises and give one to Faraday, who paced a short line, back and forth, hyper-ventilating on the cigarette, tapping it every two or three seconds. He stopped suddenly and barked at me: "Go on, ask me what we were doing round at Victoria Cottage."

I shrugged with open hands, waiting to catch anything he threw at me.

"Consider it asked."

"The Wyeths' car, right? She'd lied to us, day after the shootings. She said it was in to have the exhaust fixed. The same car body shop you spoke to told us she pranged it."

"Allan did. He was driving."

"Whatever. So, we put this to her, it being a loose end. Our guvnor's a bugger for tying up his loose ends. This matter has been dealt with, says Lady Muck, by Nathan Hawk and your superior."

"Well, I did sort of..."

He swung round at me.

"You didn't tell us there was a third person up on The Ridge, night of the murder. On a fucking motor-bike!" He threw his cigarette down on the pavement as if trying to spark a firecracker. He yelled at Quilter.

"Can't you lot smoke ordinary fags, for God's sake?"

Quilter turned away, as if he might cry and didn't want us to see. I shrugged as apologetically as I thought my oversight warranted.

"I didn't tell you because your boss doesn't believe what I say. For example, guns in the loft."

"*I* believed you. *I* checked it out. Isn't that enough?"

"Have you found them yet?"

There was a silence, hopeless rather than embarrassed. I'd reminded them of their biggest problem.

"They're my department," said Quilter, "and we reckon they won't be found."

He had a soft, pleasant voice, the sort which goes with a man who does five years in the job and gives up for want of being heard.

"Of the two men who fired the shots," he went on, "at least one of them was Irish, according to Julie Ryder. Maybe that's where they've gone... back home and taken the weapons with 'em."

"So their names aren't Jackson and Evans, then," I said. "Good old Irish names though they be?"

"No," said Faraday. "They've been released."

"And this car that was nicked, night of the shooting, from... Wheatley, was it?"

Faraday nodded. "It was found in Wendover Woods. Burnt out. Joyriders."

"And the third person biker, any ideas?"

"No," said Faraday, growing weary of me pointing out that the case was unravelling before his eyes. "Have you, and you're just not telling?"

"I know he - or she - followed me last night."

"Christ Almighty! Now it's a bloody woman. Followed you where?"

"Around. Pulled up right beside me, quiet country lane. Same description Petra Wyeth will have given you. I rammed the bike, you can see it's the clean dent on the bumper."

Quilter went to examine it.

"Any news on my neighbour, Stefan Merriman?" I asked Faraday.

"Only that I wasted two or three hours digging into his past. The guy was done for possession of cannabis when the law thought it mattered. He also used his house-master's credit card to buy a computer with. Jesus, if you're going to help us, guvnor, don't waste your time on crap like him."

"He has a motor-cycle."

"Him and two million others." He placed a foot on the front tyre of the Land Rover, leaned forward into a stretch. "Where you off to, anyway?"

"To find Tom Templeman's alibi before Charnley persuades him to confess. He'll find Gizzy a bit tougher, but it's only a matter of time."

Faraday stretched the other leg and said, touchily, "Come off it, guvnor. He may be a bull in a china shop but he's nothing if not professional."

"He puts the fear of God into *you*, John. Think what he'll do to Beanpole Tommy. All that 'give it up of your own free will, lad, don't make me come looking for it.'"

Faraday nodded, slightly. There was truth in what I'd said.

"How's the stomach, sir?" asked Quilter, as I climbed back into the Land Rover.

It was a genuine enquiry, not a wind-up.

"Fine," I said, starting the engine. "How's McKinnon's fist?"

Ashenham Place, Freddie and Stella Taplin's house, was a square-built Queen Anne mansion, ten times the size of mine with only twice the number of people living in it. The figures assumed that Hideki was just passing through, albeit very slowly.

I guess Ashenham had another purpose than as a dwelling, though. It told people that its owner had been successful, that he'd sold so many packets of frozen fish he could afford a house he couldn't walk round in a single day. It sat in a long, shallow valley and was defended by sycamore, beech and horse chestnut trees, so old and tall they must've been planted the same day the builders took their leave. Behind the house, the terrain rose gently to The Ridge. The hillside to the front was the last wrinkle in the landscape before the Vale of Oxford.

As I approached the house, down the long gravel drive, two Great Danes came loping towards the Land Rover and tried to corral it into submission with barking and feinting. The Land Rover wouldn't be bullied and came to a halt beside the powder-blue Jag. The dogs conceded their defeat and greeted me with cautious approaches and retreats. One of them brought me a rubber toy to throw and friendship was declared.

Freddie Taplin called to me from a gap in the yew hedge to the West of the house.

"Must've read my mind, Mr Hawk. Just taking a breather. Beer by the fountain."

He was dressed for organising other people to do the real job of gardening: old jeans, waistcoat over a thick shirt with the sleeves rolled up. He descended, via stone steps, to a sunken garden, the Great Danes and I followed him.

Dead centre of a lawn you could play billiards on, never mind croquet, was a large, stone-built pool with a fountain playing out of the mouth of some vaguely mythological creature. The breeze occasionally whipped the spray towards flowerbeds, where dahlias and delphiniums were fading in the seasonal decline.

Two men who'd been working on the enclosing hedge, father and son by the look of them, had taken their boss's cue and settled on the edge of the lawn. The old man took a flask from a rucksack and poured tea into two plastic cups.

At the pool, Taplin reached into the water and took out a can of beer, wiped it on his waistcoat and handed it to me.

"Been warm today," he said. "Indian summer, but winter's on its way. You like the winter, Mr Hawk?"

"I can take it or leave it."

"Why not head for the sun, France or Spain? Isn't that where coppers retire to?"

"Retirement's been getting me into trouble recently," I said.

He opened his own beer and started to drink.

"Doesn't suit you?"

"We don't suit each other."

He turned to the pool where a flotilla of Koi carp had approached. He indulged them with food pellets from a waistcoat pocket.

"In The Imperial Palace, Tokyo," he said. "These guys grow to two, three feet long."

"I know. I've seen them."

"You've been there?"

"Daughter. Lives there."

The Great Danes had come over for their share of the bounty. Taplin had dog biscuits in another pocket, threw a couple in the air and the dogs leaped for them.

"You know, if you're looking for a challenge with good money attached, why not come and work for me? We're expanding, going East. We'll need someone in there, right from the start, organising security."

"I've handled security for many things, Freddie. I've body-guarded royalty, politicians, even the Pope on one occasion. I never thought I'd be asked to mind frozen fish."

He laughed. "Fish have been good to me. They could be good to you."

"They already have been," I said. "My father was in fish..."

"Oh, yes?"

"...and chips."

He smiled. "You know the rewards it can bring, then. Think about my offer. I'm serious."

I'm sure he was. However, not only was his hair colour out of a bottle, the hair itself had been around the block. It was a transplant and sprouted from the tanned forehead in clumps, much as the bristles on a toothbrush do. I wouldn't work for a man like that for all the fish in China.

"Is your wife not at home?" I asked.

"No ... no. Stella only spends two, three days a week here."

"And the rest of the time?"

He tried to make it sound normal. "We have a flat in London, easier to reach her various charities from there. Was it her you wanted, then?"

"I wanted to know why she was at Jim Ryder's funeral."

"Well, I can tell you that," he said, dragging an orange forearm across his mouth. "When Jim worked for me, Stella was his secretary. They were close."

"So close that she was crying?"

He looked away. "She's a very emotional person. There was never anything between them, if that's what you mean. Stella spent most of her time weaning him off his addictions. I'd say she was crying at the waste of it all."

He'd mentioned the addictions in hushed tones, so I guessed we weren't talking about caffeine or tobacco.

"What was he on?" I asked.

"For at least three years before he went inside Jim was pissed at ten o'clock in the morning and coked up by seven in the evening. God knows what else he did in between."

Maybe this is what Julie had wanted to tell me in The Plough, after the funeral.

"When did you marry Stella, Freddie?"

He had to think about it. "Eight years ago? Just after Jim joined the company?"

"And as the boss's wife she didn't mind being a secretary?"

"Not at all. She rather enjoyed the counterpoint. Living here, working in an Aylesbury office. Look, I know why you're asking these questions..."

"Jack Langan."

"What about him?"

"You mean his wife didn't tell you? I think he was killed by the same person who shot Jim. If you want me to explain in detail..."

As I did so, he rose from the fountain-side, put his back to the mid-morning sun and in doing so became the God of the fish fillet, dark in general form with his outline burning at the edges. I raised a hand to shield my eyes and, courteously, he moved and became mortal again. He'd been rattled, though. He'd offered me the job of Fishminder General and I'd added him to my list of possibles for Jim's murder. For lots of reason. Revenge against Jim was the obvious one. As for getting rid of Jack, well, it didn't look as though there was much of a marriage going on here at Ashenham Place.

After brief thought he said, "Look, if I'd wanted to kill Jim I'd have done the job myself and with a great deal more finesse than was the case." He gestured up to The Ridge. "I know this much: I wouldn't have shot him on my own doorstep."

"How did Jim steal the money from the company?"

Taplin shrugged. "Very simply, I'm afraid. He signed a hundred and twenty-three cheques to cash, over a period of five years."

"Even though he was pissed by ten in the morning?"

"Maybe the booze gave him extra courage or blinded him to the danger."

"And the Fraud Squad never found the cash. You know, in your shoes, if I wanted my money back, I'd be thinking Julie Ryder, Julie Ryder, Julie Ryder."

He chuckled. "So I shot her as well?"

"Someone did."

He sat down on the edge of the pool again and turned to one of the carp. He dipped a hand in the water, the fish came up to head-butt it.

"Two million? Look around. Has it made a great deal of difference to me?" he said, quietly.

I hate people who talk like that. I hate people who can *afford* to talk like that.

"Tell me about you and Jean Langan."

"Well, as you know, it's none of your business. Then again I don't want you to make a bigger fool of yourself than you've already done."

I set the can of beer down on the stone rim beside me. He spoke like he was addressing a shed full of fish-gutters, clipped and precise. And The Map was in the Land Rover.

"Jean Langan and I are old friends. And all that that implies. In your copper's mind. So, yes we did have a relationship. More years ago now than I care to remember. She was married. So was I."

"Which made it all the more fun, I suppose? How did you meet?"

He softened a little, at the recollection of time spent with Jean.

"She came to work for us as a transport fixer, soon worked her way up to boss of the department. She's a fabulous organiser. If we'd met sooner there's absolutely no doubt that I'd have asked her to marry me. Yesterday, though, at six-thirty, just after she'd heard that Giselle had been arrested, she rang me for help. I said I'd pick her up within the hour. She wanted a solicitor for the kids, to replace the one the police had offered them. She wanted the best. I got her two, a his and hers. David and Belinda Barclay."

I'd heard of them. They were young, sharp and responsible for a lot of people who should've been locked up forever, still walking the streets.

"Have they given an opinion?"

"They're seeing the kids this morning but, off the top of their heads, they say the police'll have a tough job without the murder weapons."

"Police have given up looking for them. I haven't."

When he smiled, his mouth twisted all the way up to his right ear. "I see. You're on both sides, are you? Police and ours?"

"No, but I agree with the Barclays. Without the guns no one goes to court."

I drained the rest of the beer and thought I could taste fish pool. I told myself it was my imagination. I rose.

"When you speak to the Barclays again, tell 'em I've gone in search of the kids' alibi. Kate Whitely. Fingers crossed that I find her."

He shrugged. "Don't let me keep you."

- 15 -

I got to Oxford roughly at noon, parked at Westgate and walked down to Foley Bridge. You can't really tell, unless you're on foot, but the bridge itself, while straddling the Isis, arcs over an island. You reach this via a gap in the balustraded stonework and descend to a gaggle of buildings clinging to the water's edge with Venetian conceit.

Blenheim Stalk was a newish, tower-like development, five or six stories high. At bridge level there was an art gallery, trading in stuff by artists whose only talent was for taking the piss. Below the gallery, at river level and reached by a narrow flight of steps, was an Italian restaurant. The upper levels of the tower were so-called studios and Studio 5, so a brass plate beside the gallery entrance declared, was the home of Foley Bridge Intros.

I pressed the buzzer and a young, female voice sang out, cheerfully.

"Hi! Come on up, we're on the third floor."

The door gave a long, electronic groan and I entered.

Studio 5 overlooked the uptown side of the river and, beyond that, had a view right up to Carfax. The girl who welcomed me was in her late twenties, with rolling, reddish hair and a great deal of make-up which she really didn't need. I guess she didn't like the pale complexion, and maybe the freckles which came with her God-given colouring. I did. Her smile was automatic, like one of those security lights which floods the area whenever you walk under it. She gestured for me to sit in one of the steel and black leather chairs.

"So, you're Mr.?"

"Waterman," I said. "Will Waterman."

God knows why I chose Will's name, rather than make one up. Maybe I fancied that here was a chance to get back at him.

"I'm Claudia Merton," she said. "Coffee?"

"Thanks. White, no sugar."

She went to the Cona and poured two cups.

"Actually, I was told to ask for Kate," I said.

There was a momentary lapse in her composure.

"Who told you to do that?"

I hesitated. I guessed that Claudia was a girl who didn't like silence and would do most of my talking for me, if I played it right.

"Another client?" she suggested, to cover the silence.

She handed me my coffee and I nodded.

"Who was that, then?"

I hesitated again. "Well, he..."

I looked away. There were two identical desks in the room. The vacant one had a wooden pencil holder on it in the shape of a K. No work had been done at the desk for a week or more. It was pin neat but a film of dust had settled on the surface and caught the light which came in from the all-window south.

"He asked you to keep it under your hat? Yes, well, we're very big on discretion here. Kate's away at the moment but I can help you, Mr Waterman. May I call you Will?"

"By all means."

"What exactly are you looking for, Will?"

"I'm not really sure..."

And, God knows, that was the truth. Kate being 'away at the moment' didn't really confirm that she was alive and kicking, anymore than it told me where I might find her. Nor could I tell, at that point, what Claudia and K, presumably Kate, did for a living. The word Intros on the brass plate had given me a few hints and now Claudia was developing them.

"Well, let's take a few details, shall we, then we can try matching them to a Target Profile. Are you wanting the gay or the straight database?"

If she'd she asked the question of most coppers of my generation they'd have thrown her against the opposite wall.

"Straight," I managed to say without incident.

"Are you married?"

"Yes."

She ticked a box on a form in front of her.

"How old are you, Will?"

"Forty-nine."

"Late forties. And what do you do for a living?"

"I'm the security officer for a company. We deal in frozen fish."

"That sounds very interesting," she said without a flicker of irony.

"Takes me all over the world," I said. "Wherever fish go, there go I. Where's Kate gone, by the way? For her holiday?"

"Abroad," she said. "Where do you live?"

I hesitated again.

"If you prefer," she said, "you can give us a mobile phone number as a contact point but it does mean you'll have to pay us with a credit card. Is that acceptable to you?"

"Highly."

"So, are you looking for a platonic relationship beyond your marriage, or would you be looking for a sexual one as well?"

For some reason, not entirely mysterious, my eldest daughter appeared to enter the room and regarded me from beneath the arched eyebrows people said she'd inherited from me. Ellie was right behind her, about to mouth off. Clearly the Enrique thing had been sorted out between them and they'd decided to turn their attention to me.

"Mr Waterman?" said Claudia.

"Sorry, drifted off. Platonic. To begin with." I glanced at the girls. They were leaving, though I had a feeling that they might return. When they were safely out of earshot I added quietly: "I'm not saying that's how it would stay."

"Of course not," said Claudia, ticking another box. "What age range?"

"Forty-three. Or thereabouts."

"And large or petite?"

"On the ... chunky side."

"Blonde? Brunette?"

"Dark hair. Very dark eyes"

She smiled at me. Her own smile, I think, not the business one. "You seem very sure of what you want."

"I didn't know I was but ... yes." I was coming out of my shell a little. "I'd also prefer someone professional. A doctor, say, someone like that?"

She leaned back in her chair and tapped her posh biro on the leather edge of a redundant blotter.

"You know, we can't always guarantee to match expectations precisely but we do have quite a selection of ladies in your Target Profile range. If anything stumps us it'll be the doctor, the professional thing, though we do have a beautician, a lady farmer and a chiropodist on our list. Would they be professional enough?"

"I'm sure they would."

"Perhaps at this stage we should talk about how it works?"

"Let's do that," I said. "You know I could do with a bit of a holiday myself right now. I was thinking ... Japan, somewhere like that. Where's Kate gone?"

"Europe. Round and about."

That could mean anything from Finland to Turkey via Galway Bay but I nodded enviously. It was beginning to look as if Kate was still alive and Claudia had been told to keep her trap shut about where she was staying.

"The way it works is this," she said. "We publish your details, together with a photo if you think that's appropriate, in a monthly magazine, posted to all clients. The Foley Bridge Bulletin. This contains between two and three hundred contacts, male and female, at least a hundred of whom are new every month. All correspondence between clients who wish to meet each other is done through this office..."

She patted a tray of letters beside her. They were ready to be signed and sent.

"... that's for security reasons. You'll know all about that, being in fish. Once you've exchanged the first letter, obviously, what follows is up to the clients concerned."

"When do I pay you? Only I haven't got my credit cards with me."

My eyes went back to the correspondence tray. Some of the letters were already in envelopes. Some of the envelopes had been stamped.

"You can phone the card number through to me when you get home. As soon as you've paid, your details will be included in the Foley Bridge Bulletin and a copy will be sent to you."

"And what do you charge?"

"Two hundred and twenty pounds a month, plus V.A.T."

I went right back into my shell again. In genuine amazement I asked, "Jesus! Who owns this business?"

"Kate does. She bought it about nine months ago when it was on the ropes and she's turned it around. You must've seen our advert in *The Oxford Times*."

I shook my head. Kate had kept Foley Bridge Intros a secret, at least from most of her family and the Winchendon Gestapo. That was just as well given the nature of it, planned adultery. But Gizzy had obviously caught a whiff of the money Kate was raking in which is why she'd asked her sister's advice about borrowing the stuff.

So, was Kate in Europe, round and about? Or was there more to her sudden disappearance than getting a late sun tan? As the boss of this outfit she'd want to keep in touch, surely, wherever she'd gone, for whatever reason. She could do that by phone or e-mail. But there'd also be things to physically check, cheques to write, letters to sign...

I spent another quarter of an hour giving Will Waterman's details to Claudia and, when it came to his hobbies, I told her about the goats but left out the photography. Claudia's summary was that I'd be intro'd within the first month. I left on a cloud of superfluous hope, promising to ring her with my credit card details the moment I reached home.

On the bridge, maybe fifty yards from Blenheim Stalk, there was a double pillar box. I walked along to it and checked the collection times, in the childish belief that the Post Office still sticks to them. The next was two fifteen. There was a clear eyeline between the box and the Italian restaurant, down on the riverfront, and with it being lunch time I was feeling peckish anyway.

Spinatori's did food in the modern style. Very little of it and served on a plate you could put to sea on. I went for the cannelloni and twenty minutes later wondered if they'd understood me. Can you mistake the words: "I'll have the cannelloni, please" for "Nothing for me, thank you"?

Out on the river, Salters the boat people were having a good day. An armada of punts was slopping up and down, manned by day-trippers, mainly couples with teenage kids of seventeen or eighteen. I guessed there was an open day at some of the colleges. These hopeful parents would be passing off life in this golden stepping-stone city as a matter of boating, boozing and opposite sex-ing, with an occasional essay thrown in for good manners. They would confess, with half-embarrassed smiles, their own misdemeanours all those innocent years ago.

The view inside the restaurant was pretty gentle too. The place was busy with hurrying scoffers from nearby offices and an easy going bunch of academics discussing the wine they were drinking. A sedate, elderly couple, fresh from the shopping malls, were smiling on a good-looking girl and her partner with a small baby. Closer to me an open day family was on its best behaviour. The proud father was chatting to three late summer visitors. They were Dutch, the bald one told him. They were told in return how clever the English daughter was and that she'd been offered a place at Somerville. The Dutch guy said something about The Communards and I stopped listening...

The focal point of the place, especially to everything male in the room, was tall with dark skin, dark hair and dark eyes. Her Italian was perfect though not so her English. Maybe that's why I was still waiting for the cannelloni. As a waitress she made a beautiful, full-figured reminder of the things I'd lost when Maggie died. I guess I felt that partly because of what I'd been through, albeit in Will Waterman's name, up at Foley Bridge Intros. The woman I'd described as being ideal had been Laura Peterson. I glanced round for Fee and Ellie. No sign. But they would be there, in Maggie's name, the first time I tried to kiss Laura. I knew it. They would stand in a corner, arms folded, while I unbuttoned her blouse and tried to re-run some youthful night, thirty years ago. They would turn to each other, in amused disbelief, and say: "But he is our *father*!" They would stop me, dead in my tracks, at the second button down.

The cannelloni still hadn't come. I took my glass of Lambrusco and a bread-stick out onto the pontoon. A family of swans came over to scrounge haughtily from me and then moved on with never a word of thanks. I took out my phone and dialled Laura's number. All manner of clicks and ticks re-routed me to the phone in the surgery.

"Doctor Peterson?" said the husky voice.

"It's Nathan," I said. "Didn't you recognise me?"

"How could I have done? You didn't say anything."

"I meant my number. Didn't it come up on the L.E.D? I always recognise yours."

"If I knew what the L.E.D. was, or where I might find it, I'd be able to tell you but, as of this moment, no."

"I'm sorry. Start again. Laura, it's Nathan. What are you doing tomorrow, Saturday?"

"You tell me."

"Would you like to go out for the day?"

"Where to?"

"I don't know yet. Europe definitely."

She interrupted with a giggle. "That could mean Milan or Milton Keynes. What are you drinking?"

Up on the bridge I saw Claudia leave Blenheim Stalk with an armful of post and head towards the pillar box.

"I'll call you tonight."

I switched off the phone and watched as Claudia reached the box and began to feed Foley Bridge Intros mail into it. I glanced at my watch. One fifteen. I went back into the restaurant where the cannelloni had finally arrived.

The waitress had also brought me another glass of wine, compliments of the house, to apologise for the long wait. She was beautiful, no doubt about it, but she was hardly my Target Profile. She had dark hair and very dark eyes but she wasn't forty three. She wasn't professional and on the chunky, awkward side... with something about her.

The postman arrived to empty the pillar box, ten minutes late. I wanted to point that fact out to him but it didn't quite go with the anxious clerk I was trying to impersonate. I hurried up to him as he reached in and started hand-shovelling mail into a sack.

"I'm sorry," I said, "I've made a balls up. If you could just..."

I was reaching into the mail myself now. The postman was puzzled but easy.

"Problem?"

"I've sent the letter, didn't include the contract. They'll think I'm mad... Ah! There it is."

I'd seen the name Kate Whitely above an address. I grabbed the envelope and held it close to me as if my life, or at least my job, depended on it.

"Next post, five-thirty," said the postman. "Should still get there tomorrow."

"Thanks, mate. Take care."

I headed back to Westgate and the Land Rover.

It wasn't Milton Keynes and it wasn't Milan. It was an address in Walberswick, on the Suffolk coast. When I phoned Laura that evening to tell her, she was delighted.

"Wonderful," she said. "I love that part of the world. What time do we leave?"

"Well, it's not quite that simple."

"Oh?"

"It depends on you and how presumptuous you think I'm being."

There was a pause while she tried to break that down into understandable parts. It didn't make things any clearer.

She said: "The telephone isn't a good way of us communicating, is it."

"The problem is this: it's too much of a slog to go there and back in one day. We'd have to stay over."

There was another pause, quite a long one for Laura, while she considered the implications of a night on the East coast with me.

"Fine," she said, eventually. "So what time do we leave?"

"Eight o'clock. There was one other thing..."

"Yes?"

"Can we go in your car? It's a bit of a long haul in a Landrover. And can I drive?"

"I'll pick you up, ten to eight."

The phone went dead.

- 16 -

I can remember going to Southwold as a kid, eight years old, with my parents. There's not much I do remember from childhood but I could guide you along the path from Southwold to Walberswick as if I'd walked it yesterday.

It ran in a shallow curve behind a grass covered dyke, twice as tall as my father. We could hear the waves breaking on the shingle beyond it and on a windy day the spray would gust over the defence, flatten our hair, sting our faces and dowse the old man's cigarette. He'd curse and my mother would laugh.

To our right, draining a bunker-studded golf course, ran a wide ditch, alive with frogs and tall with reeds. Warblers clung to them, gorging themselves on the feathery heads as they swayed in the breeze. In the dense undergrowth beneath, my father told me, there would be golf balls, knocked there by ponces who had never done a day's work in their lives. Sure enough, as we prodded with our sticks, we'd uncover them, pluck them from their muddy hiding place. With a wipe on the grass verge, a final polish on our trousers, they would shine like new stars.

As we approached Walberswick, and the mouth of the River Blyth, the dyke sloped away and gave us, fresh each day, that thrill which comes from a first sighting of the sea. If the wind was cold my mother would blame the Russians and their Steppes. The path began to wind its way around sculpted inlets, spurred off from the estuary, all tongues and loops, like the unfinished edge of a jigsaw puzzle. The incoming tide brought with it the smell of ozone and seaweed to our North London noses and as the water rose it lifted from the mud the stranded wooden boats, angle-beached along the high tide mark. As they regained their upright dignity, so they were filled with the promise of places I'd only seen on postage stamps, or heard my father talk about as places he'd been to in the war. Hoist the sail on any one of those tiny craft, slip the muddy chain that held them to the bank and by nightfall I could have been in Malaya, Indonesia, the Cocos Islands.

Near the river bank the stone path gave way to narrow wooden planks held up by rough oak timbers. The path reached all the way to the water's edge, where it became a jetty, and took us over the silt brought down each day from the hinterland. Mum would take my hand in case I fell into it, Dad would speak of a Bailey bridge farther up river, left there by the army like the tank traps still standing on the beach itself. I didn't know what he meant. It just sounded so good.

At the end of the jetty a ferry waited, a simple rowing boat owned by two brothers, the oldest men I had ever met. I can see them now, one large and jolly, the other slighter and bad tempered. Ernie and Bob. They would help us into the boat and row us across. My father would pay them sixpence.

At the other side, two girls used to come running to meet us, heavy shoes clumping on the broken concrete road, cardigans flying behind them like tail feathers. They had green eyes, both of them, and pudding basin haircuts and yet I could sense it, even at eight years old: their dawning femininity.

They would walk up to the pub with us. The Bell. There was a forge near or beside it, where horses were shod in the traditional manner. I can still hear the sizzle of bone as the red hot shoe burned into the hoof, I can taste the sickly smoke as it rose...

There it ends. I've no other memory of the place apart from the wife of an old army friend my father had come to see. She was tall and seemingly built of incongruous parts: long thin legs, wide hips, a short and narrow torso. The head was small and fierce with black hair cut short either side of a bony face. She had small eyes and an accent I didn't understand.

Could Laura and I find that wretched path, the dyke, the bridge my father talked about? We could not. But we did find the Bell Inn and had lunch there, after which we found the cottage Kate Whitely was living in. It was called Herondale and was out on the road to Blythburgh.

It was the smaller of a pair of semi-detached cottages with a sharply pitched roof covered in big, shovel-like tiles. A square bay window stood out from the front of the house, so large that it took up most of the front garden. The front door, enclosed in a glass porch, was round at the side, giving out onto a narrow driveway.

Somebody was definitely at home. The local radio station was blathering away with the lunchtime news. The smell of a casserole drifted out through an open window. I rang the doorbell. A moment later we heard Kate's voice.

"Who's forgotten their key then? Who's a silly Billy?"

She flung open the door and was about to say something witty, or teasing, to whoever stood before her. Instead, she gawped, from one to the other of us.

"Hi, Kate!" I said.

The gawp turned to anger as, no doubt, she scoured her mind for the name of the person who'd betrayed her. Claudia must've been top of the list.

"You know Laura Peterson, don't you?" I said.

"Hallo, Kate," purred Laura. "How are you?"

"Is that a medical question?" she asked, frostily.

Laura smiled at her. "It's a small-talk, personal question. How are you?"

"I was just fine, till a few seconds ago."

"Can we come in?" I asked.

She didn't reply, in fact she stood stock still, in a kind of limbo, as if there were still a chance that she could deny her presence here. As if her quip to someone about forgetting their key had been a sound bite on the radio. As if the casserole in the oven were meant for someone she'd never met. As if Laura and I might go away and forget that we'd ever been here.

She stepped aside and gestured for us to enter.

The house was markedly different to Beech Tree, or Maple, Kate's own in Winchendon. There was light here. Daylight, through larger windows than ours, hitting white walls which, in this instance, had not yet been hung with mirrors and pictures. In fact they were freshly painted, or so the smell and the sheen on them told us. There were cardboard boxes all over the place: in the hall, under the stairs, on the stairs. There were even a few in the front room Kate led us to.

"Setting up house?" I said.

She wasn't answering leading questions. "Why are you here, Nathan? It is me you want to see, I take it?"

"Who else?" I asked, as pointedly as I could manage.

"Well, I don't know," she said, fiercely. "You're the one who's travelled all this way..."

"For several reasons," I said. "First is, I have bad news."

"For me?"

If she'd had it tattooed on her forehead, it couldn't have been clearer. There was someone else knocking about in her immediate life and she was hoping to keep them a secret.

"It's about your Uncle..."

"Jack?"

"You have other uncles?"

"Nathan, please, what has happened?"

I paused and lowered my voice. "Listen, Kate..."

Unable to bear the thought of me using Kate's impending grief as a weapon against her, to determine guilt or innocence, Laura stepped in.

"I'll do this bit, Nathan. Kate, I'm afraid Jack has passed away."

Kate stood for a moment, staring into Laura's face. Then she screwed up her eyes and whispered, "You mean ...died?"

"I'm afraid so."

Kate began to shake her head. Her hands went up to her face and she tried to cover it, as if forming a cave in which to hide.

"No, no... please."

"I'm afraid it's true."

Laura went over to her, opened her arms and Kate stepped back, holding up her hands as a barrier. In a whisper she asked what had happened and Laura explained the circumstances of Jack's death more tactfully than I could ever have done.

Half an hour later, we were seated at the kitchen table. Laura had made a pot of tea and Kate had begun to properly absorb the news of Jack's death and to realise some of its implications.

"Is Jean alright?" was the first question she asked.

"She's taken it on the chin," I said. "But then she would. I think she'd like you there, though, when it comes to the funeral."

She nodded. "Of course, of course. I'll come back."

"Kate, I'm afraid I've other bad news," I said.

She looked at me, as if whatever I was about to tell her would be my fault. "Is it as bad as Jack dying?"

"It's Gizzy and Tom. The police have arrested them."

Kate looked at me and mouthed: "Jesus, what for?"

"Nor *for* anything. In connection *with*..."

"You mean that's better?"

"...in connection with Jim's Ryder's murder."

She reached out for the ball of tissues she'd fashioned and held it to her eyes.

"Kate, they didn't do anything," I said, taking her hand, "and you're the one who can prove it. That's why I'm here. They lied to the police, said they were at The Plough when they weren't. They were with you. You're their alibi."

"Will the police accept that as proof?" said Laura.

"It's a start. It'll need more, but..."

Kate twisted her hand out of my grip and said, angrily:

"Why do I need an alibi as well? Do they think I had something to do with Jim's murder?"

She rose quickly, sending the chair backwards, tipping it over. Laura stood up and righted it. Kate prowled back and forth. The Whitely strop had come into its own and I was pleased to see it.

"I don't get you, Nathan. I don't understand. You're here and comforting me one minute, the next you're saying..."

"So prove me wrong, Kate. Friday night, the seventeenth, Gizzy and Tom came over to see you. Why?"

"They wanted to borrow money from somewhere. They thought I might know who to approach."

"Did you help them?"

"No, I didn't want to."

"Why not?"

She flared up. "Christ, is it really any..."

I swung round in my chair and looked up at her.

put them there. I didn't move them. There is no man living here with me."

"So you pee standing up?"

"What?"

"Downstairs toilet. The door was ajar when I passed it. The seat is up. Anatomy. Go check."

She didn't, because she didn't need to. Laura did. While she was out of the room I said, quietly, "She doesn't like me talking to you this way. But then I don't like whoever it is that killed your uncle. I plan to have their guts for it."

Laura came back into the room.

"You thought I was lying?" I asked.

"Strategically." She turned to Kate. "He wasn't."

Kate looked down at the floor for a moment or two, then said:

"Come and meet him."

We walked, the three of us in procession, along the bank of one of the inlets. The tide was high, the water made choppy by a breeze coming in from the east. The Russian Steppes, no doubt. Over on the far side a large flock of birds, geese I think, flew close to the ground, the careless flick of a darkened brush on an otherwise perfect skyscape.

"How did you find me?" Kate asked.

"Turner's gave me your new business address. Blenheim Stalk. I went to it."

She smiled. "Did we fix you up?"

I glanced back at Laura. "Kind of. Then I waited for Claudia to go to the post box. An hour later I intercepted the guy collecting."

"Can you do that?" she asked, indignantly.

"You can do anything if your neck's long enough. Ask that swan over there."

A hundred or so yards off-shore, three sailing boats were moored to orange coloured buoys. Kate stopped at the nearest point to one of them and turned to us.

"My turn to surprise you, I think."

"Nothing surprises me, Kate. Shocks me, yes, but nothing surprises."

She cupped her hands to her mouth and called out to one of the boats.

"Ahoy there The Merlin! Show your face!"

We saw the boat rock a little as a man emerged from below decks, a paint can in one hand, a brush in the other. He waved to Kate before he fully realised that we were with her. Then he recognised me. Kate turned to look at me.

"Is there a halfway point, between shock and surprise?" I asked.

"Who is it?" said Laura, pretending to not really care. "I've left my glasses in the car."

"It's Martin Falconer," I said. "Sharon Falconer's husband."

Kate watched Laura for a reaction, hackles raised.

"Good choice," said Laura, maintaining the peace.

On board The Merlin, Martin had padlocked the hatch and climbed into the dinghy tied alongside. He rowed the hundred yards to the shore, against an ever-stiffening breeze. When he reached the bank, he threw the painter to Kate and she tied it to a metal stake, angled into the grass verge.

"So that's it," said Martin, scrambling ashore, looking at me. "She's found me." His tone of resignation was replaced by concern when he saw that something pretty dreadful was on Kate's mind. "What's happened? Why the face?"

As she told him about Jack, he wrapped his arms around her and muttered sympathetically. Finally he came over to us, shook hands with Laura first, then with me.

"I thought it would be Sharon," he said, "the reason for you being here, I mean. She'll catch up with me one day, I just don't want it to be... Why are you laughing?"

"I'm not," I said. "It's just that last week she asked me to track you down. Offered good money."

"So, now I suppose you'll..."

"Suppose nothing. Does anyone fancy a drink?"

We all fancied a drink.

We sat round a table in the warmth and comfort of The Bell and, with it being early afternoon, we had the place pretty much to ourselves. I tried to ask Martin and Kate the question uppermost in my mind.

"How did you two ... well ..."

Nobody was willing to complete the sentence for me, though they all knew what I was trying to say.

"As a couple, you two..." I began again.

I crossed two fingers, a universal sign of attachment, surely, but not to the three people I was with. They waited. Martin and Kate were even beginning to enjoy my discomfort.

I don't know why I was being so reserved about the matter. Something to do with the age difference between them, maybe, or the fact that Laura and I weren't...

I couldn't even finish the thought.

"You and Martin..." I said, making a circular motion with my hand, an invitation for someone to pick up the story and run with it.

"For God's sake!" said Laura, as anxious as I was to know the details. "How did you two become an item?"

The answer to Laura's question was this: Martin and his wife had been together for twenty years and, halfway through the jail sentence, as he put it, the marriage had gone as stiff as a board. Rigor mortis of the heart. Not just in bed, he said, anxious to give us a complete picture, but in every other respect. They agreed on nothing about the farm, how to run it, politics, the children, what new car to buy, what colour to paint the front door. And the head on collisions were wearing them out. He began smoking, she stopped eating, which made things worse. Three years ago they gave up talking to each other, except for the bare necessities, on the understanding that as soon as the kids were old enough they'd call it a day. He wanted that badly, Sharon wasn't so keen but agreed reluctantly.

God knows where that left their kids. Unable to form decent relationships for the rest of their lives, I imagine.

Then, eight months ago, Martin saw the Foley Bridge Intros advert in *The Oxford Times* and it gave him fresh hope. It said that he wasn't alone, in fact it assured him that he was in very good company. If he went along to the agency, in confidence, and coughed up two hundred and twenty quid for the privilege, they would find him the Target Profile of his dreams. A woman in the same boat. Someone to talk to. Someone to make the last twenty years fade into oblivion.

So off he went, dressed up, nervous as hell, cash in pocket. He arrived at Blenheim Stalk, rang the buzzer and was invited up to Studio 5. In through the door he sailed and wham! The poor sod came face to face with a neighbour. A beautiful, young, recently divorced neighbour. Right there, still holding onto the door-handle, he had three choices: run, bluff or see it through. He chose the latter and poured his heart out. By the end of the interview he and Kate were in love and who was I to doubt it? Here they were, in Walberswick eight months later, setting up house to prove it.

"And Herondale?" I asked. "When did you buy that?"

"I bought the cottage ten years ago. I paid for it with a win I had. A Premium Bond came up, nothing spectacular but enough. It was the first thing of mine that Sharon didn't know about."

He turned to Kate, looked all around her face. He had landed on cloud nine and didn't care who knew it.

"And one day, maybe, I'll have the guts to tell her ... that the last two weeks have been the happiest in my life."

To fend off embarrassment, I imagine, Laura raised her glass and said, awkwardly, "Here's to the next two. And as many after that as you wish, of course."

I drank to it, hoping it would change the subject.

"So, what about you?" said Kate. "How long have you two been..."

She smiled and put her two fingers together, as I had done. I searched for an ambiguous reply but Laura jumped straight in.

"We're not," she said, as unambiguous as you please. "We're the proverbial. Just good friends."

We glanced at each other, and quickly away again. Martin judged that this would be a good moment to buy another round of drinks.

When he returned from the bar we talked about his probable future. He'd already made farming contacts round here, he said, and would never be short of a bob or two but that wasn't really the point. He fancied doing something less dogged by routine or blighted by uncertainty. It might involve the boat which Kate had recently bought for them, though he wasn't sure how. Trips to France and Holland, maybe, for budding sailors. Or maybe a pie factory, up in the sky, I wanted to say.

"You're right about one thing, though," said Laura. "Sharon will have to know."

Martin nodded, a far-off look in his eyes, all the way to a day of reckoning. A day of divvying up, accepting failure and paying lawyers to end one reality while, eyes closed, he leaped into another.

"I'll come back with Kate," he said. "Set things in motion."

We drank in silence for a few moments and then I asked:

"The night Jim was shot. What time did you and Sharon leave The Plough?"

He couldn't remember precisely. "Ten, quarter past?"

"And you went home, back to the farm?"

He chuckled, involuntarily. "Heh, just a second. You're asking me, in case I..."

Kate came to his rescue. "Nathan, back at Herondale you asked me what I was doing between eleven and eleven thirty-five that night? I was talking to Martin. His mobile, my phone at Maple Cottage."

"The landline?"

She nodded. "You could check."

"Good. Good. And where were you, Martin?"

"The yard. I phoned to tell Kate how dinner with Sharon had gone. I'd meant to tell her the whole thing, about us planning to move up here but I bottled out."

I nodded. "There were two blokes in The Plough that night. Strangers. Sharon told me they were scruffy. What's your take on them?"

He smiled. "Scruffy. It's a very Sharon remark. Fined thirty pounds for scruffiness. Next case." He shrugged. "Navvies usually are scruffy. Bit like farmers."

Laura was fractionally ahead of me.

"Navvies? How do you know they were navvies?" she said. "Did you know them?"

"No, I didn't know them, but that's what they were. Their boots were white, ground-in white, the bottoms of their trousers too. Chalk."

In case you're wondering what happened that night, behind the closed door of Room 7, The Bell Inn, Walberswick, let me put your mind at rest. Nothing happened and that had not been the intention, on either of our parts, I think.

I'd been worried, right from the start, of course. The last time I made love to a woman for the first time was in 1971 and that is a hell of a long time ago. It didn't help that the double room I'd booked us into had two divan beds, each no wider than a window sill. Then, over dinner there was a daft exchange. I won't call it an argument because it never really soared to those heights. I expressed a certain interest in Laura's description of us as 'just good friends'. She hadn't wanted the whole world to know our business, she said.

We soldiered on and, after a few glasses of the necessary, things took a fluffier turn. Then, just as I was about to metaphorically fake a yawn, an old boy at the corner table pulled the plug on me. I'd had half an eye on him all through the meal, basically hoping that when I got to his age, sixty-five as it turned out, I'd look a damn sight healthier than he did. After downing his third brandy he stood up, clutched at his chest and keeled over.

Wading through spilled wine and broken crockery, the *Maitre D* asked if there was a doctor in the house. Laura was already on her feet, hurrying across the restaurant and scattering intervening by-standers.

"Ambulance," she snapped to one of the waiters.

Then, dropping to her knees beside the man, she told the potential widow to outline his medical condition. As the woman did so, Laura fell on the man and gave him the kiss of life through a napkin, with disappointing results: it brought him round. No sooner was he groaning in a chair and his wife hailing my date as a miracle worker, the old boy closed his eyes and hit the deck again.

There was a problem with the ambulance, the waiter told Laura, who was again mouth to mouthing her patient. She came up for air and yelled at me, "Nathan, the car! We're taking this man to Lowestoft."

We returned to The Bell at about four in the morning, both shattered. Laura had saved another life. It was becoming a habit.

We checked out of The Bell at about ten-thirty the next morning, with no charge and a bunch of flowers so big we could hardly get it into the car. We drove out of the village on the Blythburgh Road and stopped off at Herondale.

Kate had already phoned her Aunt Jean and was planning to return to Winchendon later that day. Martin would go with her and face up to Sharon but right now he was upstairs, assembling a new bed in the spare room. Kate called him down and, complaining about instructions written by Taiwanese schoolchildren and there not being enough screws to finish the job with, he made us real coffee. You do that, I remember, when you first set up house: you make real coffee.

"I'm glad you dropped in," he said, setting the pot down on the table. "More than just for the pleasure of your company, I mean. Tell him, Kate, go on."

"We were talking it over last night," said Kate. "You know you asked me, yesterday, about guns in the loft at Maple Cottage?"

"Sure."

"Well, the answer's still the same. Not mine... but..."

She faltered, glanced at Martin who said, "She feels disloyal, saying it. Nathan is a pro, love, let him pick the bones out of it."

Kate leaned towards me and spoke intensely, hands painting the pictures alongside the words.

"You know in those old cottages, Nathan, yours, mine, yours too Laura; there's always gaps and crinkly bits where the plaster meets the beams, specially in the ceiling?"

I nodded encouragement. "Usually with a draught coming through."

"Well, one day, about a month ago, I came home from the office, went upstairs to change and noticed stuff on my bed. Bits. Dust and little chunks of plaster. A nail, even. They'd fallen from above. I'd seen it before, bits on the duvet, but never in those quantities. It was like..."

"Like someone had been up there," said Laura.

Kate nodded. "Like they'd walked about in the loft, disturbed the beams."

Martin took her hand. "What she means..."

"I know what she means," I said. "It's so obvious I missed it. Someone else, in that row of cottages has been using *her* part of the loft."

- 17 -

We got back to Winchendon at about seven o'clock that evening and, with it being Sunday, the village was comatose. I asked Laura to come in and have a scratch supper but she pleaded exhaustion. I said she couldn't possibly be tired, having slept most of the journey back. She denied that she had but *if* she had it was her unconscious mind's way of ignoring the speed I'd driven at.

We left it there. We were getting good at that, ditching disagreements before they became arguments. However, we usually did so with Laura having had the last word. She drove away at damn near thirty miles an hour and I went straight up to the cabin and dialled a number in South Devon. I should've done it the morning after Jack Langan died but, well ... hindsight's a wonderful thing.

A voice at the other end answered and, polite as ever, said: "Yeah?"

"Steve?" I said, masking my voice a little.

"He's not here."

"Yes you are, Steve."

There was a pause as he searched the memory banks, trying to put a name to the voice.

"Who is this?"

"You go first."

"Okay, it's Steve. Who the fuck are you?"

"Nathan Hawk."

The manner changed completely.

"Blimey, guvnor, you had me going."

"Did you think they'd caught up with you at last?"

He had a whisky drinker's laugh, kept nice and rough with forty fags a day. "Well, you never know who's about. How are you?"

"I'm fine," I said. "And if the conversation we've had so far's anything to go by, you're the same as ever."

His name was Steven Yates. He was forty-five and a Coroner's Officer. Dead bodies suited him. Less back chat. We exchanged news. His kids, my kids; his dog, my Dogge; his new love interest, my ... friend, Laura. In the end he said:

"So what can I do for you, Nathan? I mean we only ring each other when we need something."

I told him briefly about the two murders and Jack Langan finding shotguns in the loft of Maple Cottage. He agreed to run a check on them for me, to see who they might be licensed to.

"I'm not saying the kids in this squad are careless," I explained, "but they're pushed, time-wise, number-wise. And they don't do it like, you know ... the phrase we said we'd never use?"

"Like in the old days?"

"Yeah. All I've got are initials, on the box, plus the fact that they're Purdeys. The initials are Juliet Alpha Mike. Jam today. If, on the way, any names crop up they might be one of the following: Waterman, Merriman or Castellone." I spelled out Bella's surname for him.

"Who's your favourite?"

"At the moment, Merriman. Although the first two initials aren't his, the guns could've been handed down in the family."

"Purdeys? Moneyed folk?"
"No idea."
"Right," he said. "May take a day or two, with using just initials, but it will be done. Be in touch."

Maybe I chose that time of night to go round to the Langans' cottage because I didn't want Jean to see my face, at least not the fine details of contrition. Even so, I needed a glass or two of Con's Port to make the journey. Not that cover of darkness or booze made a ha'porth of difference in the end because Jean invited me in and we sat in the neon kitchen where she read every scrap of discomfort in my face. She made it worse by saying:

"Nathan, thank you. I honestly don't know what to say..."

"What are you talking about?"

"You finding Kate, of course. She rang about ten minutes ago, they're at Stevenage, on their way here ... though why anyone would stop off at Stevenage I can't imagine."

"Did she mention...?"

"Martin? Yes." She shrugged. "We can deal with that one later, right now I'm just so glad that she's safe."

"And, er.... you know she doesn't work at Turner's anymore?"

"She kind of mentioned that this morning. It's her life."

"I didn't really come here for any of this, Jean."

"No, I know."

"Do you?"

She smiled.

"Course I do. Me and Freddie Taplin, that's where your great long beak is taking you."

"Nor that, but since you mention it, Stella Taplin hooking up with Jim Ryder I can just about believe, but you and Freddie?"

She looked away, not searching for the truth so much as a polite way of expressing it.

"Stella and Jim. She liked him. He bullied her and she liked him for it. She indulged him to the point of, well, anything he wanted. Booze, coke, trips abroad..."

"That still isn't why I came round."

She smiled at me, a touch flirtatiously. "Well, I'm all out of ideas, Nathan, so I'll stop guessing."

"I came to apologise. Things I said about you and Jack. Accused you of ... I'm sorry."

She frowned, pretending to search her memory. "What things?"

- 18 -

Next morning I drove over to Penman Stables at six in the morning. Given that I'd spent the weekend wrecking any case they had against Gizzy and Tom I thought I should be the one to break the bad news to Charnley's people.

As I walked up through the trees to the stable, the lights were on inside and I could see Charnley striding back and forth, reading the riot act, underlining various clauses in it with a big fist slamming down on passing tables.

The deer had gone. Butchered and divided up, according to rank, presumably. Best cut to the guvnor, offal to the kids. The pelt was still there though. It had been removed from the carcass almost perfectly by someone who knew what they were doing. It had been pinned up under the veranda to continue drying out.

I could hear Charnley, distinctly as opposed to just the noise of him, from twenty yards away. It was mainly hungover abuse with a hint of genuine grievance.

"...what am I that I'm landed with a bunch of pricks like you lot? We're a fucking fleet, you're all captains of your own boat. One lets us down we all fucking sink. Am I making myself abso-fucking-lutely clear?"

There was a thump and a pause. Then some muttered agreement.

"Well so far, so good. I am intelligible to you. So, whoever messed up on digging out the sister, Kate Whitely, has cost us time, money and slammed us right back in the fucking drawer marked ground zero, start again..."

The kids' solicitors, David and Belinda Barclay, had probably phoned him last night and told him about Kate and her status as an alibi. I knocked on the door, though there didn't seem much point, and entered. The place fell deadly quiet, partly with relief, partly in expectation of worse trouble to come. I waited about five seconds, a long time when eyes like that are on you, before I spoke.

"You heard about Kate, then?"

Charnley came towards me. John Faraday stepped into the space between us.

"We heard," he said.

I looked past him to Charnley.

"And it all checks out? Her on the phone to Martin Falconer at eleven thirty-five?"

Charnley nodded, grudgingly. "Her at Maple Cottage, him at his farm. His wife says he went out in the yard to make a call, saying he couldn't get a signal in the kitchen. Is Kate back home?"

"Her car was in Morton Lane, if that's what you mean."

He turned to members of the squad. "Statements. Drew, Quilter, do Kate Whitely. Bailey, McKinnon, Martin Falconer. My desk here by lunchtime. If it pans out, the kids are free to go. Move."

McKinnon was the only one I watched. He grabbed his jacket, swung it round over his shoulders before slipping his arms into it. As he passed by me he paused and stared at me. Bailey took him by one arm and steered him out of the stables. I turned to Charnley.

"Was I mentioned in the Barclay dispatches?" I asked him. "As the bloke who did your job for you?"

"There was a passing reference to you but not out of admiration. They need someone to blame if it's all bollocks. Sit down. John, get him a coffee. Me too."

I took a seat, in the Elvis Presley position, back to the wall and facing the door. Charnley reached down into his cupboard for a bottle of whisky, poured a capful into his coffee. He must have read my look as criticism, not sympathy.

"Irish coffee," he said. "Thins the blood."

"Yeah, well, talking of Irish, I've got more news for you."

He sniggered, leaned back in his chair and flung his feet up on the corner of the table. He sipped his coffee and smacked his lips. For fear that his blood wouldn't be thin enough he added another capful of whisky.

"What is your problem?" he said, after testing the result. "Last count, you'd found someone to keep you warm at nights, so what are you doing, running a one man inquiry?"

"You want to hear or not?"

He motioned me to speak if I wanted to.

"The two guys who did the shooting are Irish, one Belfast, the other Dublin. One's called Billy. They're navvies."

Charnley pulled a sarcastic face. "Age, address, mother's maiden name?"

I stood up and turned. "Fuck you."

Faraday the peacemaker was standing in my way, hands pleading.

"Guvnor, there's a ton of shit poised to fall on our heads, any day now..."

"I can see that, and the worst part of it is a boss who's pissed at six in the morning, right?"

"That isn't fair." He gestured to Charnley, trying to broker a conversation between the three of us. "You mind if I speak, boss?"

"Be quick about it."

Faraday gestured for me to re-take my seat and said:

"When you were working cases like this, what did they give you? Men to do the job with, all the men you wanted. Now they give us computers and a squad at half strength. Less. We cut corners. Make mistakes. So no, we haven't found the sodding weapons, no we don't know who fired them and yes, we pulled in the wrong people."

"I always hated that speech, John."

He shrugged. "It's been a bad day. Tomorrow may be a better one. Now, let's hear about these two in the pub."

I took a deep breath and turned to Charnley.

"Navvies. White boots, white trouser bottoms. Chalk would be my guess. These two were traipsing about in it all day."

"A road," said Charnley, moving his feet off the table.

"You see, even with blood as thin as yours, you're still able..."

Faraday shrieked at us. "For Christ's sake, can we drop the one-upmanship!"

The sudden outburst came as a shock to all three of us and, no doubt, to whoever else was in the room. Faraday looked away.

"I'm sorry, it's just that every time we..."

Charnley didn't want an apology or worse still a lecture. Right now, three weeks into a murder inquiry, his Sergeant knew him better than his wife did: good stuff, bad stuff and everything in between. He wanted all of it kept strictly between the two of them, certainly not shared with me.

"Any big roadworks round here?" he asked.

Faraday thought for a moment. "Well, yeah, but there are roadworks all over."

"Yes, but there's a bloody huge one at Wheatley," I said. "That's where the car you reckon they used was nicked from."

Faraday, looked at his boss for signs of enthusiasm. "The new roundabout, just above the M40, and it's a five minute walk from the road camp to the village."

"So where does that get us?" asked Charnley.

"Allan Wyeth pranged a car up on The Ridge," I explained. "The car the killers were driving, he clobbered its front off-side wing."

Charnley swung round to a filing cabinet behind him. He pulled out a folder and flicked through the contents, eventually finding black and white photos of a burned out car. He spread them out, like a winning hand, on the table.

"There it is!" said Faraday, jabbing at one of the photos.

The car was a small Mercedes, burnt to brown, the windows blasted out. On the front off-side wing there was a dent, the size of a dustbin lid.

Charnley thought for a moment. "Worth a look," he said, quietly.

"By the way," I said, swilling round the last of my coffee. "Who skinned the deer for you?"

Charnley smiled, the first time in a year by the feel of it. "Tommy Templeman. Butchered it too. Made a nice job."

As I walked down the drive, back towards the Land Rover, John Faraday drew up beside me in his car.

"I'm off to Wheatley now, guvnor. Fancy the ride?"

I nodded and got in beside him.

We flitted from one neutral subject to the next, ranging from the weather to his sister's children, whom he'd taken to Alton Towers one day last summer and lost. Not permanently, just for half an hour or so, enough to frighten him to death. Like all good kids, they turned up when they ran out of money.

All the small talk on his part was a preamble to what he

really wanted to say and as he turned onto the Thame by-pass, he came out with it. He apologised for his boss and invited me to empathise.

"He's disappointed, that's all it is."

"That he didn't manage to nail the wrong people, you mean?"

"You know what I mean."

"And getting me to go with you to Wheatley? His idea?"

Faraday chuckled. "Jesus, old coppers again! His. Believe me, it's the nearest you'll get to a compliment from him."

"I'll tell you something else of mine he's taken on board, though."

"Yeah?"

"Jack Langan's body, it's still down at the mortuary. No release for cremation."

Faraday smiled. "That's all down to you, is it?"

"Charnley's worried that I'm right about Jack being murdered."

He smiled and shook his head, not in disagreement but in a kind of comic despair.

"You still don't believe?" I said.

"I only know there are no footprints, no fingerprints. Richardsons, the firm in Corby? They did phone, to re-arrange delivery of the setts. It's about as 'No Further Action' as it gets."

We jostled the early traffic heading for Oxford and reached the Wheatley site at around half-seven. The place had been scalped by Irish Apaches, in the name of the car and the lorry. A vast amphi-theatre had been dug out, the good soil carried away leaving a white, lifeless hole half a mile across that would soon take traffic from, or deliver it to, the motorway. Faraday pulled up beside an earth-mover the size of Beech Tree Cottage where three men, in hard hats and the combat gear of road making, stood beside one of its tyres, larger than my log cabin. They turned, all three, with whitened faces, made so by the barely perceptible mist of chalk dust hanging in the air. Their boots were white.

"Where will I find the boss?" Faraday said to one of them.

The bloke smiled. An Irish smile, a Dublin accent.

"There are so many of us, my friend. The big boss, you'll find him on holiday. Florida. Gone to be with his own, the alligators."

Faraday chuckled. "We'll pass on him, then. Which boss are you?"

"I'm the site foreman but I reckon you'll be after the project manager." He gestured towards the edge of the site. "Under the bridge there, just to your left."

There was no bridge. Faraday pointed the fact out to him.

"Well spotted. When it's built, it'll carry the back road, Wheatley to Forest Hill." He described an arc with thumb and forefinger, closing one eye to get a perspective. "Just beyond, there's a camp, scooped out of the cliff. Your man's name is Birch, you'll find him in the first cabin you come to."

Faraday thanked him and made a U-turn on the rough surface, sending up a plume of dust. The three hard hats went back to the tyre.

The camp was a mixture of pre-fab buildings and caravans, set on a two acre site of worn grass, frosted over with chalk dust. Faraday parked alongside other cars and was, by now, fussing about the long-term damage to his clothes, the chalk working into the weave of the new jacket. I tried to reassure him that it would dry-clean out.

He knocked on the project manager's cabin and a voice

from within, English and rough, replied. "Come back eight o'clock."

Faraday opened the door and we entered.

The place was a tip. Dead centre of the room was a large desk that had seen better days, with a telephone directory giving extra height to a shortened leg. The desk was stacked high with maps, memos and plans, some in wire trays, others surfing the chaos freely. A couple of filing cabinets were brand new but the stuff they were meant to hold was piled high on top of them with no chance of finding a logical home. There was a hand-basin in one corner. It hadn't been cleaned since the day it was installed. The same was true of a towel, hanging from the pipe work beneath it. I could see Faraday cringing inside at the anarchy of it all.

Birch was a large, bald man with a stationary face. It was the first thing you noticed. Not a muscle moved in it, other than those he blinked or spoke with. He was boiling an egg on an electric ring, perched on an upside down swing bin.

"Did you hear what I said?" he growled.

"We did," said Faraday. "But it's eight o'clock somewhere in the world. You're Birch, right?"

"What's it to you?"

A timer rang. Birch turned off the electric ring, scooped out his egg into an egg cup and poured the boiling water onto coffee granules and milk in a mug on the desk. John Faraday was going visibly green around the gills and trying to tough it out.

"The guy won't take his salmonella straight, guvnor," he said to me. "He boils it up and drinks it."

"Safety," said Birch.

"Oh, yeah, I can see you're a stickler for that."

He gestured at the electric ring, perched on its plastic tower, right next to the wash-basin.

"You from Health and Safety?" asked Birch, knowing full well what we were. Or at least what John Faraday was.

"We're police," he said.

"Same sort of manners," said Birch. "Burst in like you own the fucking place."

Faraday turned to me. "First impressions, guvnor? I mean above and beyond it being a pig sty. Are we or aren't we going to get Mr Birch's co-operation?"

"I think we will."

If Birch felt threatened it didn't show. He took a bread roll from the filing cabinet, pulled it in half and knifed some butter from a saucer onto it.

"We're looking for two Irishmen," I said. "Mates we reckon, hard-nuts almost certainly, one from the north, one from the south. The Ulsterman's called Billy."

Birch grunted. "If I lean out this door and shout Billy, half the workforce'll turn their heads. So the answer so far is yes, they might've worked here but why should I tell you anything more?"

Faraday turned to me again. "He's got balls, I'll say that much for him."

"Listen," said Birch, tapping his egg with a dirty spoon and leaving it to stand while he dealt with us. "I don't mean to be awkward but it's a matter of security, me keeping the old trap shut. If the boys out there think I'm a man who'll share secrets, word gets around. Don't go work for Birch, he natters."

"You employ villains, then?" said Faraday.

Birch wound up his coffee. "Keeps 'em off the street. I thought that's what everyone wanted."

I made a contribution. "Listen, this really needn't be difficult. The two we're thinking of will have left here on or about the seventeenth, without giving notice."

Birch shrugged. "Can't help you."

"No records?" I said.

"Records or not..."

Faraday said as calmly as you please: "Guvnor, would you

mind looking away while I beat the shit out of Mr Birch here? I don't mind you listening but I'd rather there were no eye-witnesses."

He eye-balled Birch for a count of three, then drew back a fist. Without the slightest change of expression, Birch conceded. "Okay, okay."

Faraday stayed his fist, back against his shoulder while Birch reached into the other filing cabinet, the one he wasn't using as a larder. He came up with a shoe box marked *personnel*.

"Pick your way through it," he said. "I don't know who's who, or if they give me the right name, but they're all there."

"I'll say it one more time," said Faraday. "Two Paddies, on or about the seventeenth. You dig 'em out. We don't want to get our hands dirty."

Five minutes later we left with two names but no addresses. They'd lived in a caravan on the campsite. Patrick Steven Grogan, twenty-six years old, curly haired, good worker with a bad temper; and Michael Kenneth MacAteer, known as Billy, twenty-five. They were unique, said Birch, in that they'd both quit with money owing to them.

"We think they found other employment," I told him. "Better paid. In fact we think they've made a bit of a killing."

I went over to Hawthorn Cottage just as it was getting dark. Stef and Bella had finished supper, pizza and salad, and Stef had settled with a book on Neapolitan history. Pavarotti was busting a gut on the CD player.

Stef offered me a glass of the Chianti they'd been drinking and I accepted.

"Italian night at the Merrimans, eh?" I offered.

Bella giggled. If you could've translated it into English or Italian the giggle would've read please strangle me.

"Since we last saw you," she said, "we've been doing a bit of thinking."

There were a dozen one liners I could've used, all of them downright vicious, none of them relevant to why I'd dropped in on them.

"Oh, yeah?"

"Made a bit of a decision."

I picked up the book Stef had been reading. "*Treasure of Naples,*" I said, "by Giuseppe Marotta."

"Short stories," said Stef. "Ask any Italian to name a book set in Naples, this'll be it."

"Never 'eard of it," admitted Bella.

Stef smiled. "Ask *most* Italians."

"Planning a holiday?" I said. "Visit to the relatives?"

"More than that. We're upping sticks, going there to live. What do you reckon?"

"In your shoes, I'd have gone years ago. I mean, Christ, they have windows there too, don't they?"

"You're forgetting, Nathan, I've got a teaching certificate, as well as a history degree. I could get a job there tomorrow."

"More than *could,*" said Bella, with a determined face. "*Will.*"

I sipped the wine. It was a decent one, to compliment the big plans, I suppose.

"Sounds to me like you're in danger of joining the establishment, Stef."

He winced. "Knocking at their door, maybe. Yet to step over the threshold."

"Gently does it, eh!"

Bella sat opposite us in one of the grotty armchairs, hooked one leg over the other and let them lean at an angle. She knew they were good legs. It was a pity they couldn't speak, they would have sounded better than the voice in her throat.

As if to prove my point she said: "How much d'you think this place'll fetch, Nathan?"

"Two hundred, two twenty-five."

"Even though we've done nothing to it?" She glanced at Stef. "Blimey! You were right."

"When were you thinking of going?"

Stef shrugged. "Spring next year."

I pulled an anxious face, looked from one to the other.

"Not a good idea?" said Bella.

"I'd say seven or eight years from now, to be on the safe side."

Bella laughed. Stef cocked an eyebrow, knowing that something was up.

"Safe side?" he asked.

"Well, a life sentence is fourteen years, you could be out in seven..."

He was on his feet by now. "What are you talking about?"

"Murder. What the fuck d'you think I'm talking about?"

Bella was still way behind. "Nathan, you don't half wind people up."

"I'm serious."

Stef knew I was. He leaned back against the books on the far wall, looked up at the ceiling.

"You've got it all wrong," he said, almost in a whisper.

"The times I've heard that..."

"I know you rate yourself as a big enforcer these days, Nathan, nose into everyone's stuff, but you're way off beam."

Bella didn't like his sudden change of tone, especially directed at me. "Stefan!"

"Shutup!" he said. And she did. I invited him to continue.

"What happened, Nathan? Did you run out of footpaths to lay, arches to build, trees to plant?" I stood up and he tried to crawl into the shelves with his books. "Oh, yeah, we all know what a hard bastard you are. If that's why you're here, to beat the crap out..."

He stopped and looked at me, no doubt realising that his attitude was that of a guilty man.

"You hid shotguns in the loft," I said. "Above Kate Whitely's bedroom."

He took a sip of Dutch courage without taking his eyes off me.

"Did I?"

"Mahogany box, J.A.M. on it. Yours? Handed down through the family?"

He sniggered and turned away, reached down to a side table and took a cigarette from a packet on one of the shelves.

"We weren't that kind of family," he said. "We were housing estate, not country estate. The only thing my old man left me was my mother."

With trembling hands he lit the cigarette, smoked it with his nerves all a-jangle.

"I'm not leaving till I know who owns those guns."

"Then you won't be leaving," he said.

"Are you saying he might've killed Jim Ryder?" said Bella, catching up.

"Where's your motorbike, Stefan?"

"Sold it, months ago."

"That's true," said Bella.

He snapped at her. "You don't need to back up every word I say!"

"Especially if it's a lie," I said. "Gizzy reckons you still have the bike, you and Tommy mess about..."

"Okay, so make that a few weeks. I got rid of it a few *weeks*, ago. Better?"

"The absolute fucking truth would be 'better'."

"You're not exactly coming clean yourself, Nathan. Why would I want Jim Ryder killed?"

"The two million pounds he spirited away from Taplin Seafoods? Far easier money than you make dealing skunk out of your bedroom."

He looked at me for a moment.

"Did Will Waterman tell you that?"

"Yes."

He looked at Bella and she went over to him. She buried her head in his shoulder, the long black hair fell down his chest.

"It's time we got out of this place," she said, quietly. "You were right. I don't want you back in prison. I couldn't bear it."

He stroked the hair with his free hand, trying to calm her.

"You've been there before, then?" I asked. "You're as good as back there again. Where are the guns now?"

He eased Bella aside and looked at me, square on. He was scared of something, no doubt about it, but he acted like he had it all under control.

"I'm not saying any more. Do your worst, bring on who you like. But I'll give you this, as a friend, because in the time I've known you I've come to like you, copper or not."

"Is it a threat, warning, premonition?"

"It's advice. Go carefully."

He meant it. He was tied into these murders somehow, even if he hadn't done the dirty work or scooped any of the profits. For a second or two I recalled the kid I liked, the free spirit who had bucked the system, albeit to clean windows and deal in dope.

"If you're in trouble," I said, "I can help."

He laughed at that. "Oh, can you! With your help, Nathan, Jack Langan was murdered. I'll pass on your kind offer."

Back at Beech Tree Cottage there was a message to ring John Faraday on his mobile.

"You want the good news first or the great news?" he said.

"Start with the good."

"Tommy and Gizzy have been released. Better still, however, at least from our point of view, these two Irish boys, Patrick Grogan and Michael MacAteer, are both known to police. GBH, armed robbery. The Garda are knocking on doors, even as we speak."

I glanced at my watch. "You want a bet?"

"Well, okay, they will be tomorrow morning."

I wondered if I should tell him about Stef and the guns, his and Bella's sudden decision to leave the country, but I wasn't easy about it. I wasn't quite sure where Stef and Bella fitted in. That, too, could wait till tomorrow morning.

- 19 -

I wasn't really sure where the Taplins fitted in either. Money has always bought a good defence, I know that much, and not just in the shape of lawyers like David or Belinda Barclay, but in walls like Ashenham Place, foreign villas to jet off to, yachts to get lost at sea in. The real Freddie Taplin had disappeared behind his purchases long ago. From the hair on his head and the teeth in his jaw, to Jean Langan's affections, Koi carp and real estate in the Far East he was now the product of what he could afford. And that was substantial. The young man, who'd set out to make a name for himself in fish all those years ago, was virtually no more.

So why, when I phoned him at six o'clock the next morning and woke him, did I get the sense of an ordinary bloke, starting to worry? I had things to tell him, I said, things to ask him. A man with a clear conscience would've told me to piss off and call back later. Freddie said I should drive down to Ashenham right away. My guess was that he wanted to know if I'd tunnelled into the Taplin stronghold and made off with any secrets.

It was chucking it down as I approached Ashenham Place and the Land Rover had sprung a leak in the roof. To be honest it had sprung it six months ago when a branch from the big beech tree by the gate fell on it and cracked the roof trimming. I'd filled in the gap with an assortment of stuff, from putty to chewing gum, but the summer heat had cracked it and here I was, the first real downpour of autumn, sitting in the cab, dodging the drips which fate had aimed right at the top of my head.

I parked under a lean-to jutting out from the side wall of Ashenham and as I got out Freddie Taplin called me from a side door.

"Nathan, good to see you!"

The Great Danes came loping towards me, barking their empty threats. I told them not to waste their breath, they didn't scare me.

"Have you had breakfast?" said Freddie.

"No, have they?" I said. "What's on offer?"

He chuckled. "You reckon this is Gosford Park? Five choices under the silver tureens? It's scrambled eggs, I'm afraid, from my own fair hands. Housekeeper's away."

"Thanks, I'll just have coffee."

He showed me into the huge kitchen ahead of him. I guess these magazines which encourage innocent women to overspend on their homes would have labelled it state of the art, not that there's any real art to feeding people and washing up after them. The most I could say for the Taplins' kitchen was that it was big and expensive, from the handmade terracotta floor tiles to the hidden lighting in the ceiling, via an Aga the length of Sweden. The very latest in ludicrous things hung from butchers' hooks in the ceiling. Oversized ladles, colanders, scoops, cast-iron pans and lids were all beautifully lit by spotlights as if at any moment they would burst into song and give the performance of their lives.

The fittings, Freddie soon pointed out, were made from acacia wood. A tree on the slope up to The Ridge had blown over one night, he'd had the wood seasoned and a year later turned into units. I told him he should've gone down to B&Q, they'd have sorted him out in less than a week.

At one end of an acacia table you could've played football on and still had room for the crowd, sat Stella Taplin. A plate of half-eaten scrambled eggs and the toast it was balanced on had been pushed to one side and she was reading a tabloid newspaper. She looked up at me and took off her glasses.

"You must be Mr Hawk?" she said. "Why have you swooped on us?"

I tried to smile as if I'd never heard that before.

Freddie poured me coffee and Stella patted the table, an invitation to pull out one of the twenty chairs and sit beside her.

"Mr Hawk found Tommy and Giselle's alibi, darling. Have you heard anything more, Nathan?"

"They were released last night. Eight o'clock. Older and wiser people, I imagine."

"Shows what good men can do." He lowered his voice and flashed his money at me. "Do I owe you anything?"

"No."

"No offence."

"None taken."

My first lie of the day.

Stella said, "Does money frighten you, Mr Hawk?"

The Map crackled away in my pocket as I turned to her.

"No. The lengths people go to, to make it and then keep it, that frightens me."

I had her in profile again, just as I'd had her at the traffic lights the day of Jim's funeral. The nose was even sharper close to. It gave her the air of a bird about to hollow out a home wherever she perched which is exactly what she'd done, of course, when she landed on Freddie. Today's plumage was more colourful than last week's funeral weeds, though. She wore a brightly coloured T-shirt, addled with some half-baked thoughts of Kahlil Gibran. The jeans were ten times the price of most women's, though still made of denim.

"You may not believe this," said Freddie, "but money's not important to me either."

That was surely *his* first lie of the day.

Stella folded her paper neatly, then placed her elbows on the table and rested her chin on linked hands. A diamond the size of a barley sugar, set in white gold, dug into her jaw. From behind the comfort of it she asked: "So who committed these terrible crimes, Mr Hawk? Do you know?"

"Two Irishmen, I think, on behalf of someone who paid them, or at least promised them, a great deal of money." I looked at the barley sugar. "There aren't many rich people in the slip-stream of all this..."

Freddie interrupted me, trying to end the discussion.

"Well, I told you my thoughts on the subject..."

I interrupted him back. "No, you told me that *you* didn't do it. You were too rich to care about two million and getting revenge on the person who stole it from you."

"Did you believe him, Mr Hawk?" said Stella.

"I can count the number of people I've *ever* believed on one hand and still smoke a cigarette with ease. Listen, we could dance round this all day. I came here to check a few things and to let you know how far I've got."

Freddie glanced at his wife, an instruction I thought, to let him do most of the talking if talking were needed . She didn't agree to it and smiled.

"I don't think you know much at all," she said. "I think you're a typical knockabout copper, barge in and bullshit your way round a few ideas, see what they bring."

"I know one thing. Your name begins with S. S for Stella."

She exploded in a giggle, over the top of the barley sugar. "No prizes for that."

"I've seen it written down. On blue notepaper. 'Jim, ring me, S'. Do I get a prize for that?"

And at that she handed over the verbal side of things to her husband.

"They were old friends," Freddie answered on her behalf. "I told you that the other day. He'd just come out of prison."

"You were crying at his funeral," I said to her.

"I also told you, she's a very emotional person."

"You were Jim's secretary. You tried to break him of his addictions and failed."

Freddie rose to his feet. "I think it's time we brought this conversation to a close..."

Stella didn't take his cue. "He wasn't an easy man to persuade, Jim Ryder. He had a certain way of doing things and as much as I tried to alter..."

"You weren't trying to break his habits at all," I said. "You were getting the stuff for him. You wanted him high as a kite, right through the working day."

"Why on earth would she...?"

I turned to Freddie at last. "She needed to keep him on another planet so that she could steal from the company. Write the cheques out. Forge his signature."

"Guesswork," said Freddie, pacing the floor, avoiding the joins between the tiles.

"One of the three G's, the kindling stuff of a good inquiry. Guesswork, gossip, graft."

"Why would I steal money from my own husband?"

"I'd say that you were planning to leave him. If you'd simply walked out there'd have been no golden handshake. A divorce might've served you even worse, your husband's wealth being tied up in the business. So you stole. You wrote company cheques out to cash, signed them Jim Ryder, and banked 'em God knows where, in a private account for yourself."

She lowered her arms, the diamond disappeared from view as she held one hand in the other.

"When did you work out what had happened, Freddie? Before or after Jim got sent down?"

"Does it matter?"

"Oh, yes. You could go to prison for it."

"I don't think so," he said.

His attitude was beginning to take its toll on me. He hadn't been able to buy me, either as a fishminder for his Far Eastern development or as an odd-job alibi seeker. He was going to smug me to death by way of punishment.

"Are you above the law?" I asked him.

"No, but everything said in this room was ... never said, if you get my drift."

"Then there's no harm in you giving me an answer. When did you work out that Stella had robbed you?"

"Halfway through the trial."

He stopped pacing and perched on the edge of the table addressing his words half to me, half to the Aga.

"Those three months, well, they represent the only time in my life when I haven't been in full control and, as such, they were uncomfortable. At the beginning I believed that Jim was innocent even though the Fraud Squad was telling me otherwise. I offered him the Barclays, to build a case for him, but he wouldn't have it. Said he didn't need it because he'd done nothing wrong."

He paused as if remembering a man with one great attribute which he himself had long forgotten the value of.

"Jim was a man who couldn't lie. Not because he didn't want to, he'd have cheated his own mother if he could have got away with it, but every lie he told came up in neon letters on his forehead. So he didn't bother doing it. When he stood up in the court to defend himself he believed the jury would find him innocent. So did I."

"But the prosecution barrister had him for breakfast?"

"Yes, being Jim he tried to flirt his way round her arguments and then she played her ace card. She let him browbeat her for a while and when, in the jury's mind he'd become not only a fraudster but a man who treated women with utter contempt, she lashed back and nailed him to the floor. To try and help him I started looking round for the real culprit."

Stella laid a hand on his arm. "And when he found me, well, he could hardly send his own wife to prison, could he?"

"Where's the money now?" I asked.

"Back in the company," said Freddie. "Every last penny."

"And the tears at the funeral?"

"Guilt," said Stella. "It's a wretched thing when it hits you. Seems to come from nowhere and affects the most unlikely people. When Jim went to prison I thought that was an end of it and, in many ways, a good thing. At least he'd be dried out and go into re-hab. Then, because someone thought he, not I, had stolen the money, that he had it salted away somewhere … they killed him for it."

"And Jack Langan in the aftermath," I said. "The note said 'ring me'. Why?"

"I was going to pay him for his trouble," said Freddie.

"How much?"

He shrugged and flashed his money again. "Million? Two? Whatever he asked, I suppose."

Stella said: "What now, Mr Hawk?"

"I don't know. Must be strange having a wife who steals from you. Did you keep quiet about it, Freddie, so long as she agreed to stay with you? Is that how it went?"

"I think that's beyond the remit of this court, don't you?" he said. "What Stella meant was…"

"I know what Stella meant. She meant: who will I be telling."

He looked at me steadily for a moment or two, trying to judge my likely reaction.

"I can make it worth your while," he said, quietly. "To forget what you know."

"How much worth my while?"

"Name it. Half a million quid, start there."

I turned to his wife. "So, now you know how much you're worth."

She smiled, put her chin in her hands again and pressed the barley sugar well into her jaw.

I'd been offered money before, usually in a brown envelope sort of way, a few thousand at the most, more usually a couple of hundred. This was riches beyond my wildest dreams. But then I never dreamed about money. I dreamed about my kids. And about women.

I rose to my feet, the Great Danes slunk away feeling a rise in temperature. Freddie straightened as I walked round the table towards him. He stood his ground with difficulty. Fisticuffs weren't in his nature.

"You're not in the police force now," he said, trying to make a joke of impending danger.

"No, and I'm just beginning to relish the beauty of that," I said. "I don't have to be polite anymore to pricks like you. I can take offence as and when I please. And I just have done."

I stopped myself just as I was about to reach for those pricey clumps of nomadic hair and bring the orange head down on the acacia. I stepped back and took out The Map, unfolded it and laid it out, down table from the Taplins. I smoothed it, carefully ... it was getting frayed in certain places now, nowhere currently important, but best not to take any risks. Who knows where I might want to go in the future? I put on my imaginary glasses and down went the forefinger on an orchard in New Zealand via an e-mail I'd received that morning from Con:

"Dad, mate, guess what. This is not, I repeat *not* a request for money."

Did I say it might be?

"Rosie and me, we're off to Los Angeles next month, to see Jaikie. He's paying the fare. Our kid's got money, mate! It'll be him I tap from now on. Joke. The serious bit is why don't you come too...?"

You know, boy, I might just do that.

"...if you feel you can leave the book, that is."

Oh, I think I can leave the book for a decade or two. There were no dates on your e-mail, dear boy. You know, forward planning as in when you're thinking of going and ... why don't we get Ellie and Fee to come along as well? Plus I have a friend. Doctor. Very clever.

Sex, Dad?

Well, not yet but ... oh, I see. Female. She'd love to meet you all, I'm sure.

Stella's voice broke through. "Mr Hawk, are you alright?"

"Fine."

I folded The Map and put it back in my pocket, glasses too, and stood up.

"Anger Management Disorder," I explained. "It's a technique I use for controlling it. Where was I? Ah, yes, I was just about to beat you to a pulp, Freddie. Some other time, maybe."

- 20 -

The rain had eased off by the time I got back to Beech Tree, so I decided to fix the crack in the Land Rover roof. I hunted down the leftover gunge I'd sealed the yellow bath with.

I climbed up onto the cab roof and sat, cross-legged facing the job in hand. I applied the stuff with an old dinner knife and ten minutes or so later I'd fashioned an angry looking yellow boil, just above the driver's seat. I'd considered the depreciation on the vehicle, of course. I'd even looked up the price in last year's guide. Sixty four quid. I'd just knocked a fiver off it at least.

It really was high time I got myself a decent car. I could've bought one that very day if I'd taken Freddie Taplin's offer.

I don't know how it happened. It must've been something to do with the sun coming out, warming the whole area but I stretched out on the cab roof to gaze up at the leaves falling from the big beech tree and nodded off. I dreamed about dreaming of women and my kids. And in that order, no offence to the kids. Laura was up front in the dream, saving somebody's life. Mine. I surfaced to the sound of Hideki's voice.

"Nathan. Nathan. Where you are?"

"I up am here," I said and leaned up on one elbow, feeling guilty. "No, no, that was a joke. It's where are you and I am up here."

He didn't care. Something far beyond English grammar was troubling him and I wasn't anxious to pry for fear of him going all Japanese on me, stiff and proper.

"I'm fixing the roof," I explained. "Leak. Rain. Top of head."

I made all the right hand motions and he nodded. He was searching for the words he needed and eventually settled for a simple statement.

"I go, Nathan."

I looked round, automatically, for Nicky and Liza. They weren't there.

"Go where, mate?"

"To Asahikawa. I go home Japan."

I sat up. "Why?"

He frowned, the frown he'd learned from me.

"I live there."

"Yes ... no," I said, confusing him totally. "I meant ... is everything alright? Is your mother okay?"

If anything the frown deepened.

"I think so," he said.

"But you go." He was leaving me. "Go when?"

"Next week. Flight Wednesday, KLM. Heathrow."

He seemed all the smaller, the more vulnerable, for being seen from the top of the Land Rover.

"I shall miss you, Deki."

"I shall miss you too, Nathan."

He turned and went back into the house.

It must have been Hideki's decision to return home that sent a wave of melancholy through me. I hadn't realised how fond of him I'd become. I told myself to find a way of telling him before he left, a hands off way this time. No face patting.

I whistled up Dogge and we set off for a walk through the village but somehow found ourselves heading to the outskirts of it, along with mothers driving to meet their kids from the school. Laura lived right next to the school.

She wasn't there when we arrived so I decided to wait. Out in the flower-packed front garden I sat on the bench beneath an ageing plum tree with not a sign of fruit anywhere near it. I needed Charnley to tell me what kind it was. The only plum I knew was Victoria. Maybe that's the only plum there was.

The house was a converted barn, a small one, single storeyed. The previous owner had bought it as a wreck and salvaged it, dragged it up from the depths of ivy and roses gone wild and had it completely restored by Jack Langan. At her husband's expense. The price he paid for having married carelessly. The price she paid was to live there alone. The result, though, was a pleasing mish-mash of old shell and modern fittings. However, no sooner had the garden been retrieved from its devolutionary state by a bloke called Dave than the lady moved, selling the place to Laura about three years ago.

The kids were still being collected from school and that, plus Hideki deciding to leave, sent me reeling inwards. I wanted to tell these girls hurling their kids into big cars, these occasional blokes doing the same while answering their mobile phones, to make the very best of it. The kids you find a pain today will be on the other side of the world tomorrow and you'll be wondering who nicked the years in between.

Laura drove up at around four-thirty and, as she entered the garden, she broke into a smile, pleased to see me. She walked over and sat down on the bench beside me with a cheerful sigh.

"Good day?" I asked.

"Not bad, not bad. Not over yet. We've a practise meeting this evening."

"When do you have the *real* one as opposed to the practice one?"

She barged me gently and stayed leaning against me. I put an arm round her shoulders. A fair stretch.

"What about you?" she asked. "Haven't seen you for a couple of days."

"I kept meaning to phone, but..."

She nodded. "The phone isn't really our thing. We're hands on sort of people."

"Well, hands on was certainly my intention, but..."

She giggled. Even her giggle was husky, throaty.

"So, what've you been doing?" she asked.

I told her what I'd done since returning from Walberswick. When I got to the Taplins, I might just as well have been telling her about people from Mars. Laura had nothing to say about a woman who might've stolen two million pounds from her husband, anymore than she had empathy with the husband who'd let her get away with it.

"I can see it's brought you down a bit," she said.

"Yeah?"

"You're not quite as breezy as you usually are."

I laughed. "Breezy? I've been called a lot of things, Laura, but never breezy. And if I'm un-breezy it's to do with important people, not the Taplins or the Watermans. Hideki's going home. I don't want him to but I don't have a say in the matter. He's going."

"How long's he been with you?"

"Five, six weeks. There's something about the kid, don't know what it is." I turned and looked at her. "You know how people cross your path sometimes, you can't imagine why you bumped into each other and then ... something happens. It all becomes clear where you fitted into each other's lives."

She was looking back at me, like Fee would've done. Head slightly bowed, raised eyebrows. The waiting for me to come to my senses look.

"Yeah, alright, so it's balls. The kid's just been a substitute for Ellie. I miss her like crazy since she went to Paris."

I could feel myself descending into self-pity and I pulled back.

"Why don't we go inside, open a bottle of wine?" she whispered.

"Good idea."

The inside of Plum Tree Cottage was pure Jack Langan. Fussed over and loved for being the work of his forbears and finished with such good taste and attention to detail that you half expected him to step through a door at any moment, trowel in hand and tell you about a documentary he'd seen. On trowels. Or plums.

"Wine's in the cupboard under the sink, corkscrew in the drawer above. I'll be with you in a tick."

She roamed through the cottage, doing several things at once, while I found a bottle of Rioja among bleach bottles and washing-up liquid. I sat at the kitchen table and opened it while Laura checked her mail, then went and changed into jeans and a sweater and returned with a wicker laundry basket.

"You were right," she said, on one of her journeys back and forth. "I did sleep most of the way back from Walberswick. Nothing to do with the speed you were driving at..."

She took something out of the freezer and slammed it in the microwave to defrost.

"...it was all to do with that wretched man collapsing. You feel you have their lives in the palm of your hand. It's true, of course, you do but your own life goes up the spout *pro tem*."

She came right up to me. I suppose one of us had to make a declaration of continuing intent and, being a doctor, she was good at sorting lives out. She put her arms round me, stooped, and her hair brushed across a thinnish patch on the top of my head. I could've died. At twenty years old I had hair like an Afghan hound and in recalling it I nearly missed what she said.

"...and I had other plans that night. Hands on sort of plans. You need a couple of glasses."

She went to an old pine dresser set crookedly against a wall and from the bread bin on top of it took two goblets and brought them to the table.

"Talking of plans," I said. "How would you fancy a trip to Los Angeles?"

She looked at me. "Very much. When?"

"Next month. Can you square it at the surgery?"

"I should think so."

She sat opposite me and I filled the glasses.

"I'm going to meet my children there. All of them."

She looked away. "Well, maybe I shouldn't, not if you're..."

"Maybe you should."

She paused. A month of being on approval? I could see how that might unnerve a person, even Laura Peterson.

"Can I think about it?"

"Sure."

And then say no, I thought.

"Will you know by then who killed poor Jim and Jack?"

Yes, well, that was the big question. Would I *ever* know?

"Police are no nearer," I said, "so why should I be? And the reason we're running round like headless chickens is a classic, at least in police terms. No murder weapon."

"Are they still around, do you think?" she asked.

"No one throws away Purdeys."

"If that's what they were. You said Jack was drunk when he told you about them."

I looked around the kitchen, down at the beautifully laid floor, up at the vaulted ceiling.

"Was this house refurbished by a man who couldn't see the quality in things? If Jack said they were Purdeys then they were.

Jam today. And Jim Ryder got blown to bits by one of them."

"These two Irishmen," she said. "They were hired by someone, you think?"

"Yes, this third person the Wyeths told me about, after much cajoling. Man or woman? Well, Julie said it was a man who spoke to her in the hospital, hand on her throat. Funny voice. *'Tell me where the money is. Where've you put it?'* Could you deepen your voice enough to ask a simple question like that?"

"Yes, but then I ..." She faltered for a moment, took a gulp of her wine. "I was going to say my voice is pretty deep anyway but I don't really want to join your list of suspects."

"Moving swiftly on, then, what do I know about this third person? Not much. They've kept well out of it. They were after the money, I know that because they said so to Julie. The Wyeths knew them, that's why he or she didn't speak to them. They ride a motorbike. Thousands do. They outran me through the corridors of The Radcliffe..."

She smiled. "And you hate them for that more than anything? What I can't understand is this ... why hire two people in the first place?"

I shrugged, leaned back in the chair. Dogge took it as a sign that we were on the move. I called her over, stroked her head.

"Some of the nastiest men I ever met couldn't do their own dirty work. I believe this person was forced to, when it came to Jack Langan - the Irishmen had gone, back to Ireland probably. I believe he or she wanted to kill me as well, that's why they followed me to Chesham, middle of the night. When they caught up, as close to me as you are now, they couldn't go through with it."

"Someone you know, by the sound of it. Will they ever find these Irish chaps?"

"Fifty-fifty chance. They made off with twenty odd grand, the weekly take at The Plough. It's enough to get lost with, for a month or two, but not forever."

"But say they *do* have the guns, at twenty thousand pounds apiece?"

"They don't. Jack Langan saw them in Kate's loft, *after* Jim was murdered."

"I say, this is a lot more fun than rheumatism." I looked at her. "It was the rheumatism clinic today. Onset of winter, most of the panel over eighty. Sorry, you were saying?"

"Jack phoning me, middle of the night. He'd seen the guns in a case marked J.A.M. Four hours later he was dead, killed because of what he'd seen."

"And whoever did it took the guns from the loft?"

"Yeah, so now I ask who had access to that loft? Everyone living in the Tree Cottages for a start. Will, Prissy. Stef, Bella not to mention Kate Whitely herself. But it doesn't stop there. What about Jean Langan? She had a key, which means Tommy and Gizzy could've got in there as well. And what about Martin Falconer? An affair with Kate, he'll have been in and out of Maple Cottage like a fiddler's elbow, if you'll pardon the connotations."

She shook her head. "All for two million pounds."

"Yes, well, you say that and it rings true. Freddie Taplin says it and I cringe. He's always on about money, how much he doesn't care if the odd fortune goes missing. Suppose that's a lie. Suppose he wasn't keen to pay Jim off?"

"Or worse, suppose Jim had turned him down, said that what he really wanted was for Stella to stand trial for the crime he, Jim, didn't commit?"

"I like that, mainly because I don't like Freddie. But now ask yourself how a loft in Maple Cottage ties in with a frozen fish millionaire in whose house you could lose the Eighth Army, never mind a couple of shotguns. The closest you get is Freddie fancying the woman whose niece is Kate Whitely in whose loft, etcetera, etcetera."

"So you've no favourites on your list?"

"No one who stays put."

She rose from the table and went over to the microwave which had pinged somewhere along the line.

"You know what I've never understood?" she said. She turned and leaned back against the fridge. "Why did somebody want them killed in the first place. Jim and Julie?"

"To make it look like a robbery that got out of hand? To perfectly hide this third person? That's the best I can come up with."

"Yes, but if you're stealing money from people, money you think they've squirreled away, surely you need them alive to tell you where it is?"

She waited for me to answer the point. I couldn't. She opened the microwave.

"Two lamb chops," she said. "I was presuming you'd be able to eat one of them."

"Well, I didn't mean to put you to any…"

"You won't be. You'll be peeling the potatoes."

"Let me guess where they're kept. Coal scuttle?"

"Actually, they're still in the ground."

"Lincolnshire? I'll be as quick as I can."

"Back garden," she said. "There's a fork at the back door, and a trug. Ground's quite dry. And bring a head of broccoli."

"You're a gardener," I said, with surprise verging on shock.

"You have to push the back door at the bottom."

You did too.

At the vegetable patch, in one corner of the rounded garden, I glanced back at the house to see Laura watching me from the kitchen window. I must lift these potatoes with style, I thought, as if I were born to the task. I made a mess of it, not just because I'd never lifted a potato in my life but because I was mulling over the question she'd just put to me. It was a good one. It opened things out a bit. Why *had* someone wanted Jim and Julie dead, if it was just the money they were after?

Laura dropped me and Dogge off at Beech Tree Cottage on her way to the practise meeting.

Hideki wasn't in but he'd left a note by the kettle. It said, in capital letters, our code for urgent: "Steve phone. You phone him. H."

The voice at the other end was typical copper, at least in one sense. Nosey. Not so typical in that Steve came straight to the point.

"Who's that who answered the phone then guvnor?"

"House guest."

"Yeah, but who?"

"Japanese lad. Name of Hideki Takahashi."

There was a pause before he said, "Daughter, Japan, knows him, sends him to Dad for a cushy time. Got it."

"Spot on. He's going home on Wednesday."

"House back to yourself, then. Listen, guvnor, this shotgun licence check, took a bit of time but there is a Juliet Alpha Mike. He is ... got a pencil and paper? ... Jerome Arthur Mayhew, date of birth 7.8.37 so he's, what, late sixties. Address: Claybury Court, Bibury, Gloucestershire."

"Good work, Steve. Thanks."

"The old boy who ran the check for me, he's a miserable old sod, I've known him for years..."

"Don't tell me we're still doing this stuff by hand."

"In theory, no, but TCD, guvnor."

"What's TCD?"

"The Computer's Down, has been for weeks. This old git went back to the archives for me and told me he'd run a similar check, couple of weeks ago, for a DC Quilter, working on the Ryder case. Wasn't for Juliet Alpha Mike but for Juliet Alpha November."

"Jesus!" I said. "No wonder they didn't find anything."

We chatted for another half hour, mainly about how efficient we used to be and how sloppy the kids are now. Which is all rubbish but it made us feel better. Then Steve's wife called him away to the supper table. He pretended not to care but I've known him too long to be fooled. She spoke, he jumped. We promised each other we'd meet for a drink some day soon. It was a good idea that each of us knew nothing would ever come of but it finished the conversation.

- 21 -

Driving through Burford I realised why I hadn't been down to that part of the world for ages, fifteen years or more. When Maggie and I were going through our waxed anorak phase, the Cotswolds was this isolated, throwback place, where hay was made into ricks and sheep sheared by hand. The churches the wool paid for rose like cathedrals between green, walkable hills. The horizon was always close and perfect, untroubled by masts and pylons. Streams ran clear, with trout for the catching. There was friendship for the asking. Or that's how it seemed, anyway.

And then the people came. They'd seen the place lauded in Germany, Australia, America, on travel programmes which promised a dip into the rural past of a great nation. They came in coaches to gawp at Museum England. They flattened the hills with their feet, darkened them with fumes from their cars and turned the Cotswolds into one, giant tea room.

Claybury Court had succumbed along with many other houses in prime positions. It was a stone-built place, early Victorian, once mellow in colour and texture, now grimy, set in its own dip just outside Bibury. A notice at the gate declared that afternoon tea could be taken here, that coaches were welcome. A small meadow to the side of the house had been buried under gravel for them to park in. The day I called on the Mayhews it was empty.

Catherine Mayhew was in her sixties with white strands of hair on a jet black, unruly mass, pinned down with a tortoiseshell clip. Some of the hair had broken away and fluttered around the once beautiful face, now gouged and thickened and approaching a caricature of its former self. The eyes were dark and sunken, the whites of them bloodshot with tiredness. The hand she offered was cold and rough. It had worked hard for most of its life...

"Mr Hawk," she said, in a polished voice. "So nice to meet you. How are you? How was the journey?"

"Both good," I assured her. "How are you?"

"Much relieved that the season is nearly over. Do come in."

She guided me through the panelled hall, hung with portraits of severe looking men, her husband's forefathers.

"Tea room there," she said, pointing to a door. "We do bed and breakfast as well, breakfast room there. Kitchen's through there ... Good Lord I sound as if I'm trying to sell you the place. If only." She stopped at a recessed door marked 'Private' and turned to me with a smile. "This is forbidden territory."

We entered her private domain, her retreat from the England she'd mocked up for her visitors. A low ceiling was centrally beamed but not herringboned like Beech Tree Cottage. A French window was the main feature. Small leaded panes, diamond in shape, distorted the afternoon light and made it colour the multitude of books, in a variety of languages, lining the walls. Too much was crowded into the room, Mrs Mayhew admitted, but where else was she to keep the family favourites?

She ushered me to an armchair and turned to a middle-aged woman who had entered behind us and said:

"I'm off now then, Mrs Mayhew."

"Daisy, would you mind doing me one last favour before you go? A pot of tea for Mr Hawk and myself. Quick as you can."

Daisy was not amused. Nor had she the guts to refuse her employer. It had obviously become their style. Catherine Mayhew gave orders dressed up as requests, Daisy conceded to them as if doing her employer a favour. Neither had much option but to bear the other's manner. For Daisy there was no other work in the village; for Catherine there was no one else in the village willing to work for her. And, in spite of everything, she did make a decent cup of tea.

"You said on the phone that you had a rather delicate matter to discuss with my husband. I wonder what that might be? By which I mean, of course, I wonder what he's been up to now."

It wasn't said as a joke. She meant it and it seemed an odd thing to say of your life-partner.

"I'm not sure he's been up to anything, Mrs Mayhew. Is he around?"

"Yes, yes, he'll be somewhere," she said, as if that somewhere might possibly be China or the High Andes so why didn't I come back in another decade. Or deal with him through her.

I rose and took my tea over to the window. The garden was mainly lawn interspersed with shrubs and bushes. It had a ... dark feel to it, no doubt made so by the tall pine trees on the western side where the sun was beginning to dip behind the top branches.

"I don't mean to sound thoroughly off-putting," said Mrs Mayhew, "but is it absolutely necessary that you speak to him?"

"The world won't stop turning if I don't but..."

"Ah, well, then" she said, brightening, "ask me what you were going to ask him."

"It was about the Purdeys, Mrs Mayhew."

She thought for a moment or two. "I'm not sure we know anyone of that name."

"Shotguns. Your husband owned a pair, I believe. I wanted to talk to him about them."

She grimaced, ever so slightly. "Yes, that might be slightly difficult because he ... well, he doesn't own any guns to my knowledge."

"Did he *ever* own a pair of shotguns, Mrs Mayhew? In a mahogany box with a brass plate on them, inscribed J.A.M.?"

"Possibly, I mean they are his initials. But we've always had secrets from each other and..."

Her voice had dwindled on seeing my interest in one particular corner of the garden. Set out there, in regimental order, was a collection of ... huts the size of old police boxes, beige in colour but of a similar size. Plastic, rounded, with a full door on each of them.

"Yes, I know you can't quite believe your eyes," she said. "There are fifty of them. I thought, to begin with, you might've been the person who supplied them and were wanting payment. I simply want shot of them. Jerome ordered them four weeks ago, they were delivered last Tuesday."

"And they are?"

"Portable lavatories. For the world's press."

I turned to her. She was smiling, rather enjoying my bewilderment.

"You'll have to explain a little," I said, dutifully.

"My husband doesn't want the world's press peeing up against the rhododendrons. Indeed, who would. So he ordered the portaloos pre-emptively."

She wasn't kidding about this, either.

"Do the press come here often?" I ventured.

"They're already here, Mr Hawk, it's just that you and I can't see them. As for the logistics of it all, we can provide tea for them, we can even do B and B for some but, I quote: 'If they all want to piddle at the same time we're sunk'."

"Is that him?" I asked, quietly.

I was referring to a tall, angular man out in the garden, emerging from the pine trees. His hair was a blistering white and shoulder length, falling around the tweed jacket with its leather patched elbows. The cavalry twill trousers were tucked into heavy socks. The boots had an army look to them. He was talking in an animated fashion, large gestures and plenty of smiles as he made his points.

"He seems to be talking to someone," I said, stating the obvious. "But there isn't anyone there."

"That is correct," she said. "But try telling him that."

I nodded as if a great fog were lifting. "Who would he be talking to if someone *were* there?"

"The foremost television broadcaster of virtually any country you care to name. They're interviewing him, possibly in their own language. He's fluent in eleven and can think in four of them." She held my gaze for a moment, then she too stated the obvious: "He's mad, Mr Hawk. Come and meet him. See for yourself."

My immediate thought was that Catherine Mayhew and I could sort out the Purdey thing on our own, no need to trouble her barmy husband, but she was already unfastening the French window, top and bottom.

Today was a good day for Jerome Mayhew, his wife assured me, in that he wasn't morose or paranoid. Quite the opposite. He was ... well, breezy, would've been the word, I suppose.

"My dear fellow," he said, stretching a hand out to me. "Lovely to see you again."

"I don't think we've met before."

He raised a playful finger. "So you say, but any friend of my wife is a friend of mine, no matter what the two of you have been up to."

"Take no notice," said Catherine, quietly. "It's all a matter of one word following another, regardless of meaning. If you've questions to ask him bear that in mind."

She turned to her husband. "Jerry, say hallo to Mr Hawk."

He spread his hands, the fingers like talons, and grabbed an imaginary kill.

"Stop that at once!" she commanded.

"So sorry. Does he speak English?"

"Of course he does."

"Then good afternoon, Mr Hawk. Are you a haggard hawk or blood-feathered?"

"Jerome, I shan't tell you again," his wife warned.

"I'm merely asking how old he is without drawing attention to the fact. But there, you've gone and spoilt it."

"Blood-feathered," I assured him.

"Right, then, let's get started on the interview. I don't have a great deal of time, so professionalism is the watchword for you and your crew."

He gestured to an empty patch of lawn where, presumably, my crew was standing.

"How would you like me to conduct the interview?" I heard myself say.

"With a baton, Mr Hawk. I do hope you're not one of these modernists who do it with curled fingers and bouncing shoulders. That is not the way to conduct the Bruch violin concerto, or any other piece of music."

"Jerome, you're doing it on purpose."

"Yes, dear. Why don't you toddle off and do womanly things, like making a sandwich or two. Egg preferably. I'll show Mr Hawk round the garden."

Catherine looked at me and I nodded minimally.

"No silliness," she said to her husband. "I mean it."

"No silliness," he echoed, pointing to the pine trees. "This way, I think."

We went into the trees at a cracking pace. Jerome Mayhew skipped ahead, like a child, then stopped and peered back at me round tree trunks, pulling a face, then flitting away again with athletic ease. At one point he stopped, then came towards me treading softly on the dead twigs beneath his feet as if trying not to disturb them. He came right up to me, looked in my face as if searching it for answers to his predicament.

"I wasn't always like this, you know," he said, softly.

"Like what?"

"Stuck."

It was a handsome face. It had all the signs of having once ruled the roost. The set of his head, tilted back and looking down on lesser mortals, was that of a leader not a follower. The hands were strong and cared for, by his wife and not him, I imagine. His face was closely shaved, again her doing, not his. The eyebrows were trim, there were no rogue hairs befuddling his ears or nose. He was ... of film star quality. Yet the eyes, for all their startling blueness, were as dead as glass beads. Behind them a fine mind was disintegrating and, in occasional moments of lucidity, knew that it was doing so.

Had he once been a man who would have killed for two million pounds? I couldn't see it.

From high in the branches I could hear the gentle coo-ing of a couple of wood pigeons. I pointed up at them.

"Damn things," I said.

"Ah, yes."

"Need shooting..."

Whether he swerved away knowingly, or was simply led by the word's alternative meaning, I've no idea.

"Well, you're the man with the camera crew," he said. "Not me."

"Yes, and I think we should start the interview right now." I turned to where he'd addressed my imaginary crew. "Are we ready?"

Jerome held his hand up to them. "Take five. I've a little something to ask Mr Hawk."

He nodded as they apparently stomped off through the trees, back to the house.

He looked down at the ground and seemed to grip the air close to him, in an effort to seize reality. Getting a loose hold on it, he asked, "Can you get me out of here?"

"I'm not sure," I said. "Where would you go?"

"Anywhere. Doesn't matter. But if I stay here, it's the end. I know that."

"Catherine would be sorry."

He suddenly snapped. "Don't start all that, how she'd miss me. Jesus, you've seen the woman, there's another thirty years in her. Are you saying that she should ... that she should..."

He paused, still struggling to hang onto the thread of reason he'd found.

"Are you saying that it's the end for her too?"

"No such thing."

"I'm dragging her down. Any fool can see that."

"I don't know many fools," I said. "I knew Jim Ryder, of course. Remember him?"

"Old Jim? Well, I'm damned. It must be ... did he say how long it was, since we last met?"

"Couple of years."

He'd never heard the name in his life and shrugged, like a child, shoulders high into the air.

"Oh, well, I can't remember what I did yesterday, let alone two years ago."

"Yesterday," I said. "We went shooting."

He pretended to remember, out of courtesy.

"So we did. What did we bag?"

"Well, you did most of the bagging."

He suddenly gripped my forearm and looked at me.

"That isn't why you're here, is it? I didn't shoot the old bagging, did I?"

"Catherine? No. Why do you ask such a thing?"

He let go of my arm. The fear of what he might have done,

without knowing, had led him down some tortuous path in his buckled memory.

"I wanted to," he confided quietly. "Wanted to get shot of her. Bloody woman does nothing but carp and criticise. It'll be physical abuse next!" He pulled a comical face. "Still, if you say you've been sleeping with her I obviously missed my target. Better make sure, though."

He hurried off, back towards the house to check that he hadn't shot his wife. Feeling a touch loopy myself, by now, I followed him.

After tea and egg sandwiches, Jerome nodded off in an armchair and I explained to Catherine the full purpose of my visit. She was gracious about my white lies and sympathetic to their purpose. Nevertheless, when it came to it, she'd no more idea about how two Purdeys might have got from Claybury Court to Kate Whitely's loft than I had.

She asked if I'd like more tea and I said I would. She went to make some and I closed the French windows, bolting them top and bottom.

When I turned back into the room, Jerome was right beside me. He'd risen noiselessly and now put a forefinger to his lips. The eyes had a look in them I can only describe as madness and sanity at loggerheads. By dint of his nap, maybe, sanity had the edge.

"Wasn't sleeping. Just pretending. You won't tell her, will you. Promise me, there's a good chap."

"Tell her what?"

"That I thought about ... you know, shooting her and all that. Relieving her of the burden."

"No, of course not."

Then he looked at me, truth rising, and for just a few moments it restored him to the man he'd once been.

"I knew it would be the wrong thing to do but I was beginning to lose the battle." He pointed to his head, the place where the ongoing war was taking place. "So I got rid of them. The guns. For safety. There was an amnesty."

It took me a moment or two to remember but he was right, there'd been a firearms amnesty two years previously. Hand in your illegal arms at the local nick and no questions would be asked.

"Was that a good idea?" he asked.

"One of your best," I assured him.

- 22 -

I got back to Beech Tree Cottage at about eight o'clock that evening. Hideki was out and had left one of his messages by the kettle. "Gone Crown. Maybe you come? H."

I telephoned Penman Stables and Drew answered the phone.

"Working late?" I said to her.

"As usual. What can I do for you?"

"Is your skipper there?"

She put a hand over the receiver and called out: "Sarge, Mr Hawk, line four."

Faraday picked up the phone.

"No we haven't, guvnor."

"What?"

"We haven't caught up with Grogan and MacAteer." He paused. "Isn't that what you phoned about?"

"Not really, no. John listen ... I don't want to raise your hopes, and I'm certainly not trying to play the big I am, but I think I know who did it."

Faraday chuckled. He thought I was kidding.

"I mean it, John. I think I know who killed Jim Ryder and Jack Langan. Is Charnley there? Maybe I should speak to him."

"No, no. HQ for a bollocking. You know the sort of thing. Time and money, where's the result?"

I glanced across at Hawthorn Cottage. I could see Stef and Bella in the kitchen. She was sipping wine from a tall glass and as Stef passed by he kissed her on the neck. Minds were meeting, maybe. Long journey.

"John, why don't you come over?"

"What's the time?"

"Eight."

"Yeah, alright, only I've promised my sister's boy..."

Stef had turned Bella round and was kissing her properly now.

"Won't keep you long, I promise."

It was almost dark by the time John Faraday pulled up in Morton Lane. He knocked on the door and Dogge went mad. He knew her well enough by now to calm her with his voice.

"Good girl," he said. "Good girl, quiet now."

Her ears went back and he let her out into the garden.

He looked all in. The strain of the case and the uncertainty of working for an alcoholic boss were showing in his face. He slumped into Maggie's dad's rocker and let his head fall back against the top curve. He smiled at me, with a presumptuous glance at the fridge. I took out a beer and slid it across the table to him.

"Where's Hideki?" he asked, looking round.

"The Crown. He likes it there better than The Plough. Younger customers. More talent."

"He's right."

I went over to the window, sipping my own beer. The light had gone on upstairs in Hawthorn Cottage, the bedroom curtains had been drawn.

"You know, when I first started looking into this, these two... well..."

I nodded across at Stef and Bella's. Faraday wrenched himself out of the rocker and came and stood beside me.

"Stef and Bella, you mean?"

"Yeah, they'd have been the last people I'd have said had anything to do with Jim's murder, let alone Jack's."

"And now you aren't so sure?"

"Didn't I tell you?" I tried to think back. "It wasn't Kate who put the guns up there on the loft, it was Stef."

"You should've told me," he said, with a shrug. "We had an agreement. Any bits and pieces..."

He'd wanted to be fierce and critical about my oversight but he was too tired for that. Or too interested in what else I might have to say.

"Sorry, I must be getting old, John. Memory going. Or maybe I was too embarrassed."

He chuckled and looked away.

"Yeah, you're a regular shrinking violet, guvnor."

"I made a mistake, you see. Jack was so convinced that his niece was tied into all this, I just took his word for it..."

"Bang went the first rule, eh?" he said. "Never believe anyone. What's Stef been saying to shine a light? The guns are his?"

"Stef isn't really talking. Too scared."

"With just cause, by the sound of it."

"He's not scared of the law, John, that doesn't seem to bother him. The people who killed Jim Ryder do, however."

"Grogan and MacAteer? Well, unless he's got them in his loft as well..."

"By which he means whoever paid the Paddies to kill Jim and Julie. They used Stef as a kind of staging post, you see, a place to keep the guns, return them to after the job was done."

I'd captured his real interest at last.

"I'm not excusing his behaviour," I went on, "but they had him over a barrel."

"How?"

"He deals drugs from his bedroom."

He chuckled again, shaking his head. "Jesus Christ, guvnor, something else you've kept to yourself? I mean what about the satanic rituals and the attic full of asylum seekers? When do I hear about them?"

"He's been inside for it. Dealing. Not that it shows on his record, you told me that yourself."

"I didn't tell you, guvnor. The best computer money can buy told you."

I shrugged. "Then all I can say is that someone's been messing with the records. I got it from the man himself, or at least his partner, Bella. He did three months and she doesn't want him doing any more. It's made him vulnerable. Open to all kinds of pressure. Blackmail."

Faraday nodded, went back to the rocker and stretched out in it, full length, joints cracking.

"Okay," he said with a gentle yawn. "I'll see to it. I'll go have a word with Stef." He held up a hand, as if I'd made a protest, which I hadn't. "No hassle, don't worry. Won't use anything against him, but if he knows where the bodies are buried, so to speak."

"You don't have to ask him, John. You can ask me."

He looked at me, over the top of his beer. He played it as if worried that I'd picked up something he'd missed.

"Okay, then, I'm asking."

"Guns, for example. I know who J.A.M. is. I had an old friend in the job run a check for me."

"Terry Quilter did that. No joy."

He tried to make it sound as if the two of us were on the same side, heading for the same goal.

"No, the check he ran was for J.A.N. That isn't what was on the gun case. That was J.A.M. Quilter misheard."

He puffed out his cheeks, blew away his irritation at having the likes of Quilter on his team.

"I'll fucking kill him," he said, lightly. "Does that sound reasonable?"

"The man's full name is Jerome Arthur Mayhew. Juliet Alpha Mike."

Faraday seemed to repent a little, with regard to Quilter and pulled a face.

"Oh, well, Jam, Jan, I guess it's an easy slip..."

"Not the way we do it. We use the UN code. M for Mike, N for November. You can mistake Jam for Jan over the phone but not Mike for November."

There was a pause this time before he laughed out loud and sat up straight. "Okay, so we're fucking idiots, you're a genius. You came up with the right guy."

"It's not quite as simple as that. Somebody gave Quilter the wrong initials to check in the first place. I made a point of spelling it out: Jam today, Jam today."

He thought for a moment before squeezing his beer can, watching it deform slowly as he did so.

"I've got a nasty feeling this is going to get ... personal? Am I right?"

"You made it personal, right from the start, by being on my back every five minutes. You weren't delivering Charnley's rebukes, or picking my brains, like I thought. You were seeing how close I'd come to the truth. Not very far, as it happens, until I asked myself this question: Why, if the object of the whole game was the two million pounds Jim Ryder had salted away ... why kill him? How can he tell you where the money is from grave 47B Aylesbury Cemetery?"

"Well, since you're full of it tonight, guvnor, keep going."

"When someone dies, especially if they're murdered, it gives certain other people access to the entirety of the victim's life. I'm talking about their bank accounts, insurance policies, credit details, safe deposits, medical records, in fact every sodding detail about them. They get tossed around by the likes of solicitors, coroners, inland revenue ... and right up front coppers. I reckon someone went through Julie's house several times, top to bottom, when Jim was inside, but they couldn't find any hint of the money. So they decided to go into more detail by killing her and Jim."

He wiped his mouth with the back of his hand. It hadn't needed it. He tried to smile and failed.

"How about this, though, for real shitty luck?" I said. "They were on a wild goose chase from day one. Jim never stole that money from Taplin Seafoods."

"Then who the fuck did?"

"Stella Taplin. And that's straight from the horse's mouth." I smiled at him, about as condescendingly as I could. "You pinned the tail on the wrong donkey, John."

He looked at me and for a few moments held his emotions completely in check. I'd never seen him do it before. Then he lowered his voice. "Any second now you'll whip out the murder weapons, will you? My fingerprints all over them?"

"I've no idea where the guns are, John, but I know how you came by them."

"I'm listening."

"Mayhew handed them in to his local nick, Bibury, in a firearms amnesty. Two years ago two, just before you transferred here. You were stationed at Cirencester at the time, stone's throw away, and when the day's collection was brought in to be rendered down for scrap, you helped yourself to the Purdeys."

He drummed his fingers on the table, then pointed to the crushed can.

"Do you think I could have another?"

"Go ahead."

He walked over to the fridge, opened it and took out two more cans. He pushed one across to me as if nothing had happened, as if it had all been a game and we were simply chewing it over in the dressing room. Tactics, manoeuvres, winners and losers. After a few moments deliberation he spoke again.

"There isn't much ... bulk to it, guvnor. In the way of hard evidence, I mean. That's my first thought."

"Oh, I don't know. There'll be bits of you on Jack Langan's body, I'm sure. It's still down at the mortuary. That's the one sensible thing your boss *has* done: kept him on ice. What will be difficult, I grant you, is connecting you to the motorbike."

He laughed. "Proving that I'm this 'third person' you refer to? This creature of the night, male or female..."

"Who I chased through The Radcliffe, who stuck a gun in Allan Wyeth's ear, who followed me to Chesham in the middle of the night. It would've been nice to have Tommy and Gizzy take the rap for Jim's murder, wouldn't it?"

I waited for him to respond to that. He didn't, merely gestured for me to continue.

"You're a bit reserved on that subject, are you? Yeah, well, innocent kids, easily stitched up? Maybe you draw the line?"

Again I waited. He sipped his beer.

"Well, leave it to me to try thinking the best of you, John. That's why you got these Irish boys to do your killing for you. I mean fear of blood on your favourite jacket would be one reason but... the other is you're not quite the hard bastard you'd like to be. Or need to be. On that back road to Chesham, for example ... and I'm sure you followed me to kill me, we were as close to one another as we are now and you did nothing. I guess in the great scheme of things it means there's a slither of hope for you, though I wouldn't suggest that you banked on it..."

He held the gaze again only this time his eyes began to water, ever so slightly, with malignant sentimentality. He looked away and it was gone.

"I'd grown to like you too much," he said. "That's the trouble with these things, you never take into account the *personal* side."

He took a small bundle from his pocket and removing the protective cloth revealed a small gun, the like of which I'd never seen before. A small weapon, such as might go into a lady's handbag. He let it drop to the table, six inches to the North of the map of Australia.

"I guess I should've learned to climb over my own feelings by now," he went on. "As a copper you're meant to choke it all back at least enough to, well... who do you think killed Jack Langan? Irishmen? Fairies?"

"The Irishmen were well away by then, that's why you didn't mind taking me to Wheatley to ask Birch about them. Where are they now by the way?"

He smiled. "Unreachable."

"So how *did* you kill Jack?"

He jerked his head towards Hawthorn Cottage. "Stef told me he'd been working on Kate's loft. There was every chance he'd seen the guns so I went to his yard the next morning, intending to find out and if need be frighten him off. When I got there he was in the forge testing the drive belt on the saw. The blade was running. I didn't even have to think about it. I just picked him up and threw him on it."

"You should've left the saw running."

He winced, like some kid who'd been caught smoking in a bike shed. "I know. That's the neat and tidy bit inside me." He smiled at me, like I was a wayward friend in need of help. "Speaking of neat and tidy, what am I going to do with you?"

"Shoot me, by the look of it. With a pop gun, not a Purdey."

"Don't be fooled by its delicacy. It'll blow your brains out easy as pie. I got it from the same amnesty as the Purdeys. Funny the stuff people throw away, don't you think?" He stood up. "We'd better go."

"Where?"

"What did you think was going to happen, guvnor? Did you reckon I'd break down in tears, beg forgiveness, have you march me back to Penman Stables, hand me over?"

"We can call Charnley, get him here."

Mention of the name Charnley pressed the usual buttons and slightly unnerved him.

"Is that what you've done? Called him, asked him to drop in?"

"No, no..."

He thought for a moment, then nodded. He came round to my side of the table. I rose and backed away. He stopped advancing, I stopped retreating.

"Turn round," he said.

"And have you do me through the back of the head? I should fucking say so. You want to shoot me, you do it face on. It'll make a man of you."

He shook his head, weary of the sarcasm.

"Turn the fuck round," he said.

He grabbed me by the shoulder and turned me himself. His plan, I suppose, was to beat me over the head with ... something, and drag me off to a quieter place but he hadn't factored in, as they say, all the possibilities. He'd turned me to face the door and even as he raised his arm to chop me over the back of the neck the door opened and Hideki walked in.

I'll remember the next minute of my life forever. I could slow it down to a dead stop and write a ten page essay on every moment of it. I'll spare you that. Hideki stood there, taking stock. I remember that he looked so small and frail.

"Jesus Christ, did you have to?" Faraday said to him, wearily.

Presumably he meant did you have to come back and throw a spanner in the works. Hideki gave his 'no speak English' shrug.

I started babbling, playing for time.

"John, this is crazy. This isn't you. Let the boy go, he's going home on Wednesday. What harm can he do you in Japan? He's seventeen, for Christ's sake. His mother, father, think of them ... put yourself in their position, imagine he's your sister's boy. How would you feel? Step back for just a moment..."

I stopped talking when Faraday made the biggest mistake of his life. He thought about what I'd just said. He considered an act of mercy. And as he lowered the gun and turned to me, with a helpless look on his face, so Hideki ran at him. He rose from the floor and turned in mid-air, like a cat, still flying, until he was parallel to the ground, one knee drawn back, his expression the same as always. As he neared Faraday's face the latter raised the gun again and fired in panic, way off target. The bullet hit the floor - you can see the chip in the flagstone to this day - and went clean through a window pane. At the very same moment Hideki's heel struck Faraday in the face with all the force of the Samurai spirit. Faraday fell sideways over the table. No rock. Hideki turned again in the air and landed on his feet, crouching for further action, but Faraday was out for the count.

As you might imagine there was a lengthy pause before I was able to speak.

"Where in God's name did you learn to do that, boy?"

Ask a silly question.

"Japan," he said.

I was already rummaging in the cupboard under the sink, searching for a roll of carpet tape. By the time Charnley arrived with a few of his finest we had John Faraday trussed up like a turkey. Christmas had come early for him.

There's an e-mail from Hideki Takahashi on my computer in the 'keep' file. It says: *"Hi, Nathan. Thank you for my stay. Hideki."*

I wanted to write back saying thank you for my life but it sounded so phoney in my head, so un-seventeen. Accordingly, I wrote back rather blandly.

"Hi, Hideki! Enjoyed your company. It was great to have you staying here. Humdinger. Thanks for everything..."

Then I thought to hell with it and added:

"...especially for saving my life. Nathan."

I haven't heard from him since. I'm sure I will some day. I hope I will.

- 23 -

The husky voice was saying, "Nathan. Nathan, it's six-thirty. Why don't you sit up and drink this."

I opened my eyes. Autumn sunlight was knifing its way into the bedroom through the gap between the curtains. Laura went over and opened them. She was fully dressed for the journey ahead of us.

"You remember...?" she asked.

"Of course I do."

"Taxi's booked for eight-fifteen. And there's a man downstairs."

"What?"

"A Mr Stillman. He insisted on seeing you and wouldn't be dissuaded."

"You explained?"

"To no avail. It'll take five minutes, he said."

She stooped to the bed and kissed me on the forehead, then left. A minute or so later I heard mumblings through the floorboards, Laura being polite to our obscenely early visitor.

I drank the tea she'd brought and dug into the nearest suitcase for my razor and toothbrush. Maggie had always packed our stuff like that, in reverse order, things you need first at the top.

Through the window I could see the goats on the green, heads in buckets of fresh ... whatever goats eat, I suppose. Will and Prissy had kept pretty much to themselves, the last month or so. Fine by me. Stef and Bella had gone. Without a word. One day they were there, next day the place was empty with a *For Sale* sign in the front garden. Also fine by me. There'd be new neighbours to cope with by the time we got back, though...

Kate Whitely wasn't up yet. That had all gone pear-shaped, the thing between her and Martin and she was suffering a bit. Sharon had been a tougher nut to crack than either of them had bargained for and Martin went back to her, settling for the quieter, unhappier life.

As for the rest, well, Gizzy and Tommy had put an offer on a restaurant in Oxford and were waiting to hear the outcome. What I knew for certain was that one day Gizzy would realise her dream: Tom would be the Marco Pierre White of a restaurant where she called the tune and counted the profits. I couldn't help but admire.

Jean Langan? Well, Jean and I were ... polite to each other. Don't get me wrong, there was no latent animosity between us, in fact she was looking after Dogge while we went off to L.A. But I'd never quite recovered from the dreadful things I'd accused her of concerning Jack. All in the line of duty, of course.

I bet what you really want to hear about is the book, though. *'The History of the Hamford Crime Squad.'* Who can blame you? But you'll have to wait...

"Nathan? You haven't gone back to sleep, have you?"

No. Life was a bit too good at the moment to waste unseemly amounts of it sleeping.

John Stillman was a stick of a man, no more than sixty years old but if you'd told me he was seventy-five I wouldn't have argued. Sleepless nights followed by days of worry had taken their toll, if the hollowed out face was anything to go by. He rose to greet me as I entered the kitchen.

"Mr Hawk?"

"Yes."

"John Stillman. Freddie Taplin said I should have a word with you."

"Oh."

Stillman smiled. "Yes, your good lady said that you might be rather ... terse at this time of morning."

"Old habits," I said. "How can I help?"

"Freddie said you were superb at what you did... at well, you know..." He looked at me for assistance.

"Sticking my nose in other people's business?"

"Yes. I'd like you to stick it in mine if you would and find my daughter for me. She's been missing for six months now. I'd like to know if she's dead or alive and if the latter ... well, I need to see her..."

His words dwindled as Laura placed a rack of toast on the table and surreptitiously tapped the face of her watch.

"Something happen between you?" I asked Stillman.

"Me and Teresa? No, no, far from it." He looked away and began to rephrase the hasty denial. "I guess you mean am I in any way responsible for her disappearance? No, not that I'm aware of."

"But you're not sure?"

He wasn't too keen on being pushed for an answer.

"I understood that you were in a hurry..."

"I can eat toast and listen."

He thought for a moment. "She has a unique quality, aside from her brains and beauty. You think I'm biased, of course..."

"Men and their daughters, Mr Stillman."

"Indeed, but Teresa has something I envy. She draws people to her and has done so ever since childhood. Once they're in her affections that's where they tend to remain. I just hope one of them hasn't outstayed his or her welcome..."

"What does she do for a living?"

"She designs and builds gardens. Beautiful gardens. It brings in some serious money, I can tell you, and that in itself calls for other skills which..." He broke off, as if singing her praises any further might somehow tempt fate. He added, flatly: "Six months ago she suddenly disappeared."

"You told the police, I take it?"

"Yes, yes. In theory the case is still open but in practise, well..." He shrugged with his hands. "Will you find out what's happened to her, Mr Hawk?"

"I'm going abroad..."

"To Los Angeles, your good lady said. I didn't ask, though: business or pleasure?"

I wanted to say I'm going to see my kids, mate, but it didn't seem appropriate in the circumstances.

"Bit of both," I said. "Why don't you call me when I get back. We'll talk then."

It was meant as a polite brush-off and most people would've taken it that way. Not John Stillman. It seemed to make his day.

"I'll do just that," he said, keenly. "Thank you. Thank you."

He shook my hand across the table, then rose and headed for the front door. Just before he reached it he turned and said,

"Oh, by the way, have a good trip."

I nodded. "We will."

We did.